MW01152678

TREASURE IN EXILE

Printed in the USA.

Cover Design and Interior Format

© The Killion Group, Inc.

TREASURE
In Exile

S.W. HUBBARD

CHAPTER 1

SWEAT...SPICYBEANS...PINE-SOL...CUPCAKES ...POPCORN. The scents of the Rosa Parks Community Center roll over me in one complex wave as soon as I step into the lobby. I'm sure my dog Ethel could pick out even more subtle distinctions, but my human nose does a pretty good job of telling me what's going on at the Center this Friday afternoon. Four lanky middle school boys are horsing around near the stairs to the gym, indicating that my husband's basketball practice must have already ended. That means he'll be on the way home to start preparing for our dinner guests.

Mr. Vargas patiently pushes his mop across the dingy linoleum in his never-ending quest to maintain a modicum of order. A tribe of laughing little kids skids across the wet floor, leaving a crazy quilt of brown sneaker prints in their wake. Mr. Vargas reaches the wall and turns to go back over the swath he just washed. His pace never changes.

A muscular man strides toward the kitchen with a fifty-pound bag of rice on his shoulder, no doubt sent to the storeroom by the women preparing the weekly neighborhood dinner in the kitchen. In an hour, the fellowship hall will be jammed with parents, grandparents, and kids all seated at the long, plastic tablecloth-covered tables waiting for the chicken and rice and beans and greens to be passed.

Right inside the door, two elderly ladies sit behind a table laden with cakes, cookies and pies. A crooked, hand-lettered sign unnecessarily proclaims BAKE SALE.

"Hi, Audrey. You wanna buy a nice pie for your man?" A sweet old gal whose name escapes me tilts a sweet potato pie for my inspection. "We're raising money to fix the plumbing."

"How about a coffee cake?" Her companion slides forward a huge confection dripping with frosting, cinnamon, and nuts. "The hot water heater is about to blow, and if we don't get it fixed, the health department says they'll shut us down."

I hesitate over the coffee cake. Sean and I have pledged to reduce our sugar consumption, so he'll clobber me for bringing a landmine like this into our home. But it sure looks good.

Five dollars for the pie. Four for that fabulous cake. They'll never raise enough money for a plumber with pricing that low.

"I could let you have it for three-fifty," the baker cajoles, fixing her mournful dark eyes on me.

"Oh, it's not the money." I reach for my wallet and hand her a twenty. "I'll take that bag of Snickerdoodles, and you keep the change."

Delighted with their transaction, the ladies release me and pounce on their next target. A tall, silver-haired man in a blue blazer and red tie has entered behind me. His jacket brushes against the bake sale table and picks up a dusting of powdered sugar. He frowns at the bake sale ladies and brushes it off. One lady opens her mouth to make a sales pitch, but is intimidated into silence by the man's haughty glare.

"I'm looking for my wife, Loretta Bostwick."

I know that name. Loretta Bostwick is a rich lady who just joined the Board of Directors here.

"She's with Reverend Levi," the sweet-potato pie lady tells him.

He purses his lips. "And where might that be?"

Man, this guy's a pill. Reverend Levi Jefferson is the Chairman of the Board, but maybe Loretta's husband doesn't know that. "I'll show you," I offer, taking him off the ladies' hands. "Levi Jefferson's office is upstairs, first door on the left."

Mr. Bostwick gives me a curt nod and heads upstairs without glancing left or right. He takes no interest in the mural of Rosa Parks smiling down over the lobby, nor of a large framed photo of the founder of the Center, Levi Jefferson Senior. Levi Senior was a lion of the civil rights movement, marching in Birmingham and Montgomery and Selma alongside Martin Luther King and John Lewis. He knew Rosa Parks personally, and when he founded the Rosa Parks Center, he named it for his friend. He died when I was a kid, and I still remember the massive traffic jam in Palmyrton caused by his funeral at the Mt. Zion African Methodist Episcopal church.

His son, Levi Jr., is the pastor of that church, but by all accounts, he's not as fiery a preacher as his father. I've often met him here at the Parks Center, a distinguished, cordial man in his late fifties, but he's not a big personality. My father knows Levi better than I do, and he says the man prefers teaching to preaching. But I guess his famous father pressured him into the family business.

I stopped by the Parks Center on my way home from work because my stepmother texted that she might need a ride to our house. When I asked why, she didn't reply, so here I am. First, I head downstairs to look for my father, but the room where he runs the chess club is straightened up and empty. Perhaps he's already with Natalie, helping her put away her knitting supplies. My dad and Natalie have been married only one year longer than Sean and I, but they already seem like they've been together a lifetime. They're both so low-key, but they tend to each other with unwavering concern.

I turn the corner and see Natalie in her classroom, her elegant silver hair pinned into a loose chignon. She's putting skeins of yarn into plastic bins when I enter. My father is nowhere to be seen.

"Where's Dad?" I ask after our brief embrace.

She glances over her shoulder as if she expects him to spring from the closet. "I'm glad I have this moment alone with you, Audrey. I need talk to you."

An arrow of anxiety stabs me. Natalie is sixty-two and Dad is sixty-four. This is the decade of suspicious shadows on the mammogram and moles turned murderous. "What's wrong? Are you sick?"

She shakes her head and directs me into a plastic classroom chair. Dropping into the chair beside me, she grips my hand. "Our trip to the American Mathematical Society meeting didn't go well."

"Really? When I saw Dad on Tuesday he didn't mention—"

In an uncharacteristic show of impatience, Natalie cuts me off. It's as if she possesses a river of information that must flow out of her before my father shows up. "Your father has decided to permanently retire from Rutgers. He's giving up his professorship."

Giving up his tenure? This is huge! After his stroke, Dad took a nine-month leave of absence, then returned to teaching part-time. "Before the trip, he was all excited about returning full-time. What happened?"

"He attended a lot of sessions on number theory at the Society meeting. Afterwards...." Natalie bites her lip. "I've never seen him so dejected, so full of despair."

"Wait—you're saying he didn't understand what was going on? Number theory is his field."

Natalie's clear blue eyes get a little watery. "He wasn't totally in the dark. But number theory is a young man's game. The field is moving in new directions. Roger feels that after his stroke and more than a year out of the academic mainstream, he simply can't catch up. If he can't be on the leading edge...."

This is blowing me away. Math has been the center of my father's life as long as I've been alive. Even right after his stroke when his speech was so impaired, I always felt his mathematical mind was still ticking. How can Roger Nealon not be a full professor of mathematics? What will he be instead? "This is a hasty decision," I protest. "How can he take such a serious step after one bad meeting? He should talk to his colleagues."

Natalie strokes my hand. "He did, yesterday. And this morning his mind was made up. Your father is a proud man. He wants to leave while his work is still valued. He wants to walk out with his head held high. His greatest fear is to be pushed aside by the younger generation. To be tolerated, not respected."

I swallow hard. "He asked you to tell me?"

"Not directly. But I know he dreads telling you because he thinks you'll argue with him. That's why I wanted to talk to you before dinner. So when he does tell you, just accept it."

I nod. "But what will he do with himself? Chess is his only hobby."

Natalie brightens. "He already has a plan. In fact, he's starting to put it into effect right now." She stands up and peeks out the door into the hallway then turns back to me. "He wants to start a group for young people here to encourage a love for higher level mathematics...wants them to experience the creativity of math instead of the drudgery of doing the endless math worksheets they get in school. He's very excited--he'll tell you all about it at dinner. All he needs is approval from the Parks Center board of directors."

This cheers me up. Running the chess club here has been a great activity for my father. In fact, it's how he met Natalie. But teaching third graders which way they can move a rook is not enough to keep his mind challenged. I'm glad he's conceived a bigger project that will help both him and the kids. Maybe his retirement will work out for the best after all.

"So, do you actually need a ride to our house?" I ask Natalie.

"No, I'll wait for your father to finish his meeting with the board, and we'll come over together." She hugs me. "I hope you don't mind I brought you here under false pretenses."

I hold her for a moment longer than usual, inhaling the delicate scent of roses that clings to her. When I release her and turn to leave, I hesitate. "The Board will give him permission to do this, won't they?"

She arches her perfectly shaped eyebrows. "Of course. Who could possibly object?"

CHAPTER 2

GARLIC....BASIL....FENNEL...SOMETHING ELSE I CAN'T PIN down.

The aromas hover in the air, having drifted out the kitchen window and across the lawn to the driveway where I've parked my car. Our garage is still too crowded with unpacked boxes and construction debris to hold both my car and Sean's.

The second sign that my husband is cooking is the lack of canine greeting when I enter the back hall. No doggy kisses, no fur-depositing embrace, no sweater- snagging leap of joy.

"Hello? I'm home!" I enter the kitchen and find Ethel sitting at the foot of the stove, her eyes fixed on mounds of crumbled sausage waiting to enter a big sauté pan. Her brown tail swishes, but her gaze never leaves her target.

Sean pivots from the chopping block on the center island and tosses a pile of chopped peppers into the pan. They land with a sizzle, and he holds his arms out in welcome.

Dodging the murderous knife in his right hand, I move in for a hug. There's nothing better than resting my head against his broad chest at the end of a long day of pricing Hummel figurines and re-arranging furniture so the worn spots aren't obvious. Fridays are always long days in the estate sale business. "You must've peeled right out of the Parks Center after practice."

"Can't dally when I'm hosting a dinner party. How was your day?"

"Tiring." I pour myself a glass of wine from the bottle on the gleaming granite counter. Sean is a very clean-as-you go cook. First, I tell Sean all about what's going on with my father. Then I tell him about my day at work. "Ty and I got the Farley sale set up, but it was a lot of work with only two of us. I really have to hire a new assistant."

"Does that mean you're going to be too exhausted to go to this fundraiser tomorrow night?"

"We're definitely going." I pluck cubes of feta cheese out of the tossed salad to stave off starvation. "The estate sale Ty and I are running tomorrow ends at three and the party starts at eight. Plenty of time for a nap in between."

"I'll take my nap at the party." Sean smacks my hand away from the salad and produces a platter of appetizers. I fall on the bruschetta and grilled eggplant like a lion presented with both impalas and gazelles.

Ever since I fished the invitation out of the recycling bin, Sean has been complaining about having to go to this fundraiser for the Rosa Parks Community Center. Not that he doesn't believe it's for a good cause, but he hates the location at the tony 1780 Club, and he's not too fond of the hostess, Loretta Bostwick.

"Maura says she'd kill to be invited to a party at the 1780 Club. She says it'll be a networking bonanza."

Sean's fast-moving chef's knife reduces branches of some herb into a little green mound. "Good. Go with your best friend."

"For God's sake, Sean—it's not a UVA tailgate party, open to all crashers. The invitation was addressed to Mr. and Mrs. Sean Coughlin. You're the one they want to talk up the after school programs to the guests. I'm the plus one. But this party will be such a great opportunity for Another Man's Treasure. This is o-o-old money. These are the people who put the estate in estate sale."

"No job is worth sucking up to the Bostwicks and their friends."

It's true that what I've seen of Mr. Bostwick doesn't lead me to believe he's a fun guy, but I won't admit that to Sean. "Socializing for two hours is not sucking up." Sean and I have been around and around on this topic already. I could really use a big-ticket job—both our wedding and our kitchen remodeling project went way over budget, and Sean still has college loan debt. Not that I regret the seven-piece band for the reception or the green-accented Italian tile under my feet or Sean's education. But I want the remaining bills paid off by the end of the summer. Sean is eager for us to start trying to get pregnant, but I can't even think of bringing a child into the world while we're in debt. Wringing more profit from Another Man's Treasure Estate Sales is the only way to put our finances in the black. Normally, Sean's all about backing me up in any and every way. But he has an unshakable aversion to Loretta Bostwick and her party.

"You're carrying this grudge against Loretta Bostwick too far."

Sean's lips are pressed into a thin line. Concentration for placing his final sheet of pasta or annoyance at being challenged? I'm guessing the latter.

"I resent that Loretta was appointed to the Board of Directors at the Parks Center when she doesn't do any hands-on volunteer work there. She doesn't even like the people we serve."

"Loretta is a good person." This smooth, low voice makes us both pivot toward the door.

"Hi, Natalie." I extend my leg to block Ethel's lunge, and give my stepmother a wave. "Where's Dad?"

"His meeting at the Parks Center is running late. He sent me ahead and said he'd take an Uber." Natalie accepts a kiss from Sean and wine from me. "Why are you complaining about poor Loretta?"

"Poor?" Sean snorts. "The woman's got more money than the Pope."

"Yes, but Loretta has such an air of…." Natalie pauses to choose precisely the right word. "Yearning. She's searching for a purpose. A place to belong."

I watch Sean's face. He would roll his eyes if it were anyone else but Natalie defending Loretta. "There's plenty of work to be done at the Parks Center if Loretta were willing to roll up her sleeves and pitch in. Instead she swans around looking like she's afraid the kids will rub their grimy hands against her designer dresses."

"Where you see aloofness, I see shyness." Natalie speaks quietly, but with authority. "Loretta is insecure and uncertain how to reach out. She wants very much to do a good job as a member of the board of directors. The success of this fundraiser is very important to her."

"I met her husband briefly today. He seems like kind of a stick. Maybe she just wants to get away from him." I start setting the table. "How did Loretta end up on the Rosa Parks Center board?"

I ask, hoping Natalie can shed some light on the matter that will bring Sean around. "Wouldn't someone like her be more suited to the art museum board or the symphony board?"

"Jared Bellack recruited her," Natalie explains.

Sean looks up from layering his lasagna. "Really? He's not one of the founding families of Palmyrton like Loretta. He made all his money with an internet start-up company that he sold to Google for a gazillion dollars."

Natalie offers a sly smile. "When he gave the Parks Center a big donation to start the Coding Club, he bought his way onto the Board. Doesn't that bother you, Sean?"

My husband slides his lasagna into the oven before he answers. "It does. Before Jared and Loretta arrived, the Board was made up of average people who volunteered because they wanted to help the community. Nice people."

"Yeah, but nice doesn't pay the electric bill," I remind my husband. "How long can the Parks Center survive trying to fix that crumbling building with the proceeds from selling cupcakes and Christmas cookies?"

Sean sighs. "I know. Jared doesn't seem so bad. At least he's a business person, not a socialite."

"Exactly," Natalie says. "I've volunteered there for twenty years, and we've been skating closer and closer to the brink of financial disaster. Now, some poor investment decisions and an unexpected plumbing catastrophe are going to push us over the edge."

Natalie places just one piece of bruschetta on her cocktail napkin. "Jared figured out how to raise money to launch his tech company, so he must know what he's doing. He told Levi Jefferson that our board needed some rich people with connections to help solve our financial problems. And he recruited Loretta." Natalie stares at Sean over the rim of her wine glass. "Do you want to be on the Board, Sean?"

"Hell, no! I have no patience for their long-winded meetings and endless squabbling."

"Speaking of long-winded meetings, what's taking Dad so long?" I glance at the clock on the oven—nearly seven.

Natalie fiddles with the tortoise shell pins keeping her chignon in place. "I hope the meeting is going well."

Just as I'm about to text my father, Ethel leaves her post beneath the hors d'oeuvres and begins baying at the door. A moment later, Dad walks in. He greets his grand-dog with focused affection and then enters the kitchen.

Dad rests his walking stick against the counter so the carved goat's head grins impishly at us, but he remains standing. The only visible effects of his stroke are a slurring of certain words and a slight unsteadiness on his feet late in the day, so he's acquired a collection of jaunty sticks.

Natalie places her hand on top of Dad's. There's no mistaking the look of concern in her eyes. "How did it go?" she asks.

Dad shakes his head. Suddenly he looks small. Frail. Old.

"No money. No space. And Jared refuses to compromise on sharing the Coding Club computers. The Math Explorers won't be launching any time soon."

CHAPTER 3

THE SIDELINING OF MY FATHER'S dream for a Math Explorers club has adjusted Sean's attitude toward the fundraiser. He's still complaining about the venue and the company, but at least he accepts the necessity of our presence. The party needs a few people to talk up the work of the Rosa Parks Center to the rich guests, and Sean is both passionate and very social.

The 1780 Club is in a turn of the 20th Century mansion in what used to be known as Millionaire's Row. The Club itself predates the mansion, having been formed in 1780, the year George Washington and his troops were encamped at nearby Jockey Hollow. At that time, I imagine the club was a ragtag group of Patriots and officers in the Continental Army, drinking ale and hard cider in some smoky tavern. But over the centuries, it became a club for the sons and daughters of the founding families of Palmyrton. As the town became bigger and more prosperous, the 1780 Club outgrew its first home, and the second--a clapboard Georgian townhouse--burned to the ground when a member fell asleep in the lounge with a cigar dangling from his hand. The Club moved into its present home in the 1930s. All this I learned from Wikipedia because the 1780 Club doesn't have a website.

Anyone who has to ask questions about the club isn't entitled to know. It's not the kind of club you join; it's the kind of club you inherit a membership to.

We pull into the driveway behind a vintage Mercedes. The valet parker, an ancient fellow rather unsteady on his feet, exchanges some friendly banter with the elderly couple who emerge from the car. Then he hands over their vehicle to a much younger Hispanic man to be parked.

We've arrived in Sean's five-year-old Camry, a chariot that, despite its dings and scratches, is still better than my ten-year-old Civic. The valet attendant approaches Sean's window. "Your invitation?"

Before Sean can complain that he didn't ask for the other guy's invite, I lean across to hand it to him.

The old man glances at the parchment square, warped from my sweaty clutch, then accepts Sean's key without comment. Is it my imagination, or is there a look of barely concealed incredulity on his face?

If this were some glitzy club where people rolled up in Maseratis, I think I'd be able to laugh off my Cinderella status. But the 1780 Club exudes a discreet air of "we know rules you are totally unaware of, so don't even try to learn." I find that a bit intimidating, but Sean certainly doesn't. He places his hand on the small of my back and guides me up the stairs as if he's been coming here all his life. I guess that's the benefit of being a cop. When you've broken up domestic disturbances in fancy executive homes and revived prep school seniors from heroin overdoses, you know that no one is too exalted to have drawers full of dirty laundry.

If I were expecting glittery splendor, I'd be sorely disappointed. This is the patrician atmosphere that can't be bought with mere money; it must be acquired with time. The dim foyer is lined with large portraits of pompous looking old men through the ages. The Oriental rug is worn to the backing in spots and the heavy crystal chandelier barely casts any light. A wide, curving staircase leads to a second floor open hallway lined with an ornate balustrade. I hear the low murmur of voices from a room down the hall, but no music or laughter.

We hesitate, uncertain of where to go. Sean heaves a sigh.

As if she heard it, Loretta Bostwick materializes from the shadows, a wraith in a black sheath dress with a sheer chiffon flounce. Her Ferragamo pumps tap toward us. She's so impossibly thin, she must have her clothing custom made because I've never seen anything that tiny in a store for adults.

"Ah, welcome. *So* glad you were able to come." Her breathy voice is only audible because the foyer is so silent. She reaches out to give my arm a squeeze, causing me to fumble because I thought she wanted to shake. Her skeletal hand, ice cold on my skin, seems like it might snap under the weight of the heavy pearl bracelet sliding past her wrist. Her pale champagne hair is tightly drawn back from her spookily smooth face. "The others are in the parlor." The lids over her pale green eyes flutter and the tendons in her neck look stretched to the limit. "Robert will show you the way."

A stooped African American man in a white jacket appears at her side and leads us down a long hallway. He opens a heavy double door, and we are dazzled by light and movement. It's as if Robert has kicked open a very high-end ant colony. Waiters bearing trays of canapés move among clusters of heavy-drinking one-percenters, ice cubes clanking in their cut glass tumblers. A musician in the corner runs her long fingers over the strings of a tall, gilt harp. Scores of coifed heads pivot in our direction.

I sense an infinitesimal break in the chatter before everyone recognizes that we're nobody and returns to their conversations. A woman in a dark red dress and droopy embroidered shawl comes fluttering toward us.

"Wow, there's actually someone I know here. She's an artist who—"

But Sean is already beating a retreat. "I'll get us some booze," Sean mutters, heading for the bar before the woman can trap him.

"Audrey, darling! What a lovely surprise!"

I forget the woman's name but I remember her profession: she paints oil portraits of pets. She's come to two of my sales to buy back her own work. Because, face it, no one wants to buy a painting of someone else's Rover or Fluffy. But she can use the old portraits as sales tools to display in her gallery.

"Fabulous party! Loretta has outdone herself." She grabs my elbow and whispers in my ear. "I'm thrilled Loretta invited me. Such an opportunity for me to show my work." She whips her phone from her evening clutch. "Look at the portrait I did of Loretta's dogs, Rex and Cleo."

I'm a sucker for dogs, so I let myself be distracted from my networking mission. Rex and Cleo are brown and white English Pointers. In the painting, one sits and the other stands with one paw lifted and his nose pointing. "Beautiful. Looks like Rex is about to jump off the canvas and chase a bird."

She beams. "One of my best works. Well, if you meet anyone who wants a pet portrait, send them my way."

I slither through the crowd toward my husband's patch of red hair I can intermittently spot bobbing above shorter heads. As I slip through knots of party-goers, a strong hand grabs my elbow. "There she is! Just the girl who could solve all your problems, George."

I stop and smile through gritted teeth at the "girl" comment. Two sixtyish men in charcoal gray suits and regimental stripe ties greet me with raised glasses of scotch. One looks vaguely familiar although he's barely discernable from any of the other late middle-aged banker/lawyer types in the room. "Audrey helped a client of mine liquidate the assets in his mother-in-law's home," he explains to his companion, a mournful basset-houndy fellow.

Am I supposed to know who his client is when I don't even remember who he is? I smile to encourage more clues, and he bails me out. "Bob Cranley. I stopped by the sale with my wife because she heard there was some kind of pottery there that she collects."

"Oh, the Milhauser sale! Yes, Mrs. M had quite a collection of art pottery." Now it's coming back to me. Bob's wife was a real bitch on wheels, dickering over the price of a small Arequipa vase with Ty until Bob finally pulled a wad of bills from his pocket, tossed two C-notes at Ty, and steered his wife out of the house. Bob, however, seems to have a fonder memory of our previous encounter.

"Audrey, George here has power-of-attorney for his sister, Birdie. She…well, she had to go into assisted living this week, and she has a big house full of stuff. He's feeling overwhelmed by all the requirements of his position."

George nods. His pouchy eyes grow watery. "She's my only sibling. Early-onset Alzheimer's. I can't bear thinking about going through her things."

"I'm so sorry—that's a rough situation." Before I can utter another word of sympathy, Bob is chattering again. "You can help him with the house, right? It's in Melton."

He actually winks at me! Melton is a wealthy enclave south

of Palmyrton, so he knows I'll be interested. This is exactly the kind of business I came here to rustle up. "Of course." I smile reassuringly at George. "You keep a few mementoes and I'll handle everything else. I could come by the house and provide an estimate this week. What day works for you?"

Looking like a weight has been lifted from his shoulders, George pulls out his phone and in a matter of minutes we've exchanged numbers and made an appointment for Tuesday. Elated, I say good-bye and pivot right into Sean's cocktail-carrying hands. I grab my drink and beckon him into a quiet corner to deliver my news.

"Great," Sean downs his scotch in one gulp. "Let's go."

"No! If my first encounter was that fruitful, I've gotta trawl for more. And you haven't talked to a soul about the kids you coach and how the Parks Center helps them."

"These people couldn't care less about a bunch of black and brown and white poor kids. They've got enough worries trying to get their offspring into Ivy League schools—" Sean neatly sidesteps a tipsy woman before she douses him with vodka. "—and their wives into the Betty Ford Clinic."

I've never seen Sean so prickly at a party. I was sure once I got him here he'd enter into the spirit of the event, but clearly I'm wrong. I glance around for someone who might lighten Sean up, and my gaze connects with Jared Bellack. He heads straight for us, his shaven head shiny under the light of the crystal chandeliers.

"Sean!" he slaps my husband on the back and pumps my hand when Sean introduces me. Then he wedges himself between us. "Hey man, there's someone here I want you to meet." He glances down at me through his trendy rimless glasses. "You don't mind if I steal your date for a minute, Angie?"

Angie, Annie, Audrey—whatever. Jared hauls Sean off without waiting for either my correction or permission. They head toward a cluster of men talking to Levi Jefferson. I scan the group from the ground up: same black shoes, same gray suits, same white shirts, same sedate ties. Only above the shoulders are they different: five white faces and one black face. I wonder if it bothers Levi to be the only black man in the room apart from Robert, the butler. But Levi appears relaxed and chatty. Maybe he's used to it.

Sean and Jared join the group. Now I'm free to resume mingling.

I plunge back into the crowd. But this time, success doesn't drop into my lap. I don't recognize a soul and everyone seems totally caught up in their own conversations. I try to remember the advice from my Bible, *The Introvert's Guide to Networking*—make eye contact with someone else who's alone or stand next to your target and wait to be included in the conversation—but I don't spot any likely prospects for either maneuver. How does Maura do this so effortlessly?

After I've been wandering alone and friendless for what feels like half an hour (although it's probably only been three minutes), I spot the flash of a familiar face in the crowd.

A black face. And not Levi.

Eager for a friend, I push in that direction without fully registering who the person is or how I know him.

I dodge around a cluster of partygoers and our eyes meet from a distance of twenty feet.

It's Dennis Sykes, a guy in his late twenties who teaches martial arts at the Parks Center. He and my father sometimes talk politics and philosophy. Why would he be here? And why is he wearing that ugly tie?

Dennis's eyes widen. He ducks his head and moves away without acknowledging me. When he turns, I notice his dreadlocks pulled back in a thick ponytail.

It clicks. Dennis is working the party, not attending as a guest. He's a grad student in sociology at Rutgers. He must earn extra money as a waiter for the caterer Loretta hired for the party. Is he embarrassed to be seen passing trays of canapés to the rich and not-famous? Or is he under strict orders not to socialize with the guests?

As I contemplate my next move, a large man regaling a group in front of me steps backward right onto my peep-toe pump.

A gasp of pain escapes me, and the man turns. "Oh, pardon me. Are you all right?" He puts his hefty arm around me and draws me into his circle. "I've nearly crippled this lovely lady," he says to his companions. Before long, I'm answering interested questions about my work and providing off-the-cuff art appraisals. See, these people aren't so bad! Although I don't score a direct hit as I did in the first encounter, I do feel that several of the women retained the name Another Man's Treasure by the time the group dispersed. Good enough. As Maura repeatedly tells me, networking is a long game.

With all my nervous sipping, I've drained my wine glass, so I head to the bar for a refill. On the way, I pass Sean, who's still in Jared's armlock. The group has gotten smaller. Levi and some of the other men have moved on, and my husband is talking animatedly to a smaller group of people who seem genuinely engaged. So I press on to the bar. While I'm waiting for my wine, I eavesdrop on the two ladies next to me.

One is wearing a dress plastered with maroon, peach and green cabbage roses, a garment so ugly only a woman of astonishing wealth would have the confidence to wear it. The other is nondescript in a navy blue suit and a small gold brooch. Clearly lower on the status totem pole.

Flower Power glances over her shoulder then proceeds to speak in a voice I can easily hear. "I'm quite surprised Loretta chose to tackle such a large event."

Blue Suit speaks more softly, but I think she says, "I didn't think she had the strength, with the way she's been feeling..."

I thought Loretta just lived by the "you can never be too rich or too thin" credo, but maybe her emaciation has medical causes.

"...and with everything going on with her son..." Blue Suit shakes her head.

I keep my gaze riveted on the bartender as if I've never before seen such adroit pouring of white wine. But my ears are sharply tuned. What's going on with Loretta's son?

Flower Power emits a bosom-heaving sigh. "Crawford was such a sunny child. Now this. Stunning. You know, that's why Frederic isn't here tonight."

Who's Frederic? Oh right, the husband I encountered last night. The ladies take their wine glasses and drift away from the bar. I'm left wondering what Crawford has been up to, and why it's caused his father to miss the party. Not that it's any of my business. I take a gulp of wine to steel myself for one more foray around the room. Then I'll snag Sean and we'll head out to hear the band at Blue Monday. I could use a little R&B after all this tinkling harp music. And a bleu cheeseburger too. The mini-quiches and tiny skewers of salmon offered by the caterer aren't very filling.

I become aware the decibel level in the room has gone down a degree. The harpist is taking a break. In the moment she steps away from her instrument, we hear a short, sharp cry.

Followed by a thump.

And then a male voice. "Lord Jesus, No!"

CHAPTER 4

SEAN RUNS TOWARDS THE SOUNDS in the foyer.

I follow Sean.

A white-jacketed figure stands frozen at the end of the corridor leading to the foyer. Robert, the butler who showed us in. Sean moves the man aside, and I see a grimace cross my husband's face. A second later I squeeze past Robert and see the source of the sounds.

Loretta Bostwick lies beside the staircase, her spindly legs splayed, her fragile arms outflung.

Her head twisted at an angle not compatible with life.

"I'm a doctor!" One of the guests runs down the hall and pushes past me. He stops short as he sees Loretta's eyes staring blankly at the ceiling.

Sean turns to block him. "You can't help her. Don't move her body."

Then my husband faces the gathering crowd. "I'm a detective with the Palmyrton police department. No one leave the building. This may be a crime scene." Sean commands Robert the butler, "Secure the back door."

As Sean calls for back-up, the crowd breaks into excited murmuring. "Crime? She simply tripped coming down the stairs." "Outrageous! We can leave if we want to." "I'm a lawyer! I know my rights!"

But no one makes a move for the door. No one wants to miss the excitement.

Flower Power and Blue Suit are in the front of the pack. I notice them gazing upward. Now I see it too. Sean's trained eye must have caught it immediately. A long scrap of sheer black fabric flutters from the ornate baluster above us.

Loretta didn't trip going down the stairs.

She must've gone over the railing in that spot.

Fell, jumped, or was pushed?

That's what the police have to determine. I watch Sean craning to look upstairs. I know he wants to charge up there and search, but he can't go without backup. He doesn't even have his service revolver with him.

A patrol car must have been in the vicinity because two uniformed officers arrive within minutes. Sean leaves one to watch over the body and the crowd, and sprints up the stairs with the other cop.

I feel a stab of fear in my chest. On a normal day, I succeed in suppressing my worry about my husband's safety because I don't know what he's been doing until after he arrives home in one piece. Seeing him head into the unknown in real time scares me.

His broad back disappears into the dark reaches of the second floor of the 1780 Club. I'm left to stare at that forlorn scrap of black chiffon on the railing. Surely, a woman as petite as Loretta couldn't have accidentally fallen over such a high, sturdy balustrade?

CHAPTER 5

MONDAY MORNING, AND TY IS riding shotgun in my Honda Civic with the passenger seat pushed back as far as it will go to accommodate his long legs.

We're on our way to a huge town house development on the far edge of Palmer County to provide an estimate on a job. I've been chatting away, telling my assistant about my networking success and the tragic finale to the Parks Center fundraiser.

"Sean says she either jumped or was pushed. There's no way it was an accident." I end my story with a dramatic flourish.

Ty stares out the window.

"It might be murder," I clarify just in case Ty didn't catch my drift.

"Hmm. An' everyone always tellin' me to watch the kinda parties I go to."

While it's true that Ty is hard to shock, I was expecting a bigger reaction. Why is he so taciturn?

Two miles pass in silence. Then Ty shakes his fist at a huge boat of a Buick driving twenty miles per hour under the speed limit "Can somebody tell this dude we're in New Jersey, not Pennsylvania Dutchland?"

I try to pass, but just as I give my Honda some juice, the Buick drifts from the right lane toward the left. It ambles along straddling the dividing line.

Ty slaps the dashboard. "C'mon, man—pick a lane. You don't get both."

I turn to look at him. "What's bugging you? And don't say nothing."

He follows my order and sits in silence.

"Ty, come on. Normally you're telling me all about your weekend, and school, and Lo—"

Mention of his toddler nephew provokes a response. "I'm worried about Charmaine."

Ty's half-sister is a little needy, but I thought she was finally on the right track. "Don't tell me she lost her job?"

"No, she's doin' great there. That's why it pisses me off that she's out lookin' for trouble. And draggin' Lo into it."

"Lo?" Now I'm all ears. I love that baby. Charmaine has always seemed like a good mother to me. Could she possibly be neglecting Lo or bringing him along to wild parties?

He rubs his temples. "She wants to take him to visit our father in prison."

Given the negative fantasies blooming in my mind, this seems minor. "Oh. Does she stay in touch with your father?"

Ty nods. "Writes him. Lets him call her collect. Now she's got it in her head to take the baby clear to Trenton to show him off. As if our old man gives a rat's ass about that baby."

"But Ty, it's different for Charmaine. You have your grandmother and your aunts and uncles and cousins plus Charmaine and Lo. All Charmaine has is you and Lo. That's why she's having a hard time separating from your father. I can see why she'd want him to meet his grandson."

Ty twists in his seat to glare at me. "Don't you go siding with her!"

"I'm not taking sides. I just...well, I get where she's coming from. When you don't have a lot of family, you're reluctant to toss anyone aside."

Ty pounds his fist on his knee. "He tossed us aside. It was his job to be there for us when we were kids. Instead he chose to sell crack so he could drive some tricked out ride and be all that in the 'hood. My mother begged him to get a legit job but no, he hadda run with the gangbangers and get his sorry ass arrested. And then once he was inside, he couldn't just do his time and get back to us. No, he had to get pulled into some throw down and kill a dude and get sent up for twenty-five to life."

I've never been clear on the precise details of Ty's father's crimes; it's not a topic I've ever cared to quiz Ty on. Now he's so wound up that he's told me more than he ever has before. Probably more than he intended to.

"How long has he been in prison?"

"Since 2001."

"That's the last time you saw him?"

Ty shakes his head. "Oh no. My mom used to do what Charmaine is doing now."

"She took you to visit him in jail?"

Ty doesn't answer for a long time. His face looks strange—frozen—as if that distant painful memory is a numbing shot of Novocain. I wait, and eventually Ty speaks.

"Grams told her not to take me. But I was seven. I missed my dad. Some kid at school said I didn't really have a dad, and I wanted to prove him wrong. When my father would call, he always asked to talk to me, and then he'd end by saying, "tell your mom to bring you for a visit." So I would beg her and nag her and finally she gave in."

A slight shiver runs through Ty's powerful shoulders. His voice drops to a whisper. "Took us all day. Caught the Jersey Transit train to Newark, then switched for the train to Trenton. Took a bus from the train to the prison. Waited in a long line with other ladies and their kids. Another boy tried to make friends with me, but I wouldn't talk to him. I hung onto my mom's hand." He stops, gazing at a fawn trailing a doe through a meadow on the side of the road.

"That doesn't sound like you," I say to prod him back to the story.

"I think in some part of my brain I was shocked by what the other kids looked like. Some of them were dirty, with bad teeth and ratty hair. Unhealthy. Didn't matter if they were black or white or brown—they all looked sad and beaten down. I didn't want to be like them. Lookin' back, I can see I was mean not to talk to that kid. Wasn't his fault he looked so poor. But at the time, I just didn't want no part of him."

I take one hand off the wheel to pat Ty's knee. He's the least likely person on the planet to reject someone for not being good enough, so I can tell this confession costs him dearly.

"Finally, after what seemed like forever, we got inside the prison. I had to watch while the prison guards searched my mother like she was the criminal. Then they searched me too, and I was shaking thinking that they might arrest me for having two sticks of gum in my pocket. When we finally got to the visitation room, it was like being in Penn Station during rush hour—people yelling and crying and laughing and pushing. It smelled nasty—like sweat and cheap perfume and dirty laundry. We found my father, and all I wanted was to be connected to him—hold him, sit on his lap, touch him. But he just patted me on the back and told me to man up—I was too big for that. Then he started talking real quiet and intense to my mom. I couldn't hear what he was saying, but I watched my mom's face. She looked scared and worried and she kept shaking her head."

Ty has begun to crack his knuckles as he talks. It's almost as if he's forgotten I'm here and simply needs to speak the story aloud for his own sake.

"After a while the guard said something over the loudspeaker and everyone started getting ready to leave. Then the real crying started. Kids hanging on to their dads and having to be dragged off…women howling like cats. I wanted to hug my dad again, but I didn't think he'd like it. I started walking toward the door, following my mom. And my dad called my name. I got excited, 'cause I thought he did want to hug me goodbye after all. So I ran back to him. And you know what he did?"

Ty's eyes are shiny and hard. I'm afraid to know the end of this story.

"He pulled me towards him, put his arm around me and his mouth next to my ear. But it wasn't no hug. I smelled his sweat and his bad breath when he whispered, 'You tell your mother to take you to see Redbird. When you see him, you give him this paper," and I felt his fingers going into my pants pocket. "And if you give that paper to Redbird, he'll get you a new basketball. And then you can visit me again.' He squeezed my arm real tight and made me repeat what I was supposed to ask my mom."

"He tried to bribe you to do something illegal? Who was Redbird?"

"Some gangsta back in the 'hood. My dad had been smugglin' messages to him. Then Dad wanted my mother to go talk to the man, and she wouldn't do it, so he figured he'd get me to work on her, get me to beg her the way I begged to come visit him."

"Did it work?"

"Hell, no. I was scared outta my mind. I felt that paper in my pocket like it was a hot rock. I was so worried a guard would find it while we were on our way out.

"Once we were back on the train, and I was sure we couldn't get arrested, I gave the paper to my mom and told her what my dad said. She read it and her hands started to shake. Then she turned her head away from me and stared out the train window the whole way back to Newark. By this time it was dark, but whenever the train passed through a town, I could see the tears shining on her cheeks. I didn't really understand what was going on, but I just knew not to ask her any more questions right then."

Ty rests his head against the passenger side window. "And that was the last time I ever saw my father."

This all happened over fifteen years ago. There must be a whole new generation of criminals running the drug business now. Ty may never have forgiven his father for his treachery, but does he really think the man is up to the same trick with Charmaine and Lo?

"Why now? Why didn't taking Lo for a visit come up sooner?" I ask.

Ty flings his arms out. "Exactly! Why is he suddenly asking to see the baby? Like he cares about being a grandpa. He's got some plan. Something's in it for him." Ty taps his fists together. "His sentence in '01 was twenty-five to life. He's gotta serve at least fifteen. I don't know what his record is, but maybe he's got a shot at early release. So he's trying to show the parole board he's got a 'stable family'." Ty puts those last words in air quotes. "I told Charmaine that our old man is using her and Lo. And if he manages to get out of prison, he'll drag his shit show right to our door. But she won't listen."

Ty twists to face me, eyes blazing. "I won't let it happen! I don't want Lo to set foot in a prison—not as an inmate, not as a guard, not as a visitor. It's a bad place. His eyes don't need to see that. Ever."

CHAPTER 6

I GOT MORE THAN I EXPECTED when I asked Ty what was on his mind. The rest of the ride passes in silence.

On the horizon, peeping out above a stand of trees, I see a cluster of brown rooftops. We've finally arrived at Sutton Courte.

We pull up to a big cast iron gate. In front of it is a small brick house with a microphone on a pole.

"What's up with that?" Ty asks. "Looks like a fancy drive-through at Mickey D's."

The unnecessary "e" should have tipped me off that Sutton Courte is a gated community. Ahead of us, the guard waves through a woman in a white Mercedes. When Ty and I pull up in my dusty, dinged Honda, he peers into the car and gives me the once over: asymmetrical haircut, badly damaged manicure from ripping open cardboard boxes, slightly disheveled blouse. Then he bends his head at the neck and sees Ty: powerful dark brown arms, bright orange Jordans, Cavs cap. Ty returns his fisheye with the prison death stare.

The sales call spirals down from there. When I finally talk my way past the guard and get to the townhouse, I discover that the executor of the estate has a wildly inflated opinion of the worth of the home's contents. Where she sees luxury, I see twenty-year out-of-date suburban schlock. We'll be lucky to clear four grand from the furnishings. And the final indignity--the clean sneaker in the big, stinky dog turd of this sales call--comes when our prospective client practically throws herself in front of the door to prevent Ty from going out to the garage alone to check out the tools.

I decline to shake her hand as we stand in the foyer. "I'll get you an estimate by Thursday." I've already decided I'll be bidding high.

For the third time since I've been here, I feel my phone vibrate in my pants pocket.

Who the hell is calling me? I never pull out my phone while I'm talking to a client, but suddenly I feel anxious. Could something have happened to Sean at work? Is it Natalie calling to say Dad has had another stroke? I can't get out of this damn townhouse fast enough.

As soon as we're out the door, Ty mutters, "She buy her paintings at HomeGoods and she think she got a five-figure sale? This bitch got bugs in a bucket."

"You nailed it. Not worth our time." I pull out my phone. All the calls are from my father.

Ty shoots me a suspicious look. "You pretty quick to walk away from her bizness."

"I don't like her." I toss him my car keys. "You drive. I have to make a call."

Ty plucks the keys from mid-air with one raised hand. "Since when we gotta like people to sell their shit?"

I settle into the passenger seat. "I can tell she'll be nothing but trouble."

Ty snorts. "Trouble ain't never stopped you before."

If my father is calling me, he's definitely not dead. But what could make him so persistent?

I get ready to call back when a large, black hand obscures the screen.

"You don't have to turn down business to protect my feelings." Ty's dark gaze won't allow me to look away.

"I didn't...I wasn't..."

"I saw the way she looked at me. I saw she didn't want me going into the garage alone. I can deal with that. Been dealin' my whole life."

"Well, you shouldn't have to deal with it."

"Shouldn't have to deal with global warming. Shouldn't have to deal with pasta from Olive Garden. World's full of stuff that sucks. Gotta handle it and move on."

I squeeze his hand. "She can get another estimate. It won't be any better than ours. If she calls back, I'll take the job. But I'm not begging her for it."

Ty purses his lips and backs the car out of the driveway. "Guess now we're limitin' our business to rich old liberals and kindhearted Christians."

As we sail through the gate of Sutton Courte, I finally get to focus on my father's text message: *The Parks Center has inherited the Tate Mansion. Call me.*

CHAPTER 7

THE ROSA PARKS COMMUNITY CENTER has *inherited* the Tate Mansion, the most iconic Victorian home in all of Palmyrton? What does that even mean?

Maybe I should be worried—my father seems to be delusional.

When I call back, Dad is uncharacteristically wound up.

"What a morning! How soon can you get over here?" In the background I hear a cacophony of high and low voices, punctuated by squeals and clapping. Today is Dad's day to run the after-school chess club at the Center. He usually spends the whole day there, getting his room set up and talking to the counselors about kids with problems.

"Dad, go to a quieter room and explain to me what's going on."

The background noise lessens but doesn't disappear. Dad's voice comes into my ear skipping along at warp speed. "You must have seen in the news last week that Vareena Tate died."

"Yeah, she was like a hundred and three or something, right?"

"One hundred and one. And then a couple days later her maid died."

You'd have to be living under a rock not to have heard the story. Vareena Tate was legendary for having not left her grand old Victorian mansion since the 1960s. She had been cared for all those years by her devoted maid, an African American woman only three years her junior. When the two old gals died within days of each other, the press quickly turned the story into a legend that went viral: grand house, mysterious owner, faithful servant who died of a broken heart. It was all over social media and even got picked up by the *New York Times*.

"So what's that got to do with the Parks Center?"

"This morning Levi Jefferson got a phone call from the executor of Vareena Tate's estate. She's left all her money, the house, and the house's contents to the Parks Center. Millions of dollars! We can remodel the kitchen, fix the plumbing, expand our hours."

He pauses. It's like he's afraid to even say it out loud.

I speak for him. "So with this money coming in, there will be no more arguing about the computers. You can buy some of your own and set up your Math Explorers classroom just the way you want it."

"Exactly." As always, my father is a man of few words, but I can hear joy and relief and optimism all packed into those three syllables.

Clearly from all the excitement, this windfall came totally out of the blue. "What's Vareena Tate's connection with the Parks Center? Why did she choose it to be the beneficiary of her estate?"

"No one knows. They've been checking the donation records and she never sent us a dime while she was alive."

"Well, that's fantastic, Dad—congratulations. I'll tell Sean. Maybe the basketball team can get new uniforms, huh?"

"So, can you be here first thing tomorrow morning? The Board of Directors want to talk to you as soon as possible."

"With me? Why?"

"Didn't you listen to my voicemail messages? The executor says the interior of the house contains every stick of furniture and piece of art acquired by Vareena Tate's father-in-law and his father before him from the time the house was built in 1882. The Board wants to talk to you about handling the estate sale."

I lean back in the passenger seat and smile.

Screw you, Sutton Courte.

CHAPTER 8

THE GOOD NEWS ABOUT MY upcoming interview with the Parks Center Board has put a spring in my step as I make my second sales call of the day. I'm meeting solo with George Armentrout, my networking score from the party, while Ty goes off to his afternoon classes at Palmer Community College.

Birdie Armentrout's house is much smaller than the last house in Melton where I organized a sale. And I pray to God it doesn't contain anything as creepy as the home of the Eskew family did. But size is relative. No house in Melton is tiny-small. Birdie's house is quite spacious, if on the smaller end of grand.

Basking in the early afternoon sun, the house exudes an English village charm. There's a rose-covered trellis over the front gate, which showers me with delicate pink petals as I walk through. All along the twisting flagstone walkway are exotic flowers planted to look like a scene in a Monet watercolor. No garish petunias or geraniums—the kind of common plants even a black-thumb like me can recognize. These delicately shaded and unusually shaped creatures a gardener must order from arcane catalogs or grow from heirloom seeds.

The wide, covered front porch contains wicker furniture with chintz cushions. How nice to sit out here and read with a glass of iced tea. Before I can raise my hand to ring the bell, George has opened the door. He's wearing a tweed sports coat and a tie over saggy wide-wale corduroy pants. Not office attire, but surely not what a man would wear to pack up his sister's belongings.

"Oh, I'm *so* glad you're here." George reaches out for me as if he thinks I might run away. His eyes slant downward at the corners. Today they're red-rimmed. Allergies, or has the poor man been crying?

I step into the foyer, where a pleasant clove-y potpourri wafts through the air. But under that scent lurks an acrid, burnt smell. From what I can see, the house is immaculate, the only sign of disarray a pile of junk mail on the hall table.

George picks up a crystal tumbler from the table as he leads me to the living room. "Can I get you a drink? Scotch? Vodka?"

Good grief, I haven't even eaten lunch yet. "No thanks—I'm fine." When we sit in angled wing chairs, I see that George's hand trembles and some pale amber liquid sloshes out of the glass onto the mahogany end table.

"Oh dear!" George pulls out a handkerchief and wipes up the drips. "Birdie is very particular." He glances around and bites his lower lip. "She loved this room."

Everywhere in the room there are flowers: dried flowers, paintings of flowers, flowers in the pattern of the Chinese rug, flowers needlepointed on the pillows, flowers worked into the weave of the damask upholstery. "She's a gardener?" I ask.

George's eyes light up. My quite obvious observation has pleased him, and he tells me all about her reign as president of the Melton Garden Club and her membership in the International Orchid Society and the Perennial Gardeners Association. This burst of enthusiasm wears him out and he slumps back in his chair, throwing up his hands in dismay.

"I don't know what to do. All her lovely things. Sometimes when I visit her she's having a good day and she recognizes me and we chat. Then she cries and begs to come home." George leans forward and looks in my eyes. "I tried to keep her here at home. Hired twenty-four-hour caregivers. But she would slip out of the house at night. The second time she climbed out a window. Was missing for eight hours. The police found her wandering on Route 202, right outside Bernardsville. And when the caregiver was in the bathroom, Birdie put a plastic container on the stove and turned on the flame. Nearly burned the house down. So I had no choice...."

That explains the burnt smell. I pat his hand. "I'm sure you made the best decision to keep her safe."

"I suppose. But I can't bear for her possessions to be hauled off to the Goodwill. And I can't fit it all in my condo."

In many ways, these gone-to-a-nursing-home sales are sadder than true estate sales. George seems so forlorn and lost. If Jill still worked for me, she'd throw her arms around him and encourage him to have a good cry. Unfortunately, I'm not that capable in the presence of grief.

"Let's go through the house and I'll help you pick out a few items that you want to save as mementos. The rest, I'll sell. Everything your sister has is so well cared for. I know that people will buy it and give it a second life in their homes."

George perks up a bit. "Really? That's a nice thought. Birdie would like to know someone is cherishing her belongings."

I don't mention that the sofa may be purchased by a crazy cat lady whose ten felines will shred the cushions, and the table may soon be marked with rings from the beer bottles of some frat boys starting out on their own. George need never know the final destination of Birdie's pride and joy.

As we walk through the rooms, George tells me about various pieces: the vase purchased on a trip to Spain, the lamp received as a gift from an old friend, the painting discovered in an antiques shop. Each time he picks up an item I'm sure this is one he'll want to keep, but he always sets it down and keeps going. Finally, I realize all George really wants is to talk about his sister. The good old days of their childhood, playing golf and tennis and sailing. The happy times they shared puttering in the garden or traveling to Europe. How she comforted him after his wife left him. How she filled the void left by sons who'd grown and flown. I'm happy to be George's sounding board. In fact, it's nice to have a client who's genuinely fond of his departed relative. A refreshing change from the recent string of "how soon can you clear this out and give me my check?" clients.

I ask him a few questions about the past, admire some of the pieces. But George doesn't require much response from me—just a few uh-huhs and reallys--so my mind is busy tabulating an estimate as we move through the house. Although she has no exceptionally valuable antiques or artwork, Birdie's home has enough nice stuff in good condition to yield a low five-figure sale.

A change in George's tone jars me out of my mental math. "What do you think really happened?" he asks.

I guess my face looks blank because he continues. "At the party? To Loretta?"

Sean has told me virtually nothing about the case other than what's been released to the press. One bit of insider info I've gleaned from overheard conversations is that Loretta's fingerprints were found on the bannister in a facing out position, as if she'd been looking over the railing. Gripping the railing as she contemplated her jump, perhaps.

Or hanging on for dear life.

But I don't say that to George. "Well, the police seem pretty certain she didn't fall down the stairs."

"No one at the club wants to believe that, but I agree with the police. I'm sure Loretta didn't trip and fall," George says. "Something was bothering her that night. There was something about Loretta's manner that reminded me of Birdie. You know, when she got the news."

"News?'

George lowers his voice. "About her Alzheimer's. That there was nothing the doctors could do. Ten years ago Birdie was diagnosed with breast cancer, and she was full of fight. And she licked it. But when the doctors told her she had Alzheimer's, she knew she didn't have much time left.... And there was this resignation, this aloneness that I couldn't touch, no matter how I tried. And that's what I saw in Loretta at the party, underneath her smile."

Wow—now George has my full attention as we head to the second floor of the house. "Loretta was terminally ill?" I know the autopsy has been done and there's been no mention of this. But if she were terminally ill, that would be a motivation for suicide.

"No, I didn't mean literally the same as Birdie. Loretta has never been robust, but she didn't have cancer." George grips the handrail tightly as we walk upstairs. "Her attitude, her demeanor—she was very tense."

Was that unusual? I barely knew her, but Loretta seemed like one pat on the back would shatter her in a million pieces. I remember what Natalie said about Loretta. That she was full of yearning. "I overheard someone at the party say she had problems with her son." I say this to George's back as I follow him.

His shoulders stiffen as he continues up the stairs. "Crawford has always been a disappointment to his father. Loretta was used to being the mediator." He says no more on that matter as he climbs. So maybe the bad-boy son wasn't what was bothering her.

At the top George turns to face me. "What was she even doing on the second floor of the club? That's what's been nagging at me."

"What's up there?"

"The Board Room, a small office for the club manager, some storage rooms. The club manager was downstairs supervising the party, so why would she have gone up there?"

I'm guessing Loretta went up there specifically because she knew it would be empty. Knew that no one would be there to stop her suicide. But George doesn't seem to have made that connection.

By this time we've made it into the first bedroom. "Did you tell the police about your concerns?" George doesn't know that the lead detective on the case is my husband. And even though Sean won't tell me information about the case, I feel a responsibility to send info his way if I can.

George gazes around the room as if he's not sure where he is. He steps next to the bed and picks up the edge of a handmade quilt—wedding ring pattern—his fingers worrying the hand-sewn binding. "I was so upset after...er... it happened. Once the police established that I'd never left the parlor that evening, they let me go. That night I lay awake thinking, thinking about Loretta." His eyes well with tears.

"So you were close friends?"

"I don't remember ever *not* knowing Loretta. Our families belonged to the same country club, and to the 1780, of course." His fingers clutch the quilt, pulling it up from the bed. "And back when I was married, we socialized as couples—Loretta and Frederic, Marian and I. Our boys and Crawford went to the Bumford-Stanley school together. Oddly enough, Loretta and Birdie and I were actually distantly related. Fifth cousins—we shared the same great-great-great grandmother, I believe. Birdie was the one who discovered it. She was...is... an amateur genealogist."

I gently remove the quilt from his nervous hand before he damages it. "This has been a terrible month for you. To have to put Birdie into a nursing home, and then to lose Loretta so soon after."

George offers me a rueful smile. "Loretta was a very private person. But people tell me things. They always have, even when I was a kid. I guess I come across as harmless. Or too dull to cause trouble. That's how my ex saw me."

I squeeze his hand. "Maybe people see you as kind and gentlemanly."

He slips away from me and moves to look out the window. I can relate to George. People tell *me* things too. Sometimes terribly intimate things about their families and their finances. People are vulnerable after a death, even a death that doesn't break their heart. Now it seems like George wants to confide in me but isn't certain if he should.

I've learned a thing or two about interrogation from the man I share my bed with. I keep my mouth shut and wait.

"Loretta wasn't one to rock the boat." George begins talking so softly I have to hold my breath to hear him. "She was concerned with appearances. Didn't like confrontation. But she had a good heart. She did. She felt her wealth carried a responsibility to help others."

He says this as if he thinks I'll protest. "I'm sure she did. It was very generous of her to organize that fundraiser for the Parks Center."

George spins around. "That's what I don't understand. Loretta was never the one to take the lead in putting an event together. She wasn't bossy like some of the others. My ex-wife, for instance. Loretta was more of a loyal foot-soldier. But she was obsessed with this party. Asked my advice over every little thing. Made me promise three times that I'd come."

"And then...."

"It killed her."

CHAPTER 9

BEFORE HE WENT OFF TO his classes, Ty made me promise we could go look at the Tate Mansion from the outside when he returned. Now, as this eventful day ends, I do some Google research on the mansion as I wait for Ty.

The house was built in 1882 by Edgar Vernon Tate, Sr. Tate's son, Edgar Vernon Tate Jr., took his father's modestly prosperous metal fabricating business and turned it into a manufacturing powerhouse. In 1910, he married, and the young couple moved into the mansion on Silver Lane. Then tragedy struck. In 1913, Mrs. Tate gave birth to Lawrence and died in childbirth. Edgar Tate never remarried.

World War I was good for Tate's business, and in 1920 he took a grand tour of Europe buying up art and antiques from newly impoverished French and English aristocrats. I tremble with excitement anticipating what might await me inside that house. But the article deflates my expectations a bit when it implies that Tate was a philistine who might've been duped into buying low quality items at an inflated price.

What do I care? Maybe the paintings won't be worthy of the Metropolitan Museum of Art, but one landscape from the Tate mansion is bound to be more valuable than all the stuff in that gated community condo that I turned my back on. Is all that artwork still inside the mansion, or did Vareena have to sell it off bit by bit over the years?

I skip ahead to an article that references the wedding announcement of Lawrence Tate and Vareena Soares that appeared in the Palmyrton *Daily Record* and the New York *Herald Tribune* in 1942. The blurry photo shows a handsome young man in an Army Air Corps uniform and a young woman in a suit with a nipped waist. She has high cheekbones, wavy hair, and a sensuous mouth. Not conventionally beautiful, but very striking. Soares. That's a Portuguese name. I guess Lawrence Tate stepped outside the WASP tribe to marry Vareena. The article says they were married "in a small private ceremony." Was that because of the war, or because Papa Tate didn't approve?

Two weeks Later, Lawrence Tate shipped out to France.

Two months after that, his plane was shot down.

I close my laptop and gaze up at the water spot on my office ceiling. What a time that was! The whole country united in the war effort. Every man from every strata of society serving side-by-side. It's hard to imagine when all I've ever known are wars that divide. Wars that educated, wealthy young men can easily avoid. Reading Vareena and Lawrence's story so soon after my own courtship and wedding, I'm struck by how quickly they committed. Did they sense that their days of happiness were bound to be brief? Did their parents urge the young couple to wait, or were even the older generation caught up in the whirlwind of wartime drama?

I think about the weeks leading up to my wedding, when I walked around in a cloud of anxiety that this happiness couldn't last…that something was bound to come along and snatch joy from my tenuous grasp. If Sean weren't killed in the line of duty, then surely Maura, my maid of honor, would be mowed down by a truck or Dad would have a second stroke. Did Vareena feel that way when her new husband shipped off to fly missions over Germany? Or was she totally unlike me…a cock-eyed optimist, positive that her luck would hold?

Ty walks in and breaks off my morbid reverie.

"Let's roll!" His earlier low mood has dissipated. Maybe he's gotten good news from Charmaine, or maybe he's accepted that there's not much he can do about her parenting decisions. Either way, he's raring to go.

We drive toward a section of Palmyrton nicknamed Millionaire's Row. Until the mid 1800s, Palmyrton was a sleepy little farm town. Then a railroad line was built connecting it to Manhattan, and lots of industrialists built country homes here. As more wealth was drawn to the area, the town became a destination in its own right, not just an escape from the city. The houses on Millionaires Row are huge, and the ones that face Palmer Avenue are exposed to too much traffic to be desirable as homes for today's oligarchs. Most of those houses have been converted to something else: high-end offices, a banquet hall, a fancy assisted living, and the 1780 Club. But Millionaire's Row continues onto some quieter side streets. The Tate Mansion is right around the corner from these behemoths.

Ty looks up at the road sign as we make the turn. "Silver Lane?"

"Not too subtle, huh?"

We pass big, perfectly restored houses surrounded by manicured lawns as we gradually climb a hill. We clear a tall stand of hedges at the crest, and the Tate Mansion stands before us.

Ty whistles. "Two little old ladies lived all alone in there?"

The house is a rambling grey stone gothic revival, with a columned front porch and many tall, skinny windows. On the second floor, above the front door is a Juliette balcony with tall French doors. On the third floor are pointed dormers and gables trimmed with gingerbread. A three-story tower looms over the rest of the house. Thick green ivy climbs up to the roof.

Ty doesn't have to say aloud what both of us are thinking. Just a few miles away on the other side of town, entire families are crammed into one-room apartments.

Ty squints. "Kinda creepy."

The house is impressive without being beautiful. "It's definitely got an *Addam's Family* vibe going on."

"What's that little fence on top of the tower?" Ty asks.

"It's called a widow's walk. Houses on the coast of New England would have them so that women married to sailors and ship captains could keep watch for their husbands."

Ty chuckles. "I guess Vareena Tate could keep watch for when her sugar daddy got off the train from New York."

"Vareena didn't have much time to watch for her returning husband. She was a young war widow who never remarried. Her husband's grandfather built this house."

A wrought iron fence surrounds the property, with a locked gate blocking the driveway. Ty parks the car on the shoulder of Silver Lane and we get out to peer through the bars of the fence. "Vareena met Lawrence Tate at a dance for servicemen. She was an Army nurse. He was a lieutenant in training to fly for the Army Air Corps at Newark Air Field. They had a whirlwind romance and married two weeks before he shipped out. He insisted that she move into this house with his father and wait for him to come home from the war."

"She had to live alone with her father-in-law? That's kinda weird."

"Yeah, I like Sean's father fine, but I wouldn't want to live alone with him. I think that's when Maybelle came onto the scene, I guess to maintain propriety so a young woman and an older man weren't living alone together."

"So what happened to the son and the father?"

"Lawrence was shot down over Germany on his second flight. His father died a month later; I'm not sure how. And Vareena inherited the entire estate."

Ty whistles. "After only being married to the guy for two weeks?"

"Technically, they were married for two months. But they only lived as husband and wife for a week or so."

"And nobody else in the family made a play for the money?"

"If they did, I guess they didn't succeed. Lawrence was an only child."

"And after the old man died, Vareena was rarely seen. In the 1960s, she stopped going out at all."

Ty shakes his head. "Sad, you ask me. To have all that money and never go anywhere."

"Yeah—I don't know why she was a recluse. But she must have had some contact with the outside world. The house seems to be pretty well maintained." While the lawn isn't as perfectly manicured as those of the neighbors, it's not overgrown. The paint on the house's trim isn't peeling, the windows aren't dirty.

"Yeah, the outside looks pretty clean. We need to see the inside." Ty lopes along the fence, and soon disappears behind some shaggy pine trees growing next to the fence. A moment later I hear a thump and a grunt. Ty grins at me from the other side of the bars.

"C'mon. I'll help you get over."

After I boost myself on a log, haul myself over the top, and fall with no dignity whatsoever into Ty's waiting arms, we head across the lawn to the house. The houses are far enough apart that I doubt any neighbors can see us, but if we are reported, I'm pretty sure a detective's wife can talk herself out of trouble.

When we get closer to the house, we can see that the windows facing the porch are covered by thick drapes. But there's a narrow slit between the panels. Ty peers through, shining a penlight into the interior. "Got the kind of chairs and sofas nobody wanna sit on," Ty says, stepping aside so I can see. He's right: there's a Victorian settee with a high, curved back and several Eastlake parlor chairs. A couple Empire tables and a bow-front cabinet that's probably filled with figurines complete the part of the room we can see. Nowhere is there any sign of contemporary life—not a book or a magazine, or even a basket of knitting. In the Tate mansion, time stopped in 1882.

"It's like Miss Havisham's house," I murmur.

"Havisham? I don't remember that sale. Was it before I worked for you?"

"Havisham isn't a customer. She's the old lady in *Great Expectations* whose fiancé left her at the altar. She preserved the banquet room as set up for the wedding celebration. There were cobwebs across the wedding cake. Didn't you have to read that in high school English?"

Ty grimaces. "I would remember something that gross. This place doesn't look dirty."

Ty slips between a tall shrub and a bay window on the west side of the house and presses his face against the glass. "Dining room with a l-o-o-ng table and a big crystal chandelier," he reports. I squeeze in beside him and shade my eyes. I can dimly make out polished parquet floors and coffered wainscoting. Twelve ornate, tall-backed chairs surround the dining table. A huge framed mirror glints on the far wall.

"Ain't no one takin' that table home in the back of a minivan, that's for sure," Ty says.

"I wonder if Vareena and Maybelle ever ate dinner in there?" While Ty is thinking about the practicalities of selling the furniture, I'm fantasizing about the lives lived behind these grand walls.

"I bet there's a room in the back with a big screen TV, and a couple a BarcaLoungers. They probably ate mac and cheese offa tray tables every night."

"I wonder if we can see into the kitchen? Let's go around to the back."

When we turn the corner, we finally find the first sign of twenty-first century life: two folded lawn chairs with bright green webbed seats leaning against the house on an otherwise empty grand flagstone verandah.

"The poor old dears must have sat out here on nice days."

Ty looks at the chairs with disdain. "These look like the kind they sell at CVS during beach season. Couldn't they have afforded something more comfortable?"

"Vareena made the inheritance last for seventy years. I guess she was thrifty"

"Seventy years of sittin' round the house doing nothin' all day? I'd rather be a Wal-Mart greeter. At least you'd see people."

I point to a one-story addition on the left side of the house. "I bet that's the kitchen."

The curtains are wide open here, and Ty and I each take a window. "Wow! Would you look at that old stove? I bet it's the kind you have to light with a match."

While the rest of the house looks like a Victorian museum, the kitchen looks like it was state-of-the-art in the 1940s. The linoleum floor is red and yellow checkerboard. The cabinets are painted wood and there are no counters, just a rectangular wooden worktable. The refrigerator is short with rounded corners and a big chrome handle. How could that still be working in the twenty-first century?

Ty points to a pantry where the edge of something tall and avocado green is barely visible. "Looks like they hadda buy a new fridge in the eighties."

"The newest item in their house is a forty year old refrigerator. Amazing. I wonder if they were cheap, or if they just wanted to keep their world intact? Live in their own little bubble."

Ty cocks an eyebrow. "What makes you so sure they both agreed? I bet the poor maid wanted an icemaker and a microwave and a dishwasher and a Roomba."

ON THE WAY BACK TO town, I get behind the wheel.

"We doin' a job as big as the Tate Mansion, we sure as hell better get a new office assistant hired," Ty says. "Jill helpin' on the weekends not goin' to fly for this."

The departure of my sister-in-law, Adrienne, from our staff was both a relief and a trial. Adrienne, with her high-maintenance ways and her catastrophic marital problems, blew a hole in both our team spirit and our productivity. "This job at the Tate mansion definitely puts the hiring heat on, but..."

"I know—we don't want to make another mistake."

Not we. I. I was the one who made a unilateral decision to hire Adrienne. I let myself be steamrollered by Sean's family, and I never even asked Ty's opinion before I made the offer. I won't be so foolish again.

Ty pulls out his phone as I drive. "Lemme check our Monster and Indeed accounts. Maybe some new resumes have come in since Friday."

Ty scrolls in silence. Then he clicks his tongue. Then he shakes his head.

"Bad?"

"What kinda person writes her resume without any capital letters? 'Worked at Macys, lower case m, Bloomingdales, lower case b, and Nordstrom, lower case n.'"

Ty passed his developmental English class with flying colors and is now killing Comp 1. He's found proofreading religion. "If she has merchandising experience, she might be good. We just won't let her do the fliers or the ads."

Ty gives me a long, penetrating look. "She's this careless on her resume, she's not a detail-oriented person. You wouldn't let a careless dentist drill your teeth, wouldja?"

"Right. Keep looking."

While Ty continues scrolling, I agonize aloud. "I keep thinking about that woman the temp agency sent us to help with the Milhauser sale. The one who moved here from Ohio. I never should have let her get away. She had graphic design experience, knew something about antiques, followed orders without complaining."

Ty grimaces. "She was lame. How we supposed to get along with a person who won't eat sushi? That's messed up."

Ty has put his finger on the problem. Whomever we hire has to fit in. Another Man's Treasure is a team, not a soulless corporation.

"Hmmm."

"Found one?"

"She's had a lotta different jobs: hair salon scheduler, assistant manager of a make your own pottery franchise, hostess at Nonna Maria's Pizza and Pasta."

"Sounds kind of unfocused."

"Yeah…maybe, but listen to what she wrote in her cover letter. 'I would love this job so much. Nothing makes me happier than cleaning and organizing. Plus, I'm a real people person. And I'm very artistic.'" Ty squints at his phone screen. "No typos either."

"Can't hurt to interview her. Tell her to come in tomorrow. What's her name?"

"Donna Frascatelli."

CHAPTER 10

ALONE UNDER THE COVERS, I sit with my laptop propped on my knees, continuing to read about the Tate Mansion.

At the foot of my bed, Ethel lifts her head from her snooze, ears cocked. A moment later, I hear the squeak of the back door.

Sean is finally home. Ten-thirty. That's some overtime he's working on the Bostwick case.

Ethel bounds downstairs to offer her joyful greeting. No level of human enthusiasm can match a dog's, but I swing out of bed and stand at the top of the stairs in the clingy nightgown Maura bought for my shower.

When Sean reaches the landing, I throw my arms around him and pull his head down to accept my kiss, so relieved that, unlike Lawrence Tate, he hasn't plummeted to a fiery death thousands of miles away from me.

"Whoa, that's quite a welcome home." He peels me off him with a mournful expression. "I wish I wasn't so damn exhausted."

"I'll take a rain check. I just wanted you to know that I missed you."

I follow him through the bedroom and into the master bath. "Did you hear about the Parks Center inheriting the Tate Mansion?" I call out above the sound of the buzzing electric toothbrush.

He nods with toothpaste dribbling down his chin.

"Tomorrow, the Board wants to talk to me about running the estate sale."

His eyes open wide and he spits. "Fantastic!"

"I also nailed down the Armentrout job."

He gives me a thumbs up as he washes his face.

"And, on top of all that" …I pause for dramatic effect… "I did some investigative work for you."

"Aud-rey." Sean says this in the tone he uses when he's threatening to pull the car over unless his sister's kids stop squabbling.

So I quickly fill him in on the background to George Armentrout's story. "But don't worry. I didn't give away that I'm married to a cop. George thinks Loretta was despairing and hopeless. He compared it to the way his sister was when she got her terminal diagnosis."

Sean grunts as he flosses.

"And he says Loretta had no valid reason to go up to the second floor of the club."

Sean uses a wipe to clean the bathroom counter.

"And that she was obsessing over the success of the party."

Sean turns off the light and slides into bed. "Go back to sleep, Sherlock."

I'm disappointed that Sean seems to already know everything I'm telling him. "And George says it was out of character for Loretta to have planned an event like this. She was an Indian, not a Chief. Why did she get it in her head to hold that fundraiser, anyway? Did Jared pressure her to do it?"

Sean props himself on one elbow and stares at me. "Why do you say that?"

Finally, I get a reaction from him. "I don't know. George says Loretta never took the lead in that sort of thing. And you yourself said she didn't seem very interested in the people who use the Parks Center. So how did she wind up planning this fundraiser?"

"Since Jared joined the Board, he's done a thorough analysis of the Parks Center's financial position. He established fundraising goals for each of the next five years. He recruited Loretta to the Board precisely because she moves in the charity party circuit. Apparently, you can't invite rich people to these events unless they're sure they'll be mingling with all the other rich people they know. Loretta must've realized Jared was using her as bait. She'd been around the block a few times."

"So how did Jared know Loretta? What made her agree to come onto the Board if she had never volunteered at the Parks Center?"

"That's what I have to find out." Sean plugs his phone in to charge and sets his alarm.

"Well, no matter why she agreed to host the party, the turnout was great. But maybe people didn't donate as much as she expected. Loretta wouldn't have killed herself over not reaching a fundraising goal, would she?"

Sean flops onto his back and stares at the ceiling. "She didn't commit suicide."

"You know that for sure?" Now it's my turn to sit up and make eye contact.

"The autopsy revealed bruising on her upper arms." Sean reaches up and grips my biceps in demonstration. "Fingerprints."

"Someone grabbed her and pushed her over?" I switch the beside lamp back on. There's no sleeping now. "The fingerprint bruises are enough to prove it's murder?"

"Not conclusive proof. The trajectory of where she landed doesn't seem right for a jump. If she had climbed over that railing and let go, she would've dropped straight down."

"So you think she was pushed?"

"Not just pushed. I think someone picked her up and threw her. That's why she landed so far out in the foyer."

"Aaack!" I squeeze my eyes shut and hunch my shoulders. Falling is a terrible way to die, in my opinion. I get queasy when people even talk about skydiving. "So it has to be a man who killed her."

"Seems so. Although according to the autopsy, Loretta only weighed ninety-two pounds."

"Good grief! Less than the average middle-schooler."

"We told her husband this evening that we're investigating this as a murder." Sean shudders and pulls me into his arms. "I've never experienced a reaction like his."

"He was devastated?"

Sean strokes my hair. "Frederic Bostwick said a murder investigation would be *unseemly* and *tawdry*. Those were his exact words. And he asked how we could keep it out of the news. Like I was creating an enormous headache for him instead trying to find justice for his wife."

CHAPTER 11

EARLY MORNING IS NOT USUALLY a busy time at the Rosa Parks Center, but today the place is hopping. In the glass-walled main office, a cluster of people gathers around the secretary as she peers into her computer screen. High, excited voices drift out of the kitchen. "I can't believe it!" "The Lord works in mysterious ways.""Amen!"

I hesitate in the lobby, not sure where to go. Then my father appears.

"The Board is meeting in the second floor conference room. Go on up," Dad urges me.

Outside the closed conference room door, I raise my hand to knock. But loud voices within restrain me.

"You already have your mind made up," an excited male voice says.

"I don't think that's true at all," a smooth female voice answers.

"We'll hear the options. We'll take a vote." That voice, also male, sounds older than the first. There's some undecipherable murmuring.

I guess the inheritance is already causing strife. Organizations are no different than families. I go ahead and tap on the door.

The voices fall silent. A chair scrapes and the door opens. "Ah, Audrey. Come on in. We're expecting you."

Reverend Levi Jefferson puts his hand on my back and ushers me into the room. He's a tall man and projects an air of the king in his castle. "Perhaps you don't know everyone here." He addresses the group around the table. "This is Audrey Nealon. Her father, Roger, runs the chess club and her husband, Sean Coughlin, coaches our basketball team. Oh, and her stepmother,

Natalie teaches the parenting class and the knitting class." He beams at me. "Audrey's part of the Parks Center family." Then he turns to point out to me the people sitting around the table. I do know all but one, but I let him run through the introductions.

"Jared Bellack." Today he's wearing a plain gray tee shirt and jeans, and barely glances up from his two phones and wafer-thin MacBook Air. He doesn't take any more interest in me here than he did at the party when he "borrowed" Sean.

"Beverly Masterson," Levi continues.

A very attractive fortyish woman with flawless mocha skin set off perfectly by a persimmon sheath dress smiles at me. "So nice to meet you, Audrey. I hear all about you from your dad. He's such a sweetheart."

I don't normally think of my dad as a sweetheart, but I'm glad to get a friendly response from someone. I don't know what she does here at the Parks Center and don't think she was at the party. I would have remembered her.

"Iris Kallner."

A thin woman with a wild mop of silver and black hair and an armful of jangling bracelets waves to me. "Super that you were able to get here during our meeting. Thank you *so-o-o* much."

"And I'm sure you know Dennis."

Dennis Sykes is on the Board of Directors? With an intense expression on his lean face, Dennis nods in my direction. Today his dreadlocks flow freely, cascading past his shoulders. Was I wrong about him being at the party as a waiter? Was he there as a guest and just wanted to avoid me?

Of course, Loretta Bostwick should also have been at this meeting. If the rest of them are reeling from her death, they're certainly containing their grief pretty well. The inheritance seems to have pushed the fundraiser tragedy out of the spotlight.

I sit down next to Jared Bellack. He keeps tapping away on his laptop. Levi is across the table from me and leans forward. "By now you've heard all about our sudden windfall. This news couldn't have come at a better time. We are currently experiencing a slight budget shortfall that might have necessitated curtailing our programs and shortening our hours."

Dennis shifts in his chair and looks at the ceiling. "She doesn't need to know all that."

"I'm putting our situation in context." Reverend Levi continues unruffled, despite the younger man's rudeness. "Most of the value of the estate is tied up in the house and its contents. There's not that much cash."

"The old dear had been living on her father-in-law's investments for over seventy years," Beverly tells me.

"It will, of course, take quite some time to find the right buyer for that huge historic house. In the meantime—"

Jared stops typing and turns to me. "We need an assessment of what the contents of the house are worth. ASAP. And we need a plan to liquidate. How long will that take?"

"I can start cataloguing the contents tomorrow. Estimating the worth could take a couple weeks, depending on the nature of the antiques and artwork," I explain.

"Weeks? We can't wait weeks," Dennis says.

"It could be less. It's hard to say without knowing what's inside. Have you all seen it yet?" I don't want to mention that I was trespassing on the property yesterday.

"Dennis, Iris, and I just got back from the house. The executor gave us a quick tour," Levi says.

"Remarkable!" Iris peers at me over her purple and green reading glasses. "There are some *fabulous* oil paintings."

"It's like a time warp." Dennis shakes his head. "Kitchen looks like something out of an old black-and-white movie. The rest of the place is like a gloomy haunted house. I can't see how we're going to make any money off that old junk. Clear it out and get the house on the market."

Beverly and Iris exchange a glance. Then Beverly smiles at her younger colleague, the epitome of tact. She must work in human relations. "Dennis, I realize the furnishings don't appeal to a Millennial like you, but I suspect a lot of the furniture and artwork is quite valuable to collectors." She turns to me. "I don't know a lot about antiques, but the furniture is massive, and the rooms are a bit gloomy. Victorian, I guess you'd say."

"Victorian era antiques aren't the most valuable, but there's still a viable market. Sometimes it's the least likely items that become all the rage among collectors." The vision of a $4,000 hanging kerosene banquet lamp that I found in an attic pops into my mind's eye. "If it's rare, people will collect it even if it's ugly."

"Deep pockets and empty hearts rule the world," Dennis says.

"Our goal is to maximize profit in the shortest window of time," Jared barks without looking up.

"I sell the most valuable pieces to specialized dealers, and the rest goes in the general sale. Sometimes finding the right dealer can take a little time, but you earn so much more, it's worth the wait. Putting everything in the general sale is faster, but less profitable."

"Speed is what we're after," Dennis says. "The wolf's at the door."

Iris glances up from a pile of papers in a folder. "Surely the money from the fundraiser can tide us over for a few months?" She seems to direct the question at Levi, but he dodges her gaze.

"Speed matters." Jared laces his hands behind his bald head. "But we have to balance competing priorities. Dynamically actualize our revenue stream."

That means they need to make money fast. At least, I think that's what it means.

"Henry Bell can do this job, and he'll get it done fast," Dennis says.

Henry Bell? I know Henry. I've even used his services. A very nice man, but he's not an estate sale organizer. He's a clear-and-clean guy, a trash hauler. He's the man you call when you know your dead relatives have nothing but broken down, dirty junk in their homes. I shudder at the idea of the Tate Mansion's priceless contents being hauled off to the dump. But it wouldn't look good to disparage my competitor.

"I know Henry—he's a great guy. I've actually hired him to help me with some projects, but he and I don't really offer the same services."

"Henry can do what needs to be done, fast. And why shouldn't a brother get this job?" Dennis jabs a finger in Reverend Levi's direction. "How can our people ever advance to economic equality if we ourselves don't choose black-owned businesses to do the work?"

All heads swivel to Levi to see how he'll respond. I feel my big job slipping away to Henry Bell. But Levi hesitates. He glances at Jared as if to take direction from him.

"This is a business decision," Jared says. "We need to do what's best for the Parks Center."

I see an opportunity for compromise. "It's a big job. I'd be happy to collaborate with Henry."

"See, she's trying to cut him out of the action," Dennis leaps up. "Collaborate? That means she takes the lion's share and leaves him with the pickins'."

I'm so stunned by this accusation I can't even defend myself.

"Dennis, that's enough." Beverly's attractive face grows stern. "Audrey was kind enough to come in here today to make a presentation. There's no call to be insulting."

"Tyshaun Griggs works with Audrey," Levi says. "She gave him a job right after he was released from prison. Not everyone would do that."

Dennis isn't mollified. "Hired him to be her nigger--haul boxes and drive her around," he grumbles.

The N-word falls like a bomb in the room. Jared even stops typing.

Now I find my voice. "I did originally hire Ty to do the heavy lifting. But in the past two years he's learned a tremendous amount about the estate sale business. He's attending Palmer Community College—studying art history and business administration. I've promoted him and he now runs some of our smaller sales single-handedly."

Dennis's eyes narrow. "Is he a partner? Does he have an equity stake in the business?"

"Well, no…but—"

"That's my point. The capitalist overlords conspire to keep the workers from gaining ground. Ty's just a flunky. She expects him to be grateful for the crumbs she tosses him."

Capitalist overlord? Crumb-tosser? Me?

"Let's not involve Audrey in a philosophical discussion." Levi rises from the table and moves to escort me to the door. "Thank you so much for coming in, Audrey. We'll let you know the Board's decision in a day or two."

After I'm out the door, I stand in the hall for a moment. Through the door, I hear the rise and fall of voices. One is higher pitched than the others.

"Dennis has made a good point. What's the point of being an organization committed to overcoming the results of discrimination if we ourselves are practicing discrimination?" That's Iris. I can picture her big, round eyes blinking above her funky glasses. "We have to *live* our values."

I sigh. Can't argue with that.

I went into this interview so positive that I would get the job. But it looks like this one might be going to Henry Bell.

CHAPTER 12

AS I WALK DOWN STAIRS, I can see my father pacing back and forth beneath the mural of Rosa Parks. Somehow, I feel like I've let him down by not nailing this job on the spot. Like the time he came to see me in the fifth grade class play and I froze on stage and forgot my lines.

Dad pauses in his pacing, looks up and catches my eye. His face brightens, then his smile collapses. He must have read defeat in my face.

We meet in the middle of the lobby.

"What happened?"

I glance around and grab his elbow. "Not here. Let's take a walk."

As we stroll away from the Parks Center, I recreate the meeting for my father. At the end of the block, he steers me into a small playground with a rusty swing set and a third-degree burn-inducing metal slide. We sit on a park bench with a missing slat and watch two teenage boys playing a spirited game of one-on-one around a netless basketball hoop.

"I'm sorry I didn't prepare you better," Dad says. "I didn't realize Dennis and the others would be there. I thought you'd be talking to Jared and Levi only."

"Why does Dennis hate me so much? What have I ever done to him?"

"He doesn't hate you." Dad pats my knee. "He hates Jared. And he's mad at Levi for not standing up to Jared. You were caught in the crosscurrents."

"More like a rip-tide. I'm sorry I screwed this up, Dad. I know I could bring in more revenue for the Parks Center than Henry

Bell, but I wasn't in a position to criticize him."

Dad tilts his head back and gazes into the leafy branches shading our bench. "Don't be so sure you've lost the job. There's a lot going on at the Parks Center these days. The Board is in a state of flux, and Loretta's death has upset some alliances. Jared has uncovered...issues...with Levi's management." Dad raises his hand. "Nothing illegal, mind you--but no one has ever challenged Levi or the small group of donors that he's always solicited from. As the founder's son, Levi has Executive Director for Life status. Lots of people think it's time for a change, but no one agrees on what the change should be. Jared says we need to go after the deep pockets--do more fundraising from corporations, wealthy individuals, and foundation grants."

Dad gestures toward the low-rise apartment buildings and small brick and frame houses surrounding the park. "But Dennis says every time we take money from a corporation or a rich donor like Jared, we sell another little piece of our soul. Dennis thinks it would be better to scale back our programs a bit and ask the community we serve to take more ownership, get them involved in both the planning and the fundraising. Get one thousand hundred-dollar donations instead of one giant hundred-thousand-dollar donation."

I follow the direction of my father's pointing arm. These houses have held generations of working class Palmyrton families: Irish and Italian, African American, and now, Hispanic. They're not fancy, but they display a brave optimism: brightly painted elf and frog garden ornaments, American flags, carefully staked tomato plants. Are there a thousand people here with a hundred bucks to spare? "Both have some valid points. What do you think should happen?"

"I honestly don't know." Dad turns to face me. "Money is power, Audrey. Whoever brings in the money has outsize influence in how it's spent."

"But the bottom line is helping the kids. Doesn't everyone agree on that?"

Dad answers with a bitter laugh. "Look at how the computers Jared donated have turned into a bone of contention. Jared insists they can only be used to teach coding. If kids agree to take the coding class, they get extra access to the computers for other projects. Jared sees his approach as motivational. Many of us see it as counterproductive coercion. And while the adults squabble, the computers stand idle."

"When they could be used for your Math Explorers."

One of the boys on the basketball court takes a desperate shot and the ball bounces off the cracked asphalt and rolls to a stop before me. I pick it up and return it with a poorly aimed, math-nerd throw.

Dad watches the game resume. "Those boys are out here all day long in the summer. Dennis agrees with me that they need more than nonstop sports to occupy them. He loves my Math Explorers idea. He's all in favor of raising the bar of expectations for these kids. In fact, he said he'd help me recruit—show these guys the connection between free throw probabilities and higher forms of statistics."

Dad's voice rises a few notes in excitement. "These kids need to be encouraged and enticed, not threatened. I could get them hooked on the beauty of math. I know I could."

"If Dennis likes your plan, why is he so dead set against me? Why wouldn't he want to raise as much money as possible from the Tate Mansion sale? Seems like that money is neutral, not controlled by Jared or Levi or anyone else."

"Dennis has so many competing passions, it's hard to predict which one will come out ahead on any given day." Dad squeezes my hand. "Neither you nor I likes to accept circumstances that are beyond our control, Audrey. But this time, I think we have no choice."

CHAPTER 13

I'M SO DEJECTED AFTER MY interview that I can't face returning to the office to sit and stare at my computer. It's a beautiful day.Why not take Ethel to the dog park? That will cheer me up.

When I arrive home in the middle of the day and speak aloud the sacred words "dog park," Ethel goes ballistic. She tears around the kitchen twice, then flings herself at the door to the garage. When I let her out, she runs to her toy bin to grab a tennis ball. Tell me dogs don't speak English!

The Palmyrton dog park has two fenced areas: one for small dogs, where shih-tzus and cockapoos can frolic, and one for large dogs. Ethel is too big for the small dog area, not because she would hurt them—she loves everyone—but because those Yorkies and Pugs get aggressive when they meet taller dogs. But sometimes the Labs and Boxers in the big dog park bowl my slender Ethel over with their enthusiasm. Today, I'm happy to see there are only a goofy, good-natured Labradoodle and a sleek, high-speed mutt who must be part Greyhound. Ethel bounds joyfully to join them, and they all run laps around the park while I sit on a bench and make doggy small talk with the other owners. Eventually, the Grehound-mix goes home and the Labradoodle, who's still a puppy, collapses at his owner's feet. Ethel jumps on the guy as if to say, "Make your dog get up again." He laughs and pets Ethel until I pull out her ball. Now her eyes are on me, and she demands that I throw it.

Although Sean's coaching has helped me improve my form, I still throw like a math-nerd. Ethel brings the ball back and tilts her head quizzically. "I know. I'm sorry I can't make it go as far as Sean can." I throw a few more times, but on the last throw, a beautiful brown and white dog appears out of nowhere and scoops up the ball right from under Ethel's surprised nose.

"Rex!" a male voice booms. "Release!"

Rex immediately drops the ball and returns to his master.

Impressed by this obedience, I turn to wave at the owner. He's standing by the gate, looking straight ahead. I see him in profile: silver hair, jutting chin, long nose, wearing khakis and a polo shirt. He looks familiar. Maybe I've seen him here before. Then I see his dogs: two beautiful brown and white English Pointers. One sees a bird, and they both point their noses and tails and lift one paw. They look just like—just like a painting! I've seen those dogs before, in the painting the pet portrait artist showed me at the fundraiser. They're Loretta Bostwick's dogs. And yes, that man is Frederic Bostwick, the guy I briefly gave directions to at the Parks Center.

I hope he won't recognize me. I don't really want to offer awkward condolences to someone I'm barely acquainted with. He nods in my direction, and I nod back. I throw the ball for Ethel again, but she's lost interest. She'd rather run with the Pointers. They're chasing birds, but don't seem to mind that Ethel tags along. Then Mr. Bostwick whistles for them, and they immediately turn and go to him.

Ethel follows.

Rex and Cleo trot up and sit at their master's feet.

Ethel charges behind them and jumps on Frederic Bostwick with her muddy paws.

Oh, crap!

"Ethel, no! Down!"

Obedience school dropout that she is, Ethel doesn't pay me one iota of attention. Frederic Bostwick scowls at her and steps back, brushing dirt off his immaculate pants.

I arrive by his side, panting, and grab Ethel's collar. "I'm so sorry. She's not as well trained as your dogs."

Mr. Bostwick frowns at Ethel. "It's in the breeding. Pointers are bred to point out birds in the field."

Breeding schmeeding. "Ethel's a shelter dog. I guess you could say she's bred to show gratitude."

Frederic Bostwick's face changes. The indifference melts away, and I see a flash of true pain. "Maybe my son should spend some time in a shelter."

There's no response I can offer to that. Bostwick pivots and snaps his fingers at the dogs. They trot beside him to the gate while I hang on to a straining Ethel.

I bury my nose in her sweet, musty fur. "Forget about them, Ethel. They're not our type."

THAT NIGHT IN BED AS I wait for Sean to get home, I continue fantasizing about the Tate Mansion. I've allowed my father to convince me that all is not lost. Dennis might have the loudest voice in the room, but clearly Jared holds plenty of influence. Maybe I'll get inside that house yet.

My mind races with fantasies of the lives lived in the Tate Mansion. The articles on the internet have delivered the bare biographical facts. What happened after Lawrence Tate's death that caused Vareena to become a recluse? She was hardly the only heartbroken war widow in America. And why was Maybelle Simpson, her maid, willing to entomb herself in that house too? They were both so young—only in their twenties. Why wouldn't Vareena have taken the money and started over somewhere else? Why wouldn't Maybelle have found a different job, gotten married, and had kids?"

I don't want to let the possibility of my own widowhood even enter my mind. So I let an entirely different thought take hold. What if Vareena wasn't entirely heartbroken by her young husband's death? What if she discovered something about herself living alone in that big house with Maybelle? Maybe they weren't rich housewife and servant.

Maybe they were lovers.

I'm really letting my imagination run wild. Interracial lesbians in the 1950s! That would be enough to keep anyone in hiding. But if they had plenty of money and no family, why stay in Palmyrton? Why not run off to Paris or Greenwich Village and live like bohemians?

This is crazy! I glance at the clock. Nearly eleven. Why is Sean so late? Normally, I hate the idea of checking up on my husband, but thinking of the widow Vareena, whose marriage lasted only months, makes me paranoid. I reach for my phone and text.

"You OK?"

"Yeah. Home soon."

Not much information, but he's alive. I tell myself to go to sleep.

But my fevered brain keeps churning. I'm dying to explore that house and find out more about the women who lived there. I long to sell those antiques and earn a pile of fast money for the Parks Center so my dad can start his Math Explorers. I want to pay off all my bills, pump up my savings, and give Ty the bonus he deserves.

I really want that job.

On the nightstand, my phone pings the arrival of an email. I'll never get any sleep if I keep messing with my phone. But I reach out and click.

Sender: Levi Jefferson

Subject line: Tate Mansion.

Trembling, I open the email.

Audrey,

Thank you so much for taking the time to discuss this project with us. Unfortunately, the Board has voted to award the project to Henry Bell. He has informed us that he is not interested in collaborating with you but rather with an antiques dealer with whom he has a professional relationship.

Regards,

Levi Jefferson

CHAPTER 14

GROGGY FROM MY SLEEPLESS NIGHT, I stumble into the office clutching an extra large coffee from Caffeine Planet to wake me up and a cinnamon donut to console me. I don't know what time Sean finally got home last night. I guess I finally dozed off, and he was dead to the world this morning when I left the house.

I haven't yet called my father.

So no one knows my bitter news but me. The more I stew, the more agitated I get. I'm not angry that the Board gave the job to Henry Bell, but I am rather wounded that Henry specifically declined to collaborate with me. I always thought we got along well. I wrack my brain trying to recall some incident when I might have offended him, but come up blank. Who is this other antiques dealer he has a professional relationship with? I can't imagine.

I'm still fuming as Ty walks into the office. I decide not to tell him the news right now. No point in getting more agitated before we conduct this job interview.

Without consulting each other, Ty and I have both gotten dressed up for our appointment.

By dressed up, I mean I'm not wearing jeans with torn-out knees and Ty's not wearing his Lil Uzi Vert t-shirt.

Ty looks me over. "You look good in those pants," he says about the black straight-leg slacks that Maura made me spend seventy bucks on at Banana Republic.

"I've never seen that shirt before," I say of his pale yellow button-down with a subtle blue stripe. "It's a good color for you."

"I worked the outlet mall with Marcus last week. That man

surely can shop." Ty looks around the office, which has become cluttered with boxes and piles of paperwork since Adrienne's departure. "I shoulda cleared some of this shit out. Too late now."

I straighten the papers on my desk into neat stacks. "She's supposed to be impressing us." I'm feeling a little defensive. Anyone who'd be willing to work in our chaotic office probably isn't the kind of person we want to hire. But the Armentrout sale, the job I landed through networking at the 1780 Club fundraiser, is coming up this weekend and we need help badly. "Let's review the key questions we want to ask."

Ty ticks off points on his long fingers. "Gotta be willing to work weekends. Gotta be willing to get her hands dirty. Gotta know how to make crap look sweet. Can't be a bossy-ass bitch."

I'm pretty sure the last requirement is the most important. For both of us.

WE HEAR A CAR DOOR slam outside. "That's her. Now listen—no matter how much we like her, we're not offering her the job on the spot. We need to talk it over, then call her back. Agreed?"

"Gotcha."

Moments later, Donna Frascatelli makes her entrance.

There's really no other way to describe it. She raps on the door, but before Ty can answer, she's come in preceded by a strong scent that's both familiar and out-of-place.

"Hi! I found you! I was worried. I've never been on this street before. Isn't that crazy? I've lived my whole life in Florham Park, not ten miles away, and I've never been to this part of Palmyrton. Usually when we come here it's to go to Trattoria Rafaele, that restaurant on Elm. I love that place—so classy. My husband said I'd have trouble parking, but I found a spot right outside. Oh, I'm talking too much as usual. You must be Audrey. I'm Donna."

She pumps my hand, and during that tsunami of words, I've pinpointed the scent. Hairspray. Lots of it. Donna has a mane of black wavy hair that's been glued into a towering crown around her head. She's wearing skin-tight black jeans, stiletto silver heels, and a black, hot pink, and silver knit top that reveals her impressive cleavage. She offers a big smile with shiny, hot pink lips while batting eyelashes as thick as wooly bear caterpillars.

I cast a nervous glance at Ty, who is stunned into silence.

A Jersey Girl. A living, breathing stereotype.

"Uhm...thanks for coming in. This is my assistant, Ty Griggs."

"Hi! You remind me of someone. Now who is it? Oh, I know—that actor, the handsome one who got the award for that movie that everyone was talking about. But I haven't seen it because my husband hates going to the movies, so I gotta wait until it's on Netflix or HBO or something. But you look like him. I bet you hear that all the time, right?"

I jump in before Ty can utter the "What the hell you talkin' about?" that I can practically see resting on his lips. "Let me tell you a little bit about the position."

Donna droops her head. "I'm sorry. I know I'm talking too much. I do that when I'm nervous."

At least she's got some self-awareness. "Oh, no need to be nervous around us—Ty and I are pretty mellow." I explain our business and how she'd be responsible for the phones, email, and helping to promote the sales.

Before I can continue, Donna jumps in. "I checked out your website. It's very nice, but I could help you make it better... simplify the mailing list sign-up form, update your blog more often, improve your SEO."

"You know HTML?" Ty asks.

"I'm not an expert or anything, but I picked up a little when I managed the hair salon, and then my nephew Frankie—he goes to New Jersey Institute of Technology—showed me some more stuff."

Ty catches my eye and gives an approving nod. Working on the website is a chore that never seems to get done.

"Then when the sales come, we *all* work—set up, sell all day, tear down," Ty explains. "Just want to be clear on this—you gotta work weekends in this job. Your kids got soccer and Little League, you're gonna have to miss those games."

Donna's face loses some of its sparkle. "That's not a problem. I don't have kids. My husband, he's got two boys from his first marriage. But they're older. And they don't want me coming to their stuff. Their mother does that."

I look at the hot pink talons at the end of her fingers. "You know, this job involves some physical labor. Lots of packing." I hold out my own hands, with their short-clipped nails. "You're not going to be able to open and close boxes with that manicure."

"Oh, these?" She snaps off one pink claw. "They're fake. I just put them on for the interview." She shows me the stubby natural nail beneath. "I'm not afraid to get my hands dirty. Like I said in my letter, I lo-o-o-ve to clean. You hire me, and I'll have this office all fixed up in no time. No more cobwebs."

I follow the direction of her gaze and realize there is a significant gray cluster in the ceiling corner over my desk. "Oops, I never noticed that," I mutter.

"I saw it soon as I came in. My husband says I've got radar vision for dirt. My mom and my sisters have it too. All the Caponetti girls do. Genetic, I guess."

"You get a chance to see plenty of dirt in this bizness," Ty warns. "Dust, bugs, squirrels—every kind o' crusty."

"But lots of beautiful things too," I interject, suddenly worried that Ty's honesty will scare her off. I'm warming up to Donna. "Artwork, antiques, collectibles, jewelry."

"That sounds so cool. I read about the sale you did in the fancy house in Melton. I would love to go inside houses like that. You know, just to see how the people live."

Of course, that's exactly what drew me to the estate sale business: the chance to peek behind the curtain. Now, Donna is really growing on me.

"We lookin' for someone who's in this for the long-haul, know what I'm sayin'?" Ty lifts Donna's resume and turns it towards her. "You had an awful lotta different jobs the past few years."

Donna's dark eyes glance back and forth under those ridiculous fake eyelashes. "I…uhm…I know that doesn't look good. But the one company, the pottery place, went out of business."

Ty stays silent but keeps his gaze fixed on her.

Donna looks at me, but Ty is right—she needs to explain that job-hopping.

"And the salon, well, I was filling in for a girl on maternity leave. I was hoping she might not come back, but she did, so then I went to the restaurant, but that was all nights and I'm not really a night-owl, you know and so…."

Her voice drifts off and I notice her upper lip is trembling. "I dropped out of college when I was nineteen. My grades were good, but I missed home too much. I thought I'd go back, but then I got married and well…." Donna shakes her head. "I didn't realize…I thought being a hard worker was enough." She reaches across the desk and grabs my hand. Her fingers, under those spiky nails, are freezing cold. "Please. I really want this job. I'll work so hard for you. You won't regret it. I promise."

I feel myself caving. Gingerly, I slide my hand away.

Ty steps in before I can say anything rash. "We got a couple more people to interview. We'll call you by the end of the week."

Donna stands. "It's all right," she says softly. "I understand."

"Bye," she whispers as she heads for the door. "Good luck with your sales."

Ty jumps up. "Hey, I'm not messin' with ya. We really will call back."

She smiles faintly and slips out the door.

Ty stands at the window peering out the tiny gap between the shade and the frame.

"What did you think?" I ask.

"She talks too much."

"Definitely. And who dresses like that for a job interview?"

"A ho. But…."

"I kinda like her," I say.

"Yeah. There's somethin'…. Oh, no!"

"What?"

"She out there next to her car, cryin'."

I push Ty away to look. Sure enough, Donna Frascatelli's silver and pink shoulders are shaking and she's rooting through her huge purse. Now she's mopping her eyes with a tissue.

Ty lopes to the door and flings it open. "Hey! You like sushi?"

Donna turns her tear-streaked face towards us. "I love it."

"Okay, then. You hired."

CHAPTER 15

I'M FEELING GOOD ABOUT OUR decision to hire Donna Frascatelli.

Yesterday was rough, what with having to tell Ty and my father and Sean about losing the Tate job. The men in my life had wildly different reactions.

Ty was defiant. "We be fine. Just gotta work double-hard on settin' up the new online auction deal."

Dad was rational. "The Board has made an unwise decision to put politics above financial solvency."

But Sean's response to the news threw me. He wasn't upset at all. To say he was pleased would be going too far, but he did seem relieved. "That job would've been nothing but trouble. You don't need that aggravation. Focus on the Armentrout gig."

So today is the first day of our newly reformed Another Man's Treasure team. Donna was available to start work immediately, and here she is right on time bearing her Dustbuster, her microfiber cleaning cloths, and a spray-bottle of distilled vinegar and water.

"It's my secret weapon," she informs us.

Ty had warned her that setting up a sale is hard, dirty work, so the high heels and long nails of the job interview are gone. Today her curly hair is pulled back in a scrunchie and her feet are shod in Keds. Without the heavy make-up, she looks much younger. She's probably no older than I am.

While Ty and I assemble the supplies we'll need to set up Birdie Armentrout's sale, Donna bustles around the office sucking up cobwebs and sanitizing desktops. "I hope you don't mind," she says as she cleans under my calculator. "I can't think straight around dust."

On the ride to Melton, Donna seems much less nervous than during her interview. She asks me about my husband, and by the time we arrive, she knows all about Sean, Ethel, my father, and Adrienne. As we emerge from the car, I realize all I've learned about her is that her husband's name is Anthony.

When we enter Birdie Armentrout's house, Donna creeps around wide-eyed as a kid in Cinderella's castle. "Wow! Look at these gorgeous drapes. And these sweet little lamps with the fringe-y shades." She plunks out a few notes of Chopsticks on the baby grand piano. "This is so pretty, so classy." She spins around to face me. "Are we going to sell all this? Doesn't she have a family who wants to keep her pretty things?"

"Never married, no kids. Only a divorced brother with a small condo. He's taken the few things he wants to keep. Everything here goes in the sale."

"She has no sisters? No nieces and nephews? No cousins?" Donna sounds as incredulous as a flat-earther studying a globe.

"Two nephews, but they don't live in New Jersey."

Donna's face crumples, and for a moment I think she's actually going to cry. "Wow, that would never happen to me. By the time the Frascatellis and the Caponettis go through my stuff, there won't even be a bone left in the fridge."

"Well, good thing not everyone's like your people or we wouldn't have a bizness. C'mon—you and me are workin' on the kitchen. Audge'll do the pricing in here." Ty herds Donna toward the back of the house, and I get busy.

Five hundred dollars for the impeccably clean matching loveseats, one-fifty for the large coffee table. Fifty for the lamps? A little high, but we can lower it early on Saturday morning if there isn't even a nibble on Friday. As I work I can't help but fantasize about the Tate mansion. I would be pricing items there in the thousands, not the hundreds—of that, I'm sure. But even more than the monetary value, I regret missing the chance to glimpse into such odd lives: two women living totally out-of-touch with the twenty-first century. How did they spend their days? Were they happy, or at least, content? Did they relish their self-imposed exile?

One thing I'm certain of: I would be able to get to know them through what they left behind.

Already, I'm getting to know Birdie Armentrout. She was fussy, I'm sure. There isn't a stain or a spot or a snag anywhere in this room. Certainly, the possessions of the meticulous are easier to sell. But there's something sad about them too. No one ever got so animated telling a story here that he knocked over a wine glass. No pet ever pressed his nose against the window, eager to welcome home his mistress. No child ever trampled Cheerios into this carpet. Birdie's life was clean and tidy but not very lively, I think.

Still, she had her passion for gardening and birds, and that shines through, giving me a little glimpse of her soul.

I finish in the living room and move into the dining room, where floral tea services and bird-decorated dessert plates await me in great quantities. As I catalog the contents of the breakfront, I hear Ty and Donna talking in the kitchen.

"Oooo, look at this—there's a back staircase. I've only ever seen that on TV," Donna says.

"Yeah, these old houses have 'em sometimes. Keep the maids and the kids where no one can see them."

I hear the sounds of cabinets banging.

"Look at all this nice stuff from Crate and Barrel and Williams-Sonoma. It's like she has the whole showroom in here," Donna says.

"Mmmm. Them big white bowls don't bring much—maybe five bucks." I hear Ty clattering through the pots and pans.

"What are you looking for?" Donna asks.

"Pyrex, Fiesta Ware, Jadeite. Too bad she don't seem to have none of it. All new stuff."

"What's wrong with new? I think—"

"Ah! Score! Stashed away over the fridge."

"That? That looks like the dish my nonna uses to make the sweet potatoes no one wants to eat on Thanksgiving."

"Pyrex. Aqua Snowflake pattern." I hear the triumph in Ty's voice. "Not quite as good as the Desert Dawn pink daisy promotional pattern, but we'll take it. An easy five hundred bucks right there."

"Are you kidding me? Five hundred for that?"

"Mad whack, huh? Collectors will give anything to get their

fix. This bowl is crack to them."

Ty's right about that. The collectibles crowd will come to blows over a Holt Howard Cozy Kitten teapot or Eisenhower-era framed gravel art. Unfortunately, Birdie was too straight-laced to own anything intentionally funky and too neat to have saved stuff that's become funky with time.

I'm betting that one Pyrex bowl may be the extent of our collectibles here.

We all keep working for the next hour. When I finish in the dining room, I check in with Ty and Donna in the kitchen. All the cabinets are now empty.

"You good at making shit look fresh?" Ty asks Donna.

"Sure."

"Okay, help me move this table. Then I'll give you all the best stuff and you arrange it on there."

The table is solid English pine, big enough to seat eight. Ty lifts his end and I move to help Donna with the other end. But with a slight grunt, she picks it up and they carry it ten feet to the far wall of the kitchen.

Ty nods with satisfaction. "You pretty buff, girl. You been liftin'?"

"I bench press two-fifty."

Donna has peeled off her long-sleeved Jets t-shirt. Her toned arms are nicely displayed in a sleeveless dri-fit.

"How'd you get that bruise?" Ty asks.

A large purple spot is fading to mottled yellow and green at the top of Donna's arm. She glances down as if she's forgotten it's there. "Oh, that—I crashed into something in my garage. We need a better light in there."

My mind flashes briefly to the fingerprint bruises on Loretta's spindly arms, and I shiver. Donna looks a lot stronger, like she'd put up a good fight if someone tried to toss her off a balcony.

"I'm going to head upstairs. Send Donna up when she's done with the display here, Ty."

On the second floor, I open Birdie's walk-in closet and let out a low whistle. The clothes are all hung on velvet hangers facing the same direction. The blouses are grouped together by color, as are the slacks. Dresses and suits hang on the other side. It dawns on me that I don't know where, or if, Birdie worked. She must have, before her memory started to slip—even a rich garden club patron wouldn't need this many suits. And the shoes! All in their original boxes.

"Wow, that's one neat closet!" Donna offers her approval as she walks into the master bedroom.

"Check the other bedrooms for clothes, jewelry and small decorations. I want to move everything that could be easily shop-lifted into this room, and just leave furniture in the others."

"Your customers steal stuff?" Donna rubs a smudge off the light switch plate. "I thought they were all rich."

"They're definitely not all rich. But even if they were, I'd still have to worry about thieves. I once had a woman all decked out in Lily Pulitzer stash a $500 pair of Baccarat crystal candle sticks in her Louis Vuitton tote bag and head right for the door. When I confronted her, she was cool as a cucumber. Said she'd just put them in there to check if they would fit because she didn't want to buy anything she couldn't carry."

"Did she buy them?"

"Nope. Looked me right in the eye, handed them back, and said they were a little too bulky."

"Geez, she probably could've afforded to buy them brand new at Tiffany."

"Exactly. For some people, it's the thrill of doing something illegal. And some are just trying to game the system, no matter what the system is. Rich people do it and poor people do it, but rich people usually know how to steal the very best."

Donna cocks her head, reevaluating her first impression of me, maybe.

"There are good people at every level too. I didn't mean to sound so cynical."

She smiles. "It's like my Uncle Vinny always says. You could be nice to people without being a chump, right?"

"Exactly." I need to work on following the Uncle Vinny credo.

Donna and I move into the smallest bedroom. Birdie has it furnished as a home office, and George has assured me he's taken all her personal papers and financial documents.

Apart from the desk, the chair, and a lamp, the room contains only a metal filing cabinet in the closet. We pick it up easily, so it must be empty.

"Check all the drawers," I tell Donna. "Just in case George missed something."

She bangs the first three open and closed. "This bottom one is stuck." Donna gets down on her knees. "I think something's wedged between the drawers."

"See if you can get it out. No one will buy a broken filing cabinet."

While she works on it, I price the office gadgets.

"Ooof!" Donna gives the drawer a hard jiggle, and it shoots open. She falls back on her butt, laughing.

"Okay, I fixed it! Told you I was handy."

Inside the drawer, a slightly ripped file folder dangles open, spewing its papers. Donna and I scoop them up.

"Hey, look at this diagram."

I take it from Donna. "Huh—it's a family tree. George said his sister was an amateur genealogist. This must be her research." I read aloud the label on the folder: "Armentrout Family, 1730-2017."

CHAPTER 16

"YO, AUDGE—WE BREAKIN' FOR LUNCH?"

Donna's eyes light up. "I'm starving!"

We clatter down the stairs. I put the genealogy folder in my bag so I don't lose it. I'll call George about it later.

I decide to stay behind and make some phone calls, and send the two of them off to rustle up lunch. The weather is perfect and Birdie's garden is so beautiful, I decide to set myself up back there to work and await the arrival of food.

With my feet up on a chaise lounge and the butterflies and hummingbirds flitting through the flowers, I feel my eyelids drooping as I send emails to clients about significant items in this sale that might interest them. Then the phone slips from my fingers into my lap, and I succumb to the warm sun and the gentle breeze.

I'm not asleep. Not really. Just drifting…where shall Sean and I go on a winter vacation….how should we celebrate Maura's birthday….what….

Music. Piano music. How nice…..

I jolt up.

Piano music? Why is there piano music coming from inside Birdie's house?

I recognize the tune. "Moonlight Sonata." There's a slight break in the notes, then a re-do. Now I'm on my feet. That's not the radio. Someone is in Birdie's living room playing the baby grand. I sure as hell know it's not Ty, and somehow I doubt Donna's playing by ear extends to Beethoven.

I get up and press my nose against the French doors that lead from the patio to the dining room. Beyond the dining room, I can just barely discern the outline of a tall man at the piano in the living room, his hands moving effortlessly up and down the keyboard, his head bobbing to the rhythm. Did we leave the front door unlocked? Or does this guy have a key to Birdie's house?

That's a little creepy. Who walks into an empty house in the middle of the day and starts playing classical music? On the other hand, I reassure myself a professional thief wouldn't announce himself with a sonata.

I check my watch—Ty and Donna should be back any minute now. I should wait for back-up before I investigate, but curiosity pulls me toward the house. I reenter through the kitchen and make my way toward the foyer. As I pass the front door, I see that the deadbolt is in the locked position. He didn't come in that way. If I stand by the doorway from the foyer into the living room, the pianist's back will be toward me. I can see if I recognize him.

He's at a fortissimo part of the sonata, transported by the music. I could stomp and knock over a lamp, but I doubt he'd notice me.

His head swivels and bobs subconsciously. He pounds a final dramatic note and lifts his head. I can see his face clearly reflected in the mirror on the other side of the piano.

I've never met this man, but I'm quite sure who he is.

Dark blond hair, fine, chiseled features, long thin arms and legs. The resemblance to Loretta Bostwick is striking.

I applaud.

He spins around. "That's not the end."

"How gauche of me to applaud between movements. I was a little surprised to find a strange man at the keyboard."

"I know the owner." He plays a few practice chords. "She and my mother were friends."

"I'm Audrey Nealon. I'm organizing the estate sale." I approach with my hand outstretched. "And you are...?"

"Crawford Bostwick."

I was right. This is Loretta's problem-child son. "I knew your mother. I'm very sorry for your loss."

Now that I'm looking at him close-up, I notice one clear dissimilarity to his mother. Where Loretta was tightly strung and intense, Crawford is as languid as a summer day. Is that why George said Crawford was a disappointment to his father—because he's a laid back musician instead of a hard-charging businessman?

"Well, it's certainly a surprise. The police have the crazy idea that someone killed her." He shakes his head. "They don't know my mother very well."

What? She wouldn't allow herself to be tangled up in anything so tacky as murder? Before I can get him to elaborate on that, he turns his attention back to the piano. "This is a fine instrument. It could use a little tuning, but it's got marvelous tone. What will happen to it?"

"I have a few instrument dealers coming to look at it during the sale. Are you interested in buying it?"

Crawford snorts. "My current abode would not accommodate a baby grand. I couldn't get a cheesy electronic keyboard in there. Not that I'd want one."

So, he must not live with his parents. "What brings you here today?"

"I needed a place to practice. I'm persona non grata at Heatherington."

"Heatherington?"

"Ancestral home of the Bostwicks." Crawford speaks with an ironic smirk, then turns to face the keyboard again. "Don't let me distract you from whatever you're doing."

Man, I wish I could learn to dismiss people like that! What a life skill. But I'm not so easily intimidated.

"How did you get in here? Do you have George Armentrout's permission to use this piano?"

"Georgie? Oh, he won't mind. He's such a pussycat. Not like my old man." He suddenly spins back around on the piano bench. "Say, do you think I could stay here? Then I could practice every day. The house isn't sold yet, is it?"

"You mean, *live* here?" I'm so stunned by the turn the conversation has taken that I let it pass that he hasn't answered how he gained entry to the house. Is this guy homeless?

Crawford gives a vague wave of his elegant hand. "Oh, you know—just camp out for a bit. Until all this nonsense blows over. It would beat couch-surfing."

What nonsense? Surely that's not how he characterizes his mother's death? But Crawford acts like I'm fully up-to-date on all his issues. If there's one thing my work has taught me--the rich really are different. He turns his back on me and picks up the next movement of the sonata.

I retreat to the kitchen to call George. This is above my pay grade. Way above.

Just as I enter, Ty and Donna come in the back door bearing take-out.

"Who's playing the piano?" Donna asks.

I give them an update. Ty's eyes narrow, and he steps toward the foyer. "You want me to go throw him out?"

I catch the hem of his t-shirt as he passes. "Let's not be hasty. His mother was George's friend, and Birdie's too, I guess. In fact, George says they're distantly related. I'll call him to find out what to do."

When I call George and explain what's going on, he's immediately distraught. "Oh, dear! Oh, no—that won't do. That won't do at all."

"I can have my assistant escort Crawford out, if that's what you want. I just wanted to check first."

I hear a sharp intake of breath. "Crawford might prove difficult. I owe it to Loretta to do what I can to help her son. Just ignore him until I get there."

SO WE SIT DOWN AND eat our lunch listening to Crawford roll through some Chopin and Mozart, and await the arrival of George Armentrout.

"He sure does play great," Donna says. "Do you think he performs at Carnegie Hall and places like that?"

"If he played on stage, he wouldn't be lookin' for a crib to crash in." Ty collects our trash. His hand rests above Donna's Styrofoam sandwich clamshell. "You gonna eat that pickle?"

Donna looks at it longingly, but starts to rise. "Well…if lunch is over, I'll get back to work."

"Sit down." I slide her pickle back to her. "Ty eats too fast."

"You don't eat fast at Rahway, some land shark takes your food." The casual reference to his stint in Rahway State Prison slips out of Ty. I'm surprised. Has he already told Donna his story of running with a bad teenage crowd and driving the getaway car for an impromptu convenience store robbery? I know he likes her, but it's not like him to open up to strangers so quickly.

I lift up my big glass of ice tea and peek at Donna over the rim. Either the remark has sailed over her head, or she knows so much about Ty's life in prison that she feels no need to ask a question.

She catches my eye and grins. "Hey, guess what? We saw your husband on our way back here. He's cute!"

"You saw Sean in Melton? What did he say he was doing here?"

"We didn't talk to him," Ty explains. "We just drove by and saw him standing in the driveway of some big-ass house. And then a dude came out and got in a black limo and they all drove away."

I wonder what he's doing in Melton? Maybe the Loretta Bostwick investigation has spread outside of Palmyrton.

As I ponder this, I realize the piano music has stopped. How long ago did that happen? Where is Crawford now?

As if reading my mind, Crawford appears at the foot of the back staircase that leads from the second floor to the kitchen. What was he doing up there?

"I remember that cookie jar," Crawford smiles and makes a beeline for the flower-patterned Roseville in Donna's display. "Birdie always had it filled with Lorna Doones. Never ate any other cookie." He shakes his head. "I thought they tasted like dust."

What an odd young man. His mother's been murdered and he's reminiscing about cookies he didn't care for?

He looks from me to Donna to Ty and back to me again. "Where's George?"

Should I tell him that George is coming over to deal with him? Maybe not. George said to ignore Crawford. "George is at work."

"Oh, right. What day is today?" Crawford drifts around the kitchen, picking up gadgets and running his fingers over a stack of folded tablecloths.

Ty shoots me a look. "Wednesday, man. All day long."

"I lose track of time in the summer." Crawford plops into a chair.

Surely he's too old to still be in college. "You're in school?"

"I work at Bumford-Stanley."

He doesn't look like he could hold the attention of a classroom full of overachieving prep school kids hell-bent on getting into

Harvard. "What do you teach?"

"Oh, I'm not a teacher. I coach the JV girls fencing team and play the piano for the chorale. But I'm off until September. I guess."

Before Ty can blurt out, "That's a job for a grown-ass man?" I interject, "Well, we have a lot of work to do, so unless there's something I can help you with…." I wish George would show up. I don't know how close his office is. Would it be better if Crawford just wandered off the way he wandered in, or does George want to talk to him?

"Right. I'll be heading out." He stands up. "First, I need the facilities."

"There's a powder room off the foy—"

He gives me a dismissive wave as he brushes past. "Oh, I know my way around."

Ty's brow furrows as he watches Crawford disappear through the dining room. "What's up with that? He just dropped by to play piano and pee?"

"His mom was *murdered*?" Donna sets down a glass salad bowl. "Is she the one in the news who died at that party? He didn't even seem upset."

I turn back to the stacks of kitchenware awaiting pricing. "He's definitely rude. And strange."

Ty is standing stock-still, his head cocked to one side like Ethel when she senses the presence of deer in the backyard.

A low murmur of voices drifts back from the foyer. We all strain to listen.

Wheedling. "Don't you think my mother would want you to help me? I thought you were supposed to be her great friend."

Flustered. "Of course I am. But Crawford, I'm a trustee of the Alumni Council. In light of your present…er…predicament at the school, I can't allow you to stay here. It would be a conflict—"

Aggrieved. "I didn't *do* anything. She's a neurotic little bitch. This is a witch hunt."

Pleading. "No one wants this to escalate, Crawford. Just live quietly at Heatherington until—"

Belligerent. "What part of impossible don't you understand?" A crash of breaking china—Birdie's bowl of potpourri.

Ty doesn't need to hear more. He bolts through the dining

room with Donna and me on his heels.

When we skid into the foyer, we find George backed against the wall, a flume of dried flowers and china shards at his feet. "I can't live under the same roof with my father." Crawford's face is inches from George's. He's got George's tie bunched into his right hand. "I need to get away."

Ty grabs Crawford and twists his left hand up behind his back. "Time to change your tune, Jack."

George steps away from the wall and straightens his jacket and tie. He turns his mournful gaze to Ty. "I believe Crawford was just leaving."

Ty loosens his grip enough to allow Crawford to perform a ballroom dancer's turn to straighten his arm.

As our intruder saunters toward the door, I notice a bumpy bulge in his front pocket. I step right out onto the porch with him and hold out my hand, palm up. "Empty your pockets."

"Wha--? I have no idea—" He moves toward the porch steps.

I grab his thick Oxford shirt and press my mouth to his ear. "Birdie's pearls and whatever else you took from her bedroom. Turn it over, or I'll get Ty to shake it out of you."

Crawford doesn't even have the decency to blush. "Aren't you *efficient*," he drawls as a strand of pearls, a gold watch, three pairs of gold earrings, and a scarab bracelet drop into my waiting hand.

Then he skips down the stairs, a breezy "nice meeting you," floating back to my astonished ears.

CHAPTER 17

WHEW! I THOUGHT I'D NEVER see the end of this day!

I plop into a chaise lounge on my deck while Ethel runs laps around our fenced backyard. What a luxury to not have to walk her when I'm exhausted. I sip some Chardonnay and laugh as a squirrel perched on a branch above Ethel's head drops an acorn on her snout. Ethel backs away and redirects her energy at some tiny finches she finds easier to intimidate.

The scene at Birdie Armentrout's house today was too weird for me. After that big confrontation, George murmured regrets for distracting us from our work and left. No explanation. No gratitude.

And Crawford! Why does he want to live in Birdie's house? Is he afraid of his father? And why would the scion of one of New Jersey's wealthiest families want to steal some moderately valuable jewelry worth maybe a thousand bucks, tops? Had Crawford been upstairs looking for something else and just pocketed the jewelry in passing? He certainly didn't fight to keep it.

What exactly is Crawford's "predicament" at the Bumford-Stanley school? Obviously something sexual, but what?

I take another sip of wine. Really, what does it matter? None of my business.

Unless...could their sketchy behavior have something to do with the murder of Loretta Bostwick? I'm definitely going to tell Sean about this. And, in the interest of helping my spouse to the fullest extent, maybe I can seek out some additional information. The sooner he solves this case, the sooner he can get back to working normal hours.

I pull out my phone and text Isabel Trent, the only person

I know well who attended the Bumford-Stanley School. She's always too busy with her real estate clients to chat, but maybe she'll give me a few quick hints via text.

Do you know Crawford Bostwick? I hear he's in trouble with the Bumford- Stanley School.

Two seconds later, my phone is ringing.

"How do you know about this?" Isabel demands.

O-*kay*, I hit a nerve.

"I'm organizing the estate sale at Birdie Armentrout's house. Crawford showed up there and asked if he could crash in the house. Said he couldn't live under the same roof as his father. And George said no because of Crawford's predicament at the school."

"Dear Lord…those fools! We're trying to minimize this unfortunate incident."

Hmm. "Unfortunate incident" sounds like Isabel-speak for "really juicy scandal." But if I say "what incident?" she'll realize I how little I really know and clam up.

"Yes," I offer. "I imagine this accusation could be problematic for the school, given that Crawford coaches—"

"Ugh! How could he? Independent schools are in the spotlight right now with all the reports of improprieties at St. George's and Phillps-Exeter. Bumford-Stanley makes it a selling point that our reputation is above reproach. And then along comes Crawford to sully our name."

Right. I remember reading about a teacher having an abusive relationship with a student at St. George's. So Crawford must be in that sorry club. But Bumford-Stanley is legally obliged to report an incident of sex between a teacher and a student.

"Honestly, Isabel—the school needs to report this to the police. It's a crime to cover it up."

"Darling, I know. We're between a rock and a hard place. The parents, who are huge donors, insist that nothing happened."

I cough on a gulp of wine. "Wait--the parents of the abused girl don't want Crawford prosecuted?"

"They don't want the scandal. The girl, and the parents, insist that Crawford was a *gentleman*."

"So…who says he wasn't?"

"The Bumford-Stanley trustee standing behind Crawford at the front desk of the Ritz-Carlton. Never complain about room service when you're trysting with a fifteen-year-old."

Before I can ask another question, Isabel has rung off with a "Must run. Thanks for the tip about the loose lips."

As I end my conversation with Isabel, Sean's car pulls into the driveway. He lifts his hand in greeting and pulls into the garage. A few minutes later, the sound of the fridge door slamming and pots banging drifts through the open kitchen window. This doesn't sound good. Sean appears at the back door. "You couldn't have taken the chicken out of the freezer before you came out here? Did you buy the mushrooms?"

Damn! All day long I've felt like I was forgetting something. This is it. ""I'm sorry, honey. I totally forgot. I'll run out right now."

"After you've been drinking? I think not."

He pivots and returns to the kitchen. More slamming and banging ensues.

Now I'm irritated. What's the use of having a nice back yard to relax in if you can't sit down after a long day? Who cares what we have for dinner? It's not like I demand that Sean whip up a gourmet meal every night. There's a package of Trader Joe ravioli and a jar of spaghetti sauce in the fridge. What's wrong with that for dinner?

"Audrey! What did you do with my garlic press?"

What did I do with it? I don't even know how to use it. And why is he yelling loud enough that the neighbors could weigh in with suggestions of where to look for it?

I snatch up my empty wine glass and head into the lion's den.

As I enter the room, the smoke alarm goes off, triggered by a cloud of fumes from a pan full of scorched butter on the range. Sean grabs the pan off the burner with his bare hand.

"Augh!" He recoils and the pan clatters to the floor, splashing grease everywhere. My husband stands surveying the chaos he's created.

I cross the room and lead him to the sink, where I run cold water over his burned hand. "Calm down. You don't have to cook dinner. We'll eat some pasta or order a pizza."

Sean stares at the water pouring over his blistering hand. I switch from irritation to concern. All this anger has nothing to do with undefrosted chicken and misplaced kitchen implements.

"What wrong? Tell me what's really bothering you."

"Nothing."

"Did something happen at work?"

"No. Everything's fine. I'm sorry." Sean turns away from me and dries his hand.

Everything very clearly is not fine, but pleading for him to confide in me won't work. I decide to take the small talk approach to see if he'll eventually give up some information.

"Say, Ty and Donna said they saw you in Melton today. Were you following up on something in the Bostwick investigation?"

His shoulders stiffen. "No! I mean, yeah, but--" He crosses to the fridge and starts rooting around. I could swear he's using the open fridge door to block my inquiring gaze.

I review what Ty told me. Sean was standing outside of a fancy house and then a man came out and got in a limo. That image triggers a memory. A few weeks ago Sean and I ran into a colleague of his standing beside a stretch limo outside one of the big office buildings in downtown Palmyrton. Sean had raised his hand in greeting but kept walking. Once we were past, he told me the guy was working off the books doing personal security.

"Were you even scheduled to work today?"

No answer.

"Were you moonlighting in Melton like that guy we met back in June?"

Sean shuts the refrigerator door. His face is flushed, and not from the cold.

"What's going on?" I face him with my hands on my hips. "Why would you take a moonlighting job and not tell me about it?"

He walks away from me and looks out the kitchen window. "I only planned to work a few shifts."

"Is that why you've been so tired? Why you've been late nearly every night?"

He nods.

Now my voice gets stern. "Sean, your mother has told me several times how she used to worry that your dad would get killed on the job because he was so exhausted from moonlighting. Why would you take a risk like that? There's no need."

My husband spins around. "There is a need. We're short of

cash."

Have I created this worry with my endless spreadsheets and budgets? "Honey, our situation isn't that bad. We have enough—"

"We don't." His jaw juts out. "My brothers and sisters want to send our parents to Ireland for their fortieth wedding anniversary. I need two thousand dollars for my share by next week."

Two thousands bucks is a lot of money right now, but a fortieth anniversary is a big deal. My in-laws deserve a special gift. Surely he knows I wouldn't have refused this. "So why didn't you talk to me about it? I have—"

His eyes narrow. "I don't want your money. They're my parents. This is my responsibility."

"So you're saying I'm not really a member of the Coughlin family?" Male pride meets only child insecurity. "Are your brothers' and sisters' spouses also left out of this gift?"

"I didn't say that. Of course, the gift is from both of us. I just didn't want to ask you—"

"And it's not *my* money and *your* money. It's *our* money. I seem to recall taking a vow recently that mentioned something about 'for richer, for poorer.' Remind me of how that goes."

"You've been working your ass off to earn more money to pay off this kitchen." Sean thumps his chest. "I can do some extra work to help pay for this extra expense."

"O-o-h, now I see." I start banging dinner plates and silverware onto the table just to blow off some of my anger. "This is why you weren't upset I didn't get the Tate job. You didn't want me to make more money than you. You can't be king of the castle unless you earn more."

"That's not true. I just want to do my part." He reaches for me, but I slip away.

"Fine. Why did you feel you had to sneak around and do it behind my back?"

Sean plops into a kitchen chair and stares up at the ceiling. "Because I'm covering Terry's share too."

Ah, there we have it. Sean's younger brother is chronically under-employed and short of funds. "Covering" Terry's share means we're loaning money we'll never see again. I could argue about how always bailing Terry out just encourages his irresponsibility. I'd win on logic but lose on emotional support.

There may come a time that I draw a line in the sand over Terry's insolvency, but this isn't it. I sit down across the table and take my husband's hand. "Look, we have two thousand dollars in our account. Write the check. If you want to pick up a few security shifts, fine. But spread it out so you're not exhausted."

Sean squeezes my hand. "Do you have buyer's remorse about marrying into the Coughlin family?"

"Only when you throw burnt butter on the floor."

I rise, but Sean pulls me into his lap. "I'm sorry for snapping at you. And I accept your offer to write a check for the trip from our joint account. But I'm going to replenish that withdrawal and add more to it."

"And I'll make dinner tonight as long as you lower your expectations."

"Deal. I'll clean up this mess."

I pick my way gingerly to the back door. "Ethel's happy to assist with the preliminary mopping."

The dog tears in and immediately sets to lapping up the butter, while I put on a pot of water for the ravioli. Sean talks to me from his spot at the kitchen table.

"Unfortunately, I'm committed to working one more security shift this week, and it couldn't come at a worse time. He pours himself a glass of wine. "I'm under tremendous pressure from my boss to come up with some leads in the Loretta Bostwick case. But I've got nothing. No witnesses. No motive."

"Frederic Bostwick still insists that Loretta fell accidentally?"

Sean nudges the dog out of the way and gets out the mop. "The forensics don't back that up, but we have zero additional evidence pointing to suicide or murder."

"Who profits from her death? Isn't that always the prime motive?"

"You'd think that would be a straightforward question, but in the case of Loretta Bostwick, I need to talk to her estate attorney. Who is strongly resisting talking to me."

I dump a package of mushroom ravioli into the boiling water and turn to face Sean. "Rich people may not have figured out how to take their money with them when they die, but they sure do know how to control their loot from beyond the grave. If I were you, I'd unravel all the trusts and restrictions."

Sean grimaces. "Easier said than done. Frederic Bostwick is a powerful man and he's using his influence to push for having the case closed and ruled an accidental death. He's even threatened to hire some celebrity pathologist to do a second autopsy to challenge our results. And his pressure at the top is filtering down to me."

"Sounds like he's protecting someone. Could his son be involved? It happens I had a strange encounter with Crawford Bostwick today, and I found out some dirt about him."

Sean perks up. "What?"

"Did you know that Crawford Bostwick was seen at the Ritz-Carlton shacking up with a student from the Bumford-Stanley school?"

Sean lets the mop clatter out of his grasp "What? Who told you that?"

Ah, I love it when I know something my husband doesn't. I hand him back the mop and while the pasta cooks, I settle back to spin the tale of Crawford's appearance at the house, George's refusal of help, and Isabel's clarification. Sean hangs on my every word.

"What kind of parents don't want to press charges against a child molester?" Sean slams the mop back into the broom closet. "If Crawford Bostwick went after my kid, I'd want him strung up by the balls."

"Maybe the parents are afraid of going up against the Bostwick family. If he's capable of pressuring the police and the medical examiner, imagine what he'd do to civilians. You know 'Neither of us wants unpleasant publicity and here's a hundred grand for your trouble.' "

Sean nods. "I knew those people were hiding something. When I interviewed Frederic Bostwick, he was very cagey about his son's whereabouts at the time of Loretta's death. He insisted Crawford was at their house, Heatherington. But that place is as big as Yankee Stadium. Several of the servants confirm that Frederic was there all evening. They served him dinner, brought him a drink in the library"—Sean rolls his eyes—"helped him pack a bag for a trip. But only the butler claims to have seen Crawford. This guy's been an employee for years, smooth as silk. He was very vague about exactly when and where he'd seen

'Young Mr. Crawford', but he insisted he was there all night. But when I interviewed the cook and the maid, they were both nervous wrecks. They said Crawford was home, but they couldn't say how they knew."

"Did you talk to Crawford's boss at the school?"

Sean glances heavenward. "Oh, yes. I talked to the headmaster, the games coordinator and the vocal head. Otherwise known as the principal, the gym teacher, and the choir director. And don't get me started on the first names—Spalding, Woodson, and Pippy. Seriously, Pippy. No one in Bostwick-land is named Tom, Dick, or Harry. Or Mary Jane."

"So what did Spalding, Woodson, and Pippy have to say about Crawford?"

Sean suddenly realizes he's told me much more than he normally would about an active case. He strokes my arm. "Never you mind, Miss Marple. But I appreciate the lead on Crawford's preference for little girls. It'll give me something to use when I go back for round two of questioning."

His touch sends a shiver up my arm, but it's not one of pleasure. "Uh-oh. Isabel will know I told you. I don't want to wreck our business relationship, but honestly, I think the poor girl Crawford seduced deserves some police protection."

"Unfortunately, since the assault happened in Manhattan, there's not much I can do for her. But I can find out if he's hurt anyone else. And don't worry. I'll keep you and Isabel out of it. If George Armentrout and Isabel both knew about Crawford's troubles, then I bet half the Bumford-Stanley community knows. Each parent will think another parent spilled the beans, and pretty soon they'll be tripping over each other to talk to me."

"Three people can't keep a secret, right?" I quote one of Sean's favorite sayings back to him.

"Not unless one of them's dead."

CHAPTER 18

DESPITE AN ENTHUSIASTIC KISS-AND-MAKE-UP AFTER dinner last night, I still manage to make it to the office by nine-thirty. Before we all head to Birdie's house for the last of the set-up, there's some advertising to finalize for the sale, and some items I'm shipping off to longtime customers. We work in companionable silence, interrupted only by the zip of Ty's packing tape dispenser and the tap of computer keys.

Tom, our regular UPS driver appears just as Ty has finished with the outgoing boxes. Donna presents the paperwork, and by the time the UPS man leaves with his hand truck loaded, Donna has learned he has two kids, is on a gluten-free diet, and is taking his wife to Puerta Vallarta for a second honeymoon.

Through the window, Ty watches the driver's retreating figure. "I never heard that dude talk so much. In all the time I've been working here, all he's ever said to me is, "Hi, Bye, and Sign here."

Donna smiles and shrugs. "People open up to me. I just ask a question or two to get them started, then I listen."

Ty turns to look at Donna. "You *do* listen. Most people can hardly wait to interrupt and give you advice or tell you how they're sicker than you or smarter than you or righter than you. You keep your mouth shut and pay attention."

Hmmm. I wonder if I'm included in people who interrupt to offer advice? Donna looks pleased but shy at the compliment. Flustered, she asks me, "Do you want me to send an email to that record collector guy?"

"Yeah, he's in our contacts under Vintage Vinyl. The list of LPs that I thought he'd want is in my tote-bag."

Donna digs though my bag and finds the list. "You know,

you still have that genealogy folder we found yesterday in here. Should I send it to Mr. Armentrout?"

"Wow, I forgot all about that." I extend my hand for it and Donna passes it to me via Ty.

Ty opens the folder. "What are these charts and drawings?"

"The Armentrout family tree. Birdie traced the family back to 1720."

Ty studies the paper with a furrowed brow. "My family tree would have branches that twist right off the page. I bet nobody could figure it out."

He sets the open folder in front of me and points to an asterisk on a diagram that looks more like a scientific experiment than an oak tree. "What does this mean?"

The paper is covered with carefully drawn lines and boxes, and the boxes are filled with names and dates inscribed in precise printing. All of it is done in faded pencil, which has been erased and rewritten in many places. "I think it means this guy had a first wife who died, and then a second wife, and he had kids with each one." I squint at the neat but faint writing. "George said that Birdie discovered that they were distantly related to Loretta Bostwick, This shows that Loretta's maiden name was Crawford. Back in the early 1800s, a Crawford man married an Armentrout woman."

"So I guess Loretta named her son with her maiden name. That's so WASP-y," Donna says.

"What about these dotted lines?" Ty points to a box dated 1916, which is connected to a Julius Crawford with a dotted line. There's no name inside the box, only a question mark.

"I don't know. Maybe Birdie ran into a dead end."

I text George and ask him if he wants me to mail the folder or if he will pick it up from my office.

He quickly answers.

That must be a very old folder when Birdie first got started with the research. Later she switched to a genealogy software program to track all the information. I have all her electronic records and her latest print out. You can throw that folder away.

"Huh. He says it's a duplicate and he doesn't need it." I close the folder and slide it to the corner of my desk.

Donna pounces. "So throw it away. You told me you wanted

to declutter your desk."

Protectively, I slide it back toward me. "Let's just wait until after the sale to toss it. You have no idea how many times people change their minds."

"Hoo! That's fer sure," Ty agrees. " 'member that time I hadda drive clear to Newark at midnight to get back a dirty old stuffed rabbit that we sent to Sister Alice?"

"Who could forget Baxter the Bunny?" I turn to explain the Baxter saga to Donna. "Guy was a Marine lieutenant and flipped out when his sister said we could toss the toy he left behind in his childhood bedroom." I put a paperweight on top of the folder. "I'll just keep this until we close out the Armentrout sale."

Although I can tell Donna's fingers are still itching to purge, she heads out with Ty to Birdie's house in the van while I follow in my car. On my way, I stop at the post office to pick up a registered letter, a check from an overly scrupulous customer who refuses to trust standard first class delivery.

I groan as I see the line snaking through the dingy lobby, twenty people all waiting for the one clerk who works with maddening thoroughness. "Does this contain anything fragile, flammable, poisonous, or explosive?" she asks the woman at the head of the line who's placed a shoebox with a large Zappos logo on the counter.

I consider leaving, but the line is never any shorter, so I may as well gut it out. I shuffle forward, reading the *New York Times* on my phone. As I reach a turn in the maze, I see a familiar face at the end of the line: Henry Bell.

As if this trip to the post office weren't painful enough.

I hunch over my phone. Maybe he won't notice me.

"Hey, Audrey!"

Damn. I look up innocently. "Oh, hi Henry." I can't even bring myself to say, "How are you?" let alone "Congratulations." You wouldn't think he'd be so friendly to someone he just screwed over.

The line moves, and we are almost parallel to each other. The creases in Henry's forehead grow deeper as he lifts his grizzled brows. "How come you turned down the Tate job?"

My jaw nearly comes unhinged. "I didn't turn it down. The Board gave it to you."

We inch a little closer. Henry holds out his hands palms up. "I told Levi we oughta get you in to help with the antiques, but Levi said you weren't interested."

"What!" I tap my chest and my voice rises. "I suggested we work together too! Levi said you wanted to work with an antiques dealer you've worked with before."

Henry's eyes widen. "Levi said what?"

By this time, people in the line are staring at us. My turn is next. "Meet me outside."

BY THE TIME HENRY JOINS me in front of the post office, my hands are trembling with anger. I tell him what happened in my interview and show him the email I got from Levi.

Henry scratches his close-cropped head. "I don't understand. Dennis Sykes called me a couple days ago and asked was I interested in doing a quick clear-out of an old house that some elderly ladies left to the Parks Center. He made it sound like some house in the neighborhood full 'o cat shit and piles of newspapers. Then him and Levi take me to the Tate Mansion. I nearly passed out. Place is like a museum inside. I told 'em I didn't know how to sell stuff like that. And that's when I said 'Audrey Nealon would know. We could work on it together.' And Levi looked me square in the eye and told me you weren't interested."

"Unbelievable! Why would he say that? I'm dying to work on that job."

"And," Henry shoves his hands deep in the pockets of his baggy gray work pants, "Dennis told me if I needed help with the antiques, he'd send over a guy from that antiques store on Fairmont Avenue."

I feel tears prick my eyes. Dexter Abernathy is the most crooked, low-down schemer in all of Palmer County. He would cheat his own grandmother. I once heard him tell a woman that five thousand dollars worth of her Rookwood Pottery was just worthless knick-knacks, but he'd take it off her hands for twenty bucks.

"So you're working with Dexter on the job?" I can barely choke out the words.

"Give me a little credit for havin' the brains I was born with, girl. I could see as soon as he stepped into that house that he was out to cheat us. He was lickin' his lips and his eyes got all shiny like a kid at Christmas. And then he started poor-mouthin' everything. 'This here's got a scratch, this here's the wrong color, ain't nobody want this kinda table, but I'll help you get rid of it.' So I showed him the door. Then when I saw you in line today, I thought, well if Audrey don't want the job herself, she could at least tell me someone honest that could help me out."

"But I *do* want the job."

"Well, I can see that now." Henry sticks out his hand. "Whattaya say we split this job fifty-fifty? I figure I'll still come out further ahead than if I worked with that hustla, Abernathy."

I feel like Dorothy arriving in the Emerald City. I'm going to get the chance to explore the Tate Mansion after all. I grab Henry's hand and shake hard.

"What about Dennis and Levi?"

"I don't know what they're playin' at, but I don't like bein' lied to. You leave them to me."

And just like that, Another Man's Treasure is back in the game.

CHAPTER 19

“WOW!”

“Amazing!”

“Dope!”

The staff of Another Man’s treasure is finally inside the Tate Mansion. We stand in the magnificent front hall as Henry Bell watches our reaction. The walls are raised panel walnut, the floor an intricate herringbone parquet. The staircase turns halfway to the second floor where a stained glass window casts a soft glow on the landing. A six-foot marble Aphrodite stands guard at the doorway of the front parlor. Some landscape oils in heavy gilt frames hang on the walls, but pride of place goes to a larger than life-sized portrait of a stout man with bushy pork chop sideburns and a handlebar mustache.

Donna stares up at his stern visage. “Is that Vareena Tate’s husband?”

“Nope, that’s Edgar Vernon Tate, Senior, Vareena’s husband’s grandfather. He’s the one who made the family fortune and built this house in 1882. He died long before Vareena came on the scene.”

“Good,” Donna says. “I wouldn’t want to crawl into bed with him every night.”

“Yeah, it’s hard to imagine these stiff old Victorians having any kind of sex life.”

“People had kids, so someone musta been hookin’ up,” Ty says as he moves into the front parlor. “But I sure wouldn’t wanna do the nasty on that sofa.”

Donna giggles as she runs her hand over the knobby wooden

back and the scratchy horsehair upholstery. "Ouch. Maybe that was their birth control." She hugs herself and slowly pirouettes. "Two old ladies lived here all alone? I'd be kinda scared."

"Try being stacked in a house over on Findlay where a guy who works days shares a bed with a guy who works nights. *That's* scary."

"I just meant—"

But Ty has moved on, prowling the perimeter of the room. "Lots more paintings. They need a cleaning, but they're in good shape."

Heavy maroon velvet drapes cover the windows, making the interior gloomy but protecting the art from light damage. More landscapes with ornate frames hang on every wall. While Ty and I study them, Donna looks at the furniture.

"Is this where they hung out? These chairs look just as uncomfortable as the sofa."

"This is the formal drawing room, where the Tates would have received guests," I explain.

"Huh. The room is big, but it's so crowded." Donna runs her dust cloth over an inlaid table. "I don't think you could have much of a party in here without knockin' stuff over."

Parties. Did this dark, cavernous house ever contain laughing, joyful people? "Vareena moved into this house as a young bride in in the middle of World War II. This room would have been old-fashioned even then. I wonder what she thought of it?"

"I guess she couldn't talk her husband into redecorating, huh? That happened to my friend Patty. She and her husband bought the house her husband grew up in when his parents went to assisted living. Patty had all these plans to modernize, but Mario wouldn't let her change a thing. She's stuck with these 1980s vertical blinds and Laura Ashley wallpaper. Ugh!"

"Vareena and her husband hardly had a chance to live here together. He shipped out to France right after they married. A few months later, he was killed."

Donna swats at a cobweb in the corner. "Maybe after her husband died she didn't have the heart to change anything in the house."

I think of my childhood home. It was virtually unchanged from the day my mother disappeared until the day my father had a stroke thirty years later. Certainly he hadn't had the heart to redecorate.

"What's this weird thing? It looks like a wreath in a glass box." Donna holds it out to me.

"Cool--Victorian mourning hair art! The different colors are from the different colored hair of the dead people in the family."

Donna nearly drops the shadow box. "Eeeew! What are we going to do with that?"

"It's a pretty good example—should bring four or five hundred bucks."

Henry shakes his head. "White people into some strange shit, you ask me."

The back parlor is where the family should have gathered, but this room doesn't look like it's been used either. There's an elaborate onyx and marble chess set, but when I move the queen, a dust-free ring lies beneath her. A spinet piano stands in the corner, but there's no sheet music, and the ivory keys are brittle and cracked. A Victorian sewing cabinet stands beside a chair that looks less uncomfortable than those in the formal parlor. When I look inside I find a piece of fabric on which someone has started to work a cross-stitch sampler. The needle is still stuck in the brittle, yellowing fabric. "Look, it was going to be a picture of this house. Someone set it down a hundred years ago and no one ever moved it. It must have been Edgar Jr.'s wife, the one who died in childbirth. She would have been Vareena's mother-in-law if she had lived."

Was she the last person to regard this place as a real home? Apart from a light coating of dust, the Tate mansion seems like a restored historic house open for tours. Mount Vernon without the velvet ropes to keep grubby fingers off the antiques.

Except this house hasn't been restored. It simply has never changed.

Donna looks around the room and shivers. "If they didn't ever have company and they didn't sew or play games or listen to music, what did Maybelle and Vareena do all day?"

What indeed?

Henry gives a magician's wave of the hands. "All this is just for show. I think they must've spent their days back in a little room by the kitchen. There's nothing fancy in there. Old paperbacks…a radio. I'll handle that. You just pay attention to these front rooms and we won't get in each other's way."

I'm desperately curious about Maybelle and Vareena's life in this house, but I'm not about to get on Henry's bad side in my first ten minutes inside the Tate mansion.

"Will do. There's plenty to keep us busy here."

Henry nods and disappears down a long hallway.

"How did they cook?" Donna asks. "Like pioneers with kettles and a fire?"

I laugh. "The house isn't *that* old. The original kitchen would have had a coal stove and an icebox. And servants to keep them functioning. But when Ty and I peeked through the window, it looked like the kitchen had been updated in the 1940s—either right before or right after the war."

"That means there could be some McCoy pottery or some old cast iron frying pans, and big mixing bowls. And those..." Ty makes a winding gesture.

"Flour sifter." I supply. "Or did you mean an apple-peeler?"

"How do you guys know all this?"

Ty shrugs as he pulls out the iPad and prepares to start taking photos. "You pick it up. Work and learn. I didn't know nuthin'... anything...when I started. Right, Audge?"

Nothing about antiques and collectibles...plenty about life. "You were always curious. That's all it takes to learn anything new."

Donna thinks about this. "Hmmm. Maybe that's why I couldn't learn chemistry in high school. Maybe I wasn't dumb, I just wasn't curious about all those molecules and formulas."

"Chemistry might be interesting if you have a good teacher. I had Mr. Wysocki." Ty mimics snoring. "I thought the English class I'm taking now was going to be boring, you know, with poetry and shit, but the teacher is tite. We learn about all kinds of stuff. Like the other day we were talking about logical fallacies."

"What's that?" Donna asks as she helps him move a chair out of the shadows for a better photo.

"That's when you're not thinkin' straight and you're not givin' a good reason for what you're doin'. Like when I used to tell my Grams I had to hang at the playground on Fowler street instead of shootin' hoops at the Parks Center because all my homies doin' it. And she'd say, 'if all your homies gonna jump off a bridge, you gonna jump too?' See, that right there is the Bandwagon logical fallacy. Grams didn't know it was called that, but she knew sure 'nuff it was a bullshit excuse."

"I took a logic class in college." I pause in my note-taking. "There was something in Latin...post hoc ergo—"

Ty spins around and high-fives me. "Propter hoc! That means just because something happened before something else, doesn't mean the first thing caused the second thing. Like when you say, "'I got the flu right after that big snowstorm. Snowstorms cause the flu.' The snow didn't cause the flu, a virus caused the flu. Just so happens that flu season and snow season are around the same time."

"I wish I had stayed in college." Donna says softly.

"Where'd you go?"

"Sacred Heart in Connecticut. It's a beautiful school, but far away, ya know?"

I don't want to point out that for some people, two hours wouldn't be far enough away from home.

"You could go back to Palmer Community," Ty says. "It's a good school."

Donna shakes her head. "It's too late now."

"Never too late to do somethin' you really wanna do. You wouldn't be the oldest person there. I gotta dude in my class who's sixty-six. He waited 'til he retired from a factory job to go to college. He doesn't hafta go, just wants to."

"That's nice," Donna pulls out her trusty microfiber cloth and polishes a curved glass cabinet filled with Dresden figurines. "But it wouldn't work for me."

Ty and I exchange a look behind her back. He feels it too. There's something in Donna's tone that tells us to drop the subject.

CHAPTER 20

BY LUNCHTIME WE HAVE THE front and back parlors catalogued, and we're ready to move deeper into the house. I send Ty and Donna out for sandwiches, and use the break as a good reason to slip into the kitchen where Henry is working with his men.

When I walk in, they are just finishing brown bag lunches. With a quick nod, Henry indicates the break is over and the guys head back to the garage.

Henry stays seated. "I talked to Levi on the phone last night. Told him we were working together now."

I slide onto a chrome and vinyl chair. "How did that fly?"

Henry methodically folds an empty Kit-Kat wrapper. "I asked him why he didn't tell me up front that they talked to you about the job first...that you had the idea we could work together." He stuffs the lunchtime litter into one bag. "Gave me some runaround. The Board...confidentiality...blah, blah, blah."

"Did you ask him why he lied to me and told me you preferred to work with someone else?"

"He said you musta misunderstood."

"I showed you his email. Levi said it in black and white."

Henry holds up his hands to ward off my objections. "I know. But he was squirming. I felt like I had to let him off the hook."

I don't feel so compassionate. The lies he told Henry and me about each other could have ruined our working relationship. I want to squeeze the truth right out of that man.

My new partner leans across the table and lowers his voice. "Then Levi goes, 'Have you told Dennis about this? What'd he say?' Like he's worried."

Henry shakes his head. "I told Levi I don't need to be askin' permission from some kid about how to run my business. What's gotten into that man?"

"My father says Levi's under some pressure. Not everyone likes the way he's running the Parks Center."

"Hmmm. Levi doesn't like to rock the boat. He's nothin' like his old man. I guess you're too young to remember Levi Senior." Henry jumps up. "What a preacher! He knew how to make a crowd roar. Renounce Satan! A-men! Ride the school bus to the white school! A-men!" Henry's eyes shine with the memory. Then he kicks the worn linoleum with his steel-toe boot. "It's not easy to be the son of a great man. Always livin' in a shadow."

"I guess Dennis seems more like Levi Senior to some people."

"Ha! Dennis has the shoutin' down, that's for sure. But leadership is more than makin' noise. Gotta understand how people think. Gotta make 'em work together. That's what Levi Senior knew how to do. Dennis got a long way to go on that front."

BY THE TIME DONNA AND Ty have returned with our food, Henry has shown me around the kitchen. There are hardly any dishes in the cabinets. Seventy years of eating from the same crockery has reduced the supply to a few mismatched and chipped plates and bowls. The pots and pans are equally sparse and worn. Henry shakes his head. "Those old gals shoulda signed up for Meals on Wheels. There's hardly any food in this house. Looks like they lived on canned soup and instant oatmeal."

"Can we see the room where Maybelle and Vareena hung out?" Donna asks with such childlike innocence that Henry doesn't feel like we're treading on his turf.

He shrugs. "Nothin' of value in there, but if you're nosey…."

So before we eat, we follow Henry down a narrow side hall where he opens a door.

The room is no bigger than fifteen feet square, with one window and a bare wooden floor with a frayed rag rug.

"This must have been the cook's bedroom originally." Instinctively, I straighten the crooked, yellowing shade on the floor lamp. A scratched wooden table sits between two upholstered chairs. The chairs' coverings are shiny with age, and the seats have been hollowed out with the impressions of the sitters' bottoms.

"They didn't have a TV, just that old-timey radio. It still works." Henry reaches over to the big console and flips a switch. The scratchy sound of the all-news station fills the room.

"What did they do all day?"

"Guess they read books," Ty says, pulling out a romance novel from a tall, rickety bookcase jammed with paperbacks. The cover is a classic bodice ripper—a beautiful young woman in a low-cut ball gown being ravished by a dark prince with flowing locks. Ty flips to front of the well-worn book. "It's got a price penciled inside—twenty-five cents. They musta bought their books at the Saint Stephen's thrift shop."

"That's sad—they never even treated themselves to a new book?" I move in to study the books on the shelf. A book collection tells me so much about a house's occupants: intellectuals, pragmatists, romantics, dreamers. The books don't lie.

These shelves are neatly divided between fiction and nonfiction. The fiction is all romance and family sagas. The nonfiction is more diverse: biography and history, but also psychology and social science. There are even some fairly recent bestsellers like *Freakonomics* and *The Boys in the Boat*. Now who was reading that?

"Here's some hardcovers," Donna says. "Uh-oh, they're library books. A month overdue."

"Put them in my tote bag. I'll return them on the way home."

"They didn't get out much," Henry says. "The car is a 1954 DeSoto. Sixty-three years old and it has 62,000 miles on it."

'They drove less than a thousand miles a year!"

"Car still runs good. There's an oil change sticker on it from Hyler's Garage. Chuck Hyler is in his fifties and he says his dad had been taking care of that car from the time he was a teenager. Maybelle only drove the car in Palmyrton. She wouldn't drive out on the highway. Never took it on Route 287 or Route 24. Never even drove out to the big box stores on Route 10."

"Where did they buy their clothes? Surely not at Anais or The Left Bank." These days, downtown Palmyrton only has fancy boutiques. Nothing suitable for frugal old ladies.

"Look over here." Donna calls our attention to a large basket on the floor. It's full of catalogs. "Lands End, LL Bean, Burpees

Seeds, JC Penny." She digs through them. "The pages are marked with stuff they ordered. Look."

Donna shows me a Lands End Catalog. On the winter boots page, someone has written in perfect printing "one brown, size 7."

And then right below "one blue, size 8."

"They each got the same boots, one in brown, one in blue. I wonder whose feet were bigger?"

"And look here." Donna flips to the next page with a turned-down corner: fleece jackets. The same neat printing marks the page. "One wheat size small, One cerulean, size medium."

Ty peers over our shoulders at the catalog. "If Maybelle was the maid, how come she got the same clothes as Vareena?"

"I guess they were more like friends after so many years together. It would be pretty mean of Vareena to make Maybelle wear her hand-me-downs," Donna says. "And it's not like Land's End is fancy."

"Hmmm—you sure don't know much about rich people. She made Maybelle buy the books at the thrift shop. Vareena might've let Maybelle buy new boots, but I bet we get upstairs to the bedrooms, you'll see Maybelle's closet full o' rags from Saint Stephens."

"If they were hard-up for cash, why didn't they sell this old pile and move into a nice little condo?" Donna taps the cast iron radiator with the toe of her sneaker. "Something with forced air heat. This place is probably drafty and freezing in the winter. I bet that's why they holed up in this small room."

"Sean's grandfather lives in a house that's ridiculously inconvenient, but he refuses to move. I guess once a place feels like home, it's hard to leave."

"Yeah, but that's what's so weird," Ty says. "This place don't feel homey at all."

AFTER WE FINALLY EAT LUNCH, we decide to finish the day in the room Edgar Tate used as an office.

"Wow, look at that big black phone!" Donna crosses to the huge walnut desk and holds the receiver to her ear. "There's still a dial tone. Boy, is it heavy. I wouldn't want to talk to my sister for an hour on that thing."

"Who even has a landline anymore?" Ty says.

"Hardly anyone. But Vareena and Maybelle sure didn't have cellphones, so I guess this phone must've been their one connection to the outside world."

"I wonder who they called? They didn't have any friends or family." Donna sets the receiver down with a wistful expression. "I hope they didn't have to race down all those hallways every time the phone rang with a telemarketer offering them a new credit card."

I sit in the tall leather desk chair and take my turn with the phone. "Look at me—I'm a captain of industry. Edgar Tate Junior must have used this phone to wheel and deal."

I open the top desk drawer. Inside is a thick leather-bound ledger with ACCOUNTS printed on the cover in gold. I open it up. The first page says TRADESMEN and under that heading is a long list of the people needed to keep this house running. The early entries begin with, "Coal, Ice, Hay." About a third of the way down, the handwriting changes and the entries say, "Window-washer, laundress, gardener." At that point, the Tates no longer had enough servants to do all the cleaning and maintenance. Some newer additions are written in ballpoint pen in script less spidery, more modern: electrician, car repair, plumber. Each category is followed by a name and number. Sometimes a name is crossed out and a replacement entered, but for the most part, the ladies were remarkably loyal. These are the people who served Vareena and Maybelle until their death. "Looks like they got their groceries delivered by the Fairchild Market and their car repaired by Hyler's Garage. Those suppliers must have seen the ladies pretty regularly. I wonder what they thought of them?"

I flip the page and see long columns of entries and figures. Every expenditure since the house was built is entered here. "Wow, guys—look. In 1891, a load of coal cost $7.00. And in 1942, it cost $20.00."

I keep paging through the ledger. "And look—in 1945, Vareena hired Formby Architects to design the kitchen addition. The whole thing only cost five thousand dollars! I wish our kitchen remodeling had been that cheap."

"I don't think fifty years from now my grandkids are gonna give a damn how much I paid for gas and phone." Ty prowls around the office looking for items worth selling.

"WELL, I THINK IT'S INTERESTING. I'm going to save this ledger and see if the Palmyrton History Room in the library wants it."

Then my eye is drawn to a change in the columns of figures. "Look at this. In 1944, the handwriting on the ledger changes from this old-fashioned, spidery style, to this round, neat script. That must've been Vareena taking over after her father-in-law died. And in 1945 there are a bunch of entries for carpenters and plumbers and roofers. I bet that's the year they built the kitchen extension. But then in 1964, the writing changes again to this sprawling, slanted script, and it stays that way until the end."

Donna looks over my shoulder. "So you think in 1964, Maybelle took over paying the bills? What happened that year?"

"I have no idea." I close the heavy book. "But it's odd that the maid was in charge of their finances."

Donna spritzes some vinegar water on the glass front of an étagère. "Maybe Maybelle was holding Vareena hostage." She grins as she polishes the glass.

Easy to imagine in this gloomy room. "Like in that old Bette Davis movie, *"Whatever Happened to Baby Jane?"*

"Oh my God, that movie gave me nightmares for a week." Donna shivers. "That scene where she serves her sister the pet canary on a silver platter. Gack!"

"Can you two stop tellin' fairy tales and help me with this cabinet?" Ty glares at us from across the room.

Automatically, I move to help him, but my mind is elsewhere. If Sean were killed, would I give up caring about our house and my business? Would I turn decision-making about my life over to someone else? I don't think I would. But certainly my own father retreated from life after my mother died. But not to the extent Vareena did after Lawrence Tate died.

Why was his death so devastating? After all, they'd had a whirlwind romance. They barely knew each other when they married.

Maybe that made the loss even harder to bear. Vareena was mourning the life she'd been anticipating, not the life she'd had.

CHAPTER 21

"HOW'S THIS FOR A PLAN?" I'm strategizing with Ty as we drive away from our first day of work at the Tate mansion. We've dropped everything to plunge into this windfall project, but the Armentrout sale has been scheduled, and we have to juggle that too. "Donna and I will handle the Armentrout sale tomorrow while you stay at the Tate Mansion and keep working with Henry."

Ty purses his lips as he steers the balky old van around a tight corner. "That's a lot for you to manage being that this is Donna's first sale. I better come over at the end of the day to help clean up."

I laugh. "Donna could clean Versailles single-handedly, but you could help load the van with whatever doesn't sell."

Ty glances over his shoulder into the cargo area. "That girl be trippin' when she sees how dirty this van is. You better not leave anything you want in here, or it be *gone* by tomorrow."

"True." I kick through some papers floating in the footwell of the passenger seat. "Where are those old comic books I said I was going to give to Sean's nephew?"

"Think they slid under the seat." He taps the big, dusty ledger from Edgar Tate's office, which is propped against the console next to the gearshift. "If you're really going to take that old book to the library, you better move it to your car tonight. If it winds up in the back, you'll never see it again."

"Right. Don't let me forget it."

As we reach the business district, we decide to stop for gas, and as long as we're at the QuickCheck, I run into get some milk and eggs. By the time I make it through the long line and exit the store, Ty has moved the van away from the pumps and is standing beside it talking to a young man.

I start across the parking lot and realize the man is Dennis Sykes.

Good. This is my chance to confront him about the lies he and Levi told Henry and me.

I quicken my pace and watch Ty jab his index finger toward Dennis's chest. Dennis says one last thing and turns toward his own car. Ty gives a dismissive wave to Dennis's retreating figure and gets back into the van. I trot up to the driver's window just in time to see Dennis peel out of his parking spot.

"What was that all about?"

Ty blows air between his lips. "Dennis being helpful. Wanted to let me know I'm oppressed, but I'm too dumb to see it."

Ty had laughed when I first told him about Dennis calling me a capitalist overlord. Now he doesn't seem so amused. He's gazing into the distance at the spot where Dennis's car disappeared into traffic.

"Did you ask him why he and Levi lied to Henry and me?"

"He claims Henry is the one who changed his tune. That Henry wanted the whole job for himself and—"

"I don't believe that. Henry was really surprised when we talked at the post office. He couldn't have faked that."

Ty points to the passenger seat. "C'mon, let's go. No point in goin' around and around about it."

But when I get in the van, Ty still seems disturbed by his encounter with Dennis. He starts the engine but doesn't put the van in gear.

"What's wrong? What else did you talk about?"

Ty turns to face me. "Dennis wanted to know about how we know if something's worth a lot of money. Do we look at every single piece of furniture? Do we open all the drawers? Do we take the paintings off the walls and look at the backs? I told him yeah, in a house with antiques and fancy shit, we gotta do that. In a place where we can tell the pictures came from HomeGoods, then no."

"Why was he interested? He was willing to let Henry sell all the antiques in a giant garage sale, then he was willing to get ripped off by Dexter Abernathy. But now he's worried we don't know what we're doing?"

Ty frowns. "I don't think that's what was in his head. It was more like he was worried we'd be paying too much attention. He kept askin' about you...like he was tryin' to judge how sharp you were."

Ty's observation has flipped the problem one hundred eighty degrees. "You think Levi and Dennis didn't want me to have the job because they're afraid of what I'll figure out when I'm in the house? But they themselves don't know what's in there."

Ty shrugs. "You gotta rep on the street, Audge. People know you good at figurin' stuff out."

ALTHOUGH SOME OF MY HIGHEST-SPENDING regulars aren't interested in the Armentrout sale because of the dearth of antiques, there's still a sizeable crowd queuing up on Birdie's street as we drive up to open the sale. The weather is perfect: no rain, but not so sunny and clear that people are tempted to go to the shore instead of a sale.

Donna presses her nose against the passenger side window of the AMT van. "Wow, it's only seven o'clock—did they sleep here last night?"

I navigate past a mammoth Chevy Suburban parked at the corner of Birdie's driveway. "This is nothing. Wait'll you see the crowd at a really big sale."

My stomach flutters. Like the Tate sale. Man, that's going to be a trip! Even with our revenue-sharing arrangement with Henry, Another Man's Treasure will walk away with a high five-figure check. And the Parks Center will get an instant infusion of cash to tide them over until the house sells.

We left Birdie's house in good shape, so there's not much to do this morning apart from setting up the checkout area. As I arrange the cash box and receipt book, my phone rings. George Armentrout. Probably calling with a last-minute request to pull something out of the sale. These calls are quite common, but I'm surprised that lawyerly George would ask for something that's a clear violation of our contract.

"Good morning, George. What can I do for you?"

"Oh, hello, Audrey. I...er...I just wanted to check if the sale was going to take place today?" His sentence ends on a questioning up-note. "Because….."

Because what? Surely he can't be thinking that we can cancel now.

"I'm right here at Birdie's house getting ready to open the doors. The customers are lined up. I'm sure we're going to have a very successful sale." I keep my tone upbeat, not allowing the possibility of any backsliding on his part.

"Oh, I see. Yes, of course…."

Do not ask him what's wrong. Do not go there. Just thank him for calling and hang up. That's my practical businesswoman talking.

A void of dead air hangs between us. When have I ever listened to that bitch?

"What's the matter, George?"

"Oh, I know it's crazy, but I haven't slept a wink all night. Do you think I'm doing the right thing? Selling all of Birdie's precious things? Selling her house, when she's still…still…. And what about her garden? What if whoever buys the house paves over the garden and puts in a swimming pool?"

Swimming emerges as a long, anguished wail.

"Of course you're doing the right thing, George. Birdie's not going to be able to come back here. And she might live in the nursing home for a long time, so you have to get her affairs in order. And I bet whoever buys the house will want to enjoy the lovely garden and do their swimming at the country club."

I pull that last bit out of my ass, but it seems to reassure George. "True. Very true." He sighs. "I'm glad I talked to you, Audrey. I think I'll go play a round of golf until I'm sure the sale is over."

"Good idea. Just put us out of your mind, and relax."

Crisis averted.

And just in time. Ty and Donna return and we review our positions for the sale. Then Ty opens the door, and we're off and running.

An exhausted looking young Asian man in green hospital scrubs is first through the door. Probably a resident at Palmyrton Hospital saddled with medical school debt. His hugely pregnant wife plops down on Birdie's white sofa with pink flowers and beams with satisfaction. No doubt a year from now, the pink roses on the upholstery will intertwine with apple juice and baby puke stains, but I'm not here to find the ideal owners for Birdie's furniture. I take their cash, and the first of Birdie's possessions walks out the door.

A novice caterer buys the best of Birdie's kitchen equipment, ensuring her pots and pans will be working harder than they ever did in this house. And a sad-eyed divorced dad takes a chest of drawers. That's right, buddy—time to stop storing your clothes in cardboard boxes. This purchase is the first step to moving on.

Soon it gets too busy for me to philosophize over every sale, and the first two hours fly by.

At ten, the garden club ladies descend en masse. They spread throughout the first floor, snatching up floral prints, floral needlepoint pillows, floral china.

Soon a middle-aged lady in a madras plaid skirt and navy espadrilles appears at the checkout holding a pedestal cake plate bordered in purple and blue violets. Her eyes water as she hands over ten dollars. "Birdie always served her famous blueberry Bundt cake on this plate. I want it as a little memento even though I never bake cakes." She shakes her head and dabs at the corner of her eyes with a crumpled tissue. "She was my friend. I'll miss her."

Since this lady seems nicer than the flock of vultures she came in with, I enquire, "Have you been to visit her at the nursing home?"

The woman nods. "She didn't remember my name, but she did seem glad to see me. Going there"—she takes a shuddering breath—"it's not easy."

Some of the other garden club ladies don't seem so cut up. There's a cluster of them in the living room. I can hear excited female voices, but can't follow what they're saying.

"….you can't do that…"

"…waste…"

"…maybe a cutting…"

I hope I'm not going to have to referee a fight.

Finally a determined looking old gal with short iron gray hair and sensible lace-up walking shoes marches up to me. "What about the plants?"

"George took all Birdie's houseplants to the nursing home so she could enjoy them there."

"Of course, I know that. I've been there to visit her. I moved her African violets out of the direct sun so they wouldn't get scorched. I'm talking about the garden plants. Birdie had some rare and valuable specimen plants out there." She gestures to the back garden. "They should be part of the sale."

I thought I'd heard it all in this business, but this is a first. "You want to dig up her garden?"

"Not the entire garden. I have no interest in her asters or her coreopsis. I'm talking about the purple spotted toad lily and the Triteleia Rudy bicolor....and the Schizopetalus hibiscus, of course."

I'm momentarily struck dumb, so she keeps talking. "I'll dig them out and move some of her phlox to cover the hole. They're overcrowded anyway. I warned Birdie that Cabot Pink and Bright Eyes would go crazy in that exposure. And I'll pay a fair price. Of course, transplanting something so delicate is always risky, so there should be allowances for that."

I find my voice and choke out a reply. "This is highly unusual. I'd have to ask the owner."

The old bat scowls. "I talked to George about it at the country club last week. That man is always so vague. Hard to get a straight answer from him."

I know in that moment that I'm certainly not going to call George and ruin his golf game with an upsetting question from this determined old bag. So I must decide: forbid her access to the garden, or grant her wish?

She senses my wavering and goes in for the kill. "New owners won't know how to take care of those heirloom plants. They'll die, and that's a terrible waste."

This is a strange echo of George's concerns when he called this morning. Apart from the nice friend who bought the cake plate, I haven't felt that any of Birdie's things have found the ideal homes I fantasized about with George. Maybe knowing that some of the plants will live on in good hands would be comforting to him.

"All right. Show me what you're interested in. I can't have you making a mess back there. The house will be going on the market soon."

We strike a deal: a hundred dollars for five rare perennials and she'll make the garden look perfect. I go back to work.

In half an hour, I remember to check on them. "Look out the window, Donna. Are they tearing up the entire garden?"

"They've got one big bushy thing and three smaller leafy things in plastic pots, and now she's digging up some of those pink flowers and putting them in the hole where the bush was. It looks okay." Donna cranes her neck for a better view. "What's that on the sidewalk? It looks like they found a box buried in the garden."

"A box?" I finish my transaction and dart away from the checkout to take a look. I'm anticipating some big, decaying thing, but what I see on the walk is a small metal strongbox, a little smaller than the cashbox I use at sales. It's dirty, but it doesn't look old and rusty. Leaving Donna at the checkout, I head outside to investigate.

The flock of garden clubbers intercepts me on the patio. The ringleader is carrying the box. "We found this buried under the hibiscus."

"Evelyn broke the lock when she hit it with her shovel," a nervous lady explains.

"Just an old photo inside—a couple holding a baby. No reason to hide that." Evelyn taps her temple with a dirty forefinger. "Poor Birdie. Guess you'd better give it to George." She hands the box over to me and hoists the heaviest of the pots. The other ladies carry the smaller pots, and they depart down the driveway—a mother duck and her brood.

CHAPTER 22

WHEN THE LAST CUSTOMER LEAVES, Birdie Armentrout's house has been picked as clean as the turkey at the Coughlin family Thanksgiving. All that remains are a fussy floral print chair, a couple of lamps, some random knick-knacks, a toaster and some kitchenware, and a box of linens.

"We'll donate this stuff to charity." I push the chair closer to the front door. "Ty will be coming soon to help you load it all into the van to take to Sister Alice."

"Ooo, I want to meet that nun after all you guys have said about her." Donna begins sweeping. "Hey, what about this?" She hands me a small trophy.

First Prize, Hybrid Dahlia Competition, 2012 Palmer County Garden Show.

"I'm going over to George Armentrout's to give him his check from the sale. I'll take it to him. Maybe he'll want to keep it, or give it to Birdie in the nursing home."

Normally, I wouldn't offer personal delivery, but I have to admit, I'm curious to see his reaction. I've looked at the sepia-tinted photo in the box. It shows a rather somber couple—he in a suit and tie, she in a big hat and dress that stops above her ankles—holding an infant so it faces the camera. The baby's face is barely discernable inside a long, lacy white gown. Behind the couple is an ornate marble font.

A baptismal photo.

There's no date, but from the style of the clothes it seems to be from the early 20th century.

And the box contains one other thing: a credit card receipt from Staples for $10.98, the price of the box. The receipt is signed with a dramatic flourish ending in a small squiggle.

I take the box and the trophy and head out. "I'll be back in an hour to lock up."

After I start the engine, I pause and look at the box. Someone bought it specifically to hold that photo. I wonder why?

And then for no reason that's rational, I open the box, pull out my phone, and snap a picture of the old photo.

GEORGE IS STILL IN HIS golf clothes when I arrive. His condo is just what I expected: upscale, but bachelor-barren. He's clutching a scotch on the rocks and offers me a cocktail. I spy a bottle of Hendricks gin on his bar. Why not enjoy the best after a long day?

While George mixes my G&T, I report on the success of the sale and tell him about the Garden Club ladies. "I hope you don't mind that I sold them the plants, but I figured they'd take good care of them. And honestly, that woman Evelyn is hard to argue with."

"Ha! Don't I know it." George sets the drink down in front of me and notices the box I've pulled from my tote bag.

"The ladies found this buried in Birdie's garden. Evelyn broke it open with her shovel. I figured you'd want it."

"Birdie was behaving very strangely in the months before her diagnosis," George says as he sips from his drink. "Who knows why she would have buried that box." He slides the dirty box towards himself and lifts out the photo. His brow furrows. "I have no idea who these people are. They're certainly not our grandparents. Maybe some distant relatives that Birdie tracked down." He moves to return the photo to the box and his face spasms.

He pulls out the credit card receipt. "Oh, my! This is Loretta's handwriting. I'd know it anywhere." He's so surprised, it's as if he's forgotten my presence. "Loretta bought this box and gave it to Birdie? Who could these people be?" He's murmuring to himself, not expecting an answer from me.

I try to be helpful. "When is the receipt dated?"

George holds the receipt close to his eyes. "March 21."

His hand drops into his lap.

"George, you told me Loretta had been tense, not herself. Did that date back as far as March? Could this have something to do with her ...death?"

I hesitate to use the word "murder."

"No...no, how could it?" He takes a big swallow of his drink. "You say Evelyn opened up the box? Did she see the receipt?"

"I don't think she took the photo out. Her hands were dirty from digging."

"Hmmm." The furrow in George's brow deepens. "Let's hope so."

WHEN I GET BACK TO Birdie's house, Ty is loading the van. I walk inside and find Donna on her phone with her back to me.

"I have to go. It's part of my job," I hear her say. I don't think she knows I'm in the room.

"Anthony, please. I love this job. And we can't afford for me to lose it."

They seem to be arguing about Another Man's Treasure. I can't imagine why. There's a long pause on her end as she listens to her husband.

"You're being—Anthony? Anthony!"

Clearly, he's hung up on her. I cough to let Donna know I'm here. She spins around, her face tear-streaked.

"What's the matter?"

I can see she wants to say 'nothing" but knows that will never fly. She offers a shaky smile. "Husbands. You know how unreasonable they can be."

Sometimes...when they're complaining that you forgot to buy mushrooms. But mine never reduces me to tears. "I don't mean to pry, but you seemed to be arguing over your job. Is there something wrong? Because I've been very happy with your work."

Now the tears flow freely. "Thank you for saying that, Audrey. I've been trying so hard. I really love working with you guys. Anthony, he just doesn't understand my new responsibilities."

"He's mad about you working weekends?" That better not be the problem, because we made the hours clear in the interview.

She shakes her head. "I'm so dumb. I mentioned to Anthony that I was going to get to meet Sister Alice, and he freaked out. He doesn't want me driving to Newark…alone…with Ty."

Donna looks at me through watery red eyes. "He's just a little, er, overprotective."

More like a little controlling, jealous, racist. Donna's marriage is not my problem, but now that I've found a great assistant, I don't want to lose her. "Look, maybe next week you could invite Anthony to the office so he can meet us both and see there's noting to worry about. I'll go to Newark with Ty today."

"Oh, Audrey—I'm so sorry! You shouldn't have to do that. You have more important stuff to do."

I really don't like indulging Anthony's ridiculous fears, but I don't want this marital strife to put me on the hunt for yet another assistant. I need Donna for the Tate job.

"It's okay. I haven't seen Sister Alice in a while."

Donna has cleaned the house to hypoallergenic perfection, so we send her home and Ty and I head out to Newark.

"I'm not surprised," Ty says when I explain the situation. "Little things she says, sounds like the dude is kind of a dick."

"Like what?"

"Since today is Saturday, she hadda leave him his lunch in marked containers in the fridge. Like he can't make himself his own ham sandwich. And he's paranoid about crime. Got the motion-detector lights and a home security system and he keeps a gun in the nightstand drawer." Ty shakes his head. "They live in Florham Park, not the South Bronx."

I laugh. "Yeah, Sean says it's a crime wave in Florham Park when two people make an illegal left out of the Trader Joe's parking lot on the same day. So Donna might not be ready for Sister Alice's block."

"Yeah, she need more than vinegar and water to clean up all the gang tags spray-painted on the buildings."

"But none of those punks bother Sister Alice."

"They leave her be. They know she's good people."

Ty weaves through the traffic already heading to New York for Saturday night fun. He frowns. "Lotta airport traffic, too. I wanna get in and out before this road gets too nasty."

In another ten minutes, we take the exit for Newark. We bypass the high-rise office buildings and glittering performing arts center downtown, and start jolting along the neighborhood streets lined with fast food restaurants, laundromats and pawn shops. Soon we turn onto the block where Sister Alice's Resource Center is tucked between low-rise apartment buildings and crumbling brick houses. A young mother pushes a baby in a stroller. Some kids jump rope on the sidewalk under the watchful eye of a grandmother in a porch chair.

Ty glances in the side-view mirror and squints.

"What's wrong?"

"That car was behind us on Route 78. Now he's here on Sullivan Street."

I look in the mirror on my side and can barely make out a nondescript gray sedan behind us. "What makes you think it's the same car? There must be thousands of cars like that between here and Palmyrton."

"Yeah. Prob'ly." Still, Ty seems hyper-alert. Maybe all this talk of crime has made him edgy.

I text Sister Alice that we've arrived as we turn into the alley that runs behind her building. The gray car continues down Sullivan Street.

We park the van, scaring off a scrawny calico cat, and Sister Alice emerges through the scratched metal back door. She wears sensible walking shoes and khaki pants. The only sign of her religious calling is a carved wooden cross on a leather thong around her neck. "Hello, my angels! What a joy it is to see you."

Ty leans over to embrace the short, stocky nun. "Yo, sister—how you doin'?"

"Full of blessings." She turns to hug me. "Audrey! How wonderful that you've come with Ty today."

We chat briefly, but I know Ty is eager to unload and get back on the road. He unlocks the rear doors of the van. The load has shifted during the bumpy ride, and Ty deftly catches a floral lamp from Birdie's bedroom before it crashes to the street.

"Lovely!" Sister Alice says as she takes the lamp from Ty. "I know a young mother who just moved out of a shelter who can use this." She trots inside happily with her prize. Ty hands me a box full of linens and takes a heavier box loaded with random kitchenware. Locking the rear cargo door requires a key and two hands, so we leave it unlocked. We'll be right back out for the next load. And anyone from the neighborhood who wants to steal our sale leftovers probably needs them even more than Sister Alice. The nun stays inside rearranging her storage room while we return to the van for a second load.

Ty strides up to the van talking to me over his shoulder. "I wonder if—"

The sound of something being dragged and toppling comes from the van.

Ty freezes.

A black-gloved hand emerges from the van.

It holds a gun.

Ty jumps back and raises his hands. "Whoa, easy man. Ain't no need for that."

I'm stunned. We're being robbed at gunpoint? At four-thirty in the afternoon? Nothing like this has ever happened on any of our hundreds of drop-offs to Sister Alice.

The man jumps out of the van. He's thin, dressed in a long-sleeved black shirt and jeans, his face completely covered by a black ski mask. He keeps the gun aimed at Ty, but his hand trembles. "Give me the keys." The voice sounds young, panicky.

"Ain't nuthin' but old junk furniture in there," Ty protests. "You can't even sell—"

"Shut up!" the robber glances over his shoulder at the end of the alley, then up to the door to the Resource Center. His movements are so twitchy, his arm so thin—I'm sure that he's just a kid.

A jumpy, impulsive teenager who might blow our heads off.

Please don't let Sister Alice come out now. "Give him the keys, Ty. We're not getting shot over a ten year old van."

Ty makes a take-it-easy gesture. "Look man, we don't want no trouble. You can jus' take this whole van and keep everything that's in it. I'ma reach in my pocket and get the keys." Ty turns to show the kid the bulge of keys in his jeans. The kid nods and reaches out his hand for them.

Thirty seconds later, Ty and I watch the AMT van careening down the alley.

"Sorry, Audge. We prob'ly get the van back if he don't crash it." He shudders. "Amateurs with guns make me real nervous."

Shock is setting in. I've been robbed at gunpoint. Carjacked. "What just happened here?"

"I shoulda listened to my gut. I told you I thought that car was following us."

"Wait—you think this was planned? That the kid didn't just come across the van while we were inside?"

Ty shakes his head. "You see his kicks?"

"His shoes? No, I wasn't looking at his feet. I was too interested in the gun pointed at my heart."

"He was wearin' a brand new pair of Jordan's. That model goes for four hundred large. Whoever followed us out from Palmyrton paid that kid to hit us."

CHAPTER 23

FOR ONCE, TY DOESN'T OBJECT to calling the cops.

But the Newark police are quite unimpressed by our crime. An old van full of worthless junk was hijacked by a punk. No one was killed.

Yawn.

When Ty tells the cop recording our theft report that he thinks someone was following us, the guy just arches his eyebrows and keeps typing like he can't even be bothered to tell us we're crazy.

I think about mentioning that my husband is a police detective in Palmyrton, but I get the feeling these guys won't be impressed. And I'd rather tell Sean about the carjacking in person at home tonight than get him riled up with a call at work. He has enough to worry about.

In an hour, we're Ubering back to Palmyrton.

"Thank God Donna wasn't with you when this happened."

"Yeah, her old man would make her quit fer sure."

"Maybe we shouldn't even tell her about it."

"How we gonna explain why we don't have a van anymore?"

"True." I gaze out the window at the crazed New Jersey drivers surging past us. Relief at surviving this assault has been replaced by anger over having to buy a new van. "I just had that van tuned up. The mechanic said I could probably get another hundred thousand miles out of it."

"If it was a Chevy pick-up or even a Honda like yours, it would be in a chop shop by now. But I don't think there's much call for cargo van parts. It's too hot to drive it far, so they'll take what they want and abandon it. Gotta hope the cops find it before it gets totally trashed."

"Take what they want...what *do* they want, Ty? There was nothing valuable in that load. Could we have overlooked something? Some collectible? Some antique?"

"That's what I'm sittin' here goin' over in my head. I'm picturin' every single thing I loaded in there." Ty cracks the knuckle of each finger methodically. "Nuthin'. Nuthin' but old junk that no one wanted to buy."

By the time we're back in Palmyrton it's after six, but what's the point of rushing home? Sean is working late again, and I have plenty of paperwork to do at the office. I send Ty home and call my neighbor to ask if she'll let Ethel out and feed her. I file a claim with my insurance company, but I won't hear from an adjustor until Monday. In the meantime, I look up the Blue Book value of a ten-year old Chevy cargo van: $6,000. What kind of replacement van can I hope to buy with that? My van may have had some dings and scratches, but I took good care of the engine.

Then I open up my accounting program.

The profits from the Armentrout sale are totally overshadowed by the loss of the van. Now I'll have to use some of the Tate sale profits to buy a reliable used van.

I kick my trashcan. I was this close—this close—to having all my financial ducks in a row--wedding and remodeling bills paid off, Sean's debts from his first marriage and college loans settled, savings launched—when this crime blew a hole in my plans.

I don't need the van for the Tate sale since Henry has a truck, so I can get along without a van until the following week. But if the old AMT van doesn't turn up, I'm probably going to have to spend twenty grand to get a used van that's not a piece of crap.

Screw that!

I'm going to figure out why my van was stolen.

And who stole it.

And then I'm getting it back.

CHAPTER 24

"WHAT TIME IS IT?" SEAN stumbles into the kitchen on Sunday morning rubbing sleep from his eyes. He catches sight of the oven clock. "Eleven-thirty! Why did you let me sleep so late?"

"Because you were utterly exhausted." I pour him a mug of coffee. "I couldn't have woken you up even if the house was on fire."

He sips his coffee as he scrolls through the messages on his phone.

"Don't even think of accepting another moonlighting job," I warn him. "You need a break."

Sean sighs but pockets the phone. He slides his arms around me from behind as I scramble eggs. "You do realize that if I spoke to you like that, you'd turn around and do exactly the opposite of what I said."

"Me? Never!" I slide the eggs onto a plate and send him to the table. While I'm cleaning up, I chatter about the Armentrout sale and the buried box. I'm not ready to tell him about the stolen van. I'd like to have an hour or two of peace and relaxation before we have to start worrying again. I move on to a report on how funny Donna is when she cleans.

Silence.

When I turn around, Sean has his phone out with a forkful of eggs suspended in midair.

"You haven't heard a word I said." I lunge for the phone.

He holds it above his head. "I did. Donna found a box buried in the Armentrout's back yard and cleaned it off."

"Wrong." I sit down across from Sean. "What is so damn

important in these messages you get from the security job?"

"There are group texts that go out with open assignments. The first person to respond gets the gig. I don't want to miss a good one."

"What makes one better than another?"

"These German investors are visiting pharma companies in Palmer County. All I have to do escort them in and out of buildings so they think they're safe from kidnappers and terrorists." Sean rolls his eyes. "It's like picking up money off the ground."

"Pick it up some other day. I thought we'd take Ethel to hike in Hacklebarney Park and then eat at that cute restaurant with the patio seating."

"O-k-a-ay." The phone vibrates and his gaze leaves my face and drops to the screen.

"Ty and I were carjacked outside of Sister Alice's and now I don't have a van anymore."

The phone clatters from Sean's hand.

"What! Why didn't you tell me?"

"I was waiting for the right moment. Guess I found it."

Now that I have my husband's full attention, I fill him in on all the details of the crime. Sean immediately calls a contact in Newark, so the urgency of my case has bumped up a little. But I still doubt they'll be combing the streets for my van.

Unlike the Newark cops, my husband is very interested in the car that followed us out from Palmyrton. Sean makes me call Ty so he can get the details directly from the source. But Ty wasn't able to make out the license plate or even the make of the car. All he knows is that it wasn't a Mercedes or BMW or Lexus or any other model that interests him.

Now Sean starts on a second round of questioning with me.

"You think the guy was looking for something inside the van when you came back out?"

"That's what it seems like. We heard boxes being moved and stuff falling. But there was nothing but old junk left from the sale. We're sure there was nothing valuable."

Sean paces around the kitchen. "What about that buried box? It must have been important if Loretta gave it to Birdie and Birdie went to the trouble of burying it."

I study the innocent face of the cow creamer on the kitchen

table. "George and her friends seem to think her dementia made her do that, but maybe—" I pull out my phone and show him the photo of the photo. "George doesn't know who those people are, but maybe it has something to do with Birdie's genealogy research. And Loretta bought the box. That seemed to throw George for a loop."

"Who knew you had it?"

"Just Donna, Ty, and me. And George and the ladies who found it."

"So the ladies might think it was in the van," Sean says.

"You can't possibly think members of the garden club hired a punk to carjack me!"

Sean squints and points a finger at me. "What else was weird about the Armentrout job?"

"Crawford Bostwick wanting to move in…prowling around upstairs. You think he was looking for that box?"

"His mother gave it to Birdie. Seems like she wanted it out of her own house." Sean sits down across from me. "Could it have been Crawford who pointed the gun at you? You said the guy was thin."

I shake my head. "No, the voice was wrong. And Crawford is taller. I'm sure our guy is a kid."

Sean leans forward. "Crawford works at a school. And he's already shown he knows how to manipulate young people."

"Yeah, but…kids from Bumford-Stanley wouldn't do dirty work for a new pair of sneakers."

"Crawford has also been in and out of rehab. You don't know what kind of kids he has connections to."

Sean whistles for Ethel. "Let's go for our hike."

"Really?" I was sure the loss of the van would make Sean want to moonlight even more.

He pulls me in for a hug as Ethel prances around our feet. "That carjacking could have gone sideways in an instant. Money doesn't matter. All that matters is you're safe."

Sean grabs Ethel's leash. "Today we have fun. Tomorrow I'll be questioning Crawford Bostwick."

CHAPTER 25

MONDAY IS TY'S DAY OFF, a day that he spends in classes, so Donna and I will tackle the bedrooms at the Tate Mansion on our own, while Henry and his men work in the tiny servants' bedrooms on the third floor. I've decided not to tell Donna about the van right now. Maybe Sean will have it back for me by the end of the day.

We enter through the kitchen since the back door is easier to lock and unlock than the massive oak front door. Donna pauses to look around, taking in the clean but scratched gas stove and the deep porcelain sink. She sets down her caddy of cleaning supplies and runs her fingers along the wobbly wooden work table, which has been leveled with some flattened aluminum foil shoved under one leg. My assistant looks as perplexed as Ethel when Sean emerges from our pantry without a Milk-Bone in his hand. "When I saw this house from the outside, I thought living here must be like living in a fairytale castle. But now that I'm inside, this house seems more like an episode of *Survivor.* Ya know, where the people have to figure out how to make do with whatever they can find. What's the point of being rich if you don't have any luxuries? They didn't even have a dish washer."

Donna doesn't expect an answer from me. She wanders over to the avocado green refrigerator. "I wonder which one of them chose this?"

"Yeah, I've been thinking about their purchases. Maybelle seemed to do all the shopping and bookkeeping. Did she make the decisions on what they bought, decide when it was okay to spend some money?"

"It was Vareena's money." Donna giggles. "But it's not like

Maybelle went crazy with it, like my cousin Tiffany."

I GESTURE FOR DONNA TO GO ahead of me up the narrow back stairs. "Maybe the bedrooms will give us a clue."

"Whew!" Donna says as we emerge into the upstairs hall. "Those steps are steep. No wonder the old gals lived to be a hundred. They got an aerobic workout every day."

Every door in the hallway is closed. Donna looks at me. "Where should we start?"

"Pick one."

She opens the first door on the right. "Oh. My. God. Would you look at this bathroom?"

I follow her in. The room is large yet spartan.

"Look at how high that claw foot tub is! How did they climb in and out of that without breaking a hip?" Donna crosses the room. "And look at this toilet! You flush it by pulling a chain."

I have to try it. The water rushes through the pipes and circles the bowl. "Why fix it if it's not broke, eh?"

Donna opens the medicine chest. "Band-Aids, aspirin, merthiolate and toothpaste. Wow—talk about nothing but the basics!"

"Nothing to sell in here. Let's move on."

The next door Donna tries doesn't open. "This room is locked."

But when I apply a little more force, the door creaks open. A musty, mothball smell rushes out like a genie that's been contained for eons.

"Yuck!" Donna waves her hand in front of her nose as I pass her. The bedroom is wide enough to contain three of the windows that face the front of the house. They're all draped in heavy maroon velvet, blocking every ray of sunshine. An imposing four-poster bed stands against the interior wall. Was this Vareena's room? I pass through an archway into a dressing room that features built-in cabinetry. When I open the door, the mothball smell grows even stronger. Every shelf contains men's clothing: a top hat and a bowler, stiff but yellowing shirts, vests, bow ties, dark woolen suits and overcoats.

"Looks like this was the old man's bedroom, and when he died they just shut the door and never came in here again," I call out to Donna.

We quickly catalog the items of value: two paintings, some gold cufflinks, a sterling silver-backed hairbrush, and the furniture. Maybe the clothes will be of interest to a movie costume designer who's bought from me in the past. Both of us are eager to find Vareena's room.

The air behind the next door we open is much fresher. "Someone's been polishing with Pledge in here," Donna says.

This room faces the backyard. The windows are smaller and covered in a cheerful, if faded, cotton floral print. The busy green and white wallpaper looks a little less ancient than dreary maroon stripes in the master bedroom. The bed, a standard double, is neatly made with a chenille bedspread and two not very fluffy pillows. No photos, no artwork, no knick-knacks—just a vase of faded artificial flowers on a tiny corner shelf. The dresser and bedside table are heavy mahogany. I open the top dresser drawer: a stack of plain cotton panties and three sensible white bras. Next drawer: wool and cotton socks, neatly matched and rolled in balls. Three Land's End knit shirts and two cardigans, one cotton, one wool. The closet holds two blouses, two skirts, one dress, and a pair of slacks. Lined up on the floor, one pair of each: bedroom slippers, sneakers, walking shoes, snow boots. Hanging on one hook is a flannel nightgown and a bathrobe.

On another hook hangs a pair of corduroy pants with faded knees and a frayed shirt with some bleach stains. Finally, a little clue to ownership. "I think maybe this is Maybelle's room. These are the clothes she must've worn to do the cleaning."

Donna checks the labels of the hanging clothes. "All LL Bean and Land's End. She sure didn't have a lot of clothes, but everything she had was pretty nice. If this is Maybelle's room, Ty was wrong—there's nothing from the thrift shop."

On the nightstand are two books: the Bible and another library book, *The Immortal Life of Henrietta Lacks.* The story of a Black woman and her family—so maybe Maybelle. Also the story of medical research—maybe nurse Vareena.

Maybelle or Vareena? I'm still not sure. The longer I'm in the house, the less distinct their lives seem.

We move to the room across the hall. It's about the same size, but faces the front. While the other bedroom was green and white, this one is blue and yellow. Apart from that, the furnishings are virtually the same. When we open the drawers, we find the same clothing, one size larger and in slightly bolder colors. "Look," Donna says from inside the closet. "You thought the other room belonged to Maybelle because of the work clothes, but this room has a set, too."

Donna strokes the worn fabric of the shirt. "That's sweet. As they got older, they shared the work. They were like partners, not employer and employee."

I prowl around the room looking for something, anything, that indicates which of the ladies slept here.

"How could they be so old and not have any prescription bottles?" Donna asks. "My grandma takes so many pills she needs a box to sort them all out. But there were none in the kitchen, none in the bathroom, none in the bedrooms."

"Maybe that's exactly why they lived so long. They stayed totally out of the clutches of the medical industrial complex. But you're right. A pill bottle would be handy to—" I stop as my gaze falls on a worn, leather-bound book on the nightstand. When I pick it up, I realize it's not a book at all; it's a closed frame that holds two photos. "Look," I call to Donna.

On one side is a young man in an Army Air Corps uniform, facing the camera with somber resolve. On the other side is the same man smiling joyfully as he gazes into the eyes of an equally ecstatic young woman. Lawrence and Vareena.

"Wow, he was handsome," Donna says.

I notice an edge of faded blue paper behind the photo of Lawrence. Carefully, I slide it out. It's the tissue-thin paper of old-time airmail stationary. The letter is addressed to Mrs. Vareena Tate, 60 Silver Lane, Palmyrton, although the ink is so faded it would be hard to decipher if I didn't already know what it said. I can see that the letter has been unfolded and refolded countless times.

"Should we read it?" Donna whispers.

"Normally we don't read personal letters that we find; we give them to the family. But in this case, there's no one. So...."

We look like two teenagers daring each other to light a cigarette. I slip the letter out of its envelope.

"What are all those black scratch-outs?" Donna asks.

"War time censorship. The men who were serving couldn't reveal anything about their location or what they were doing in case the information got into enemy hands."

My Darling Vareena,

As I await (censored) I dream of you. I have only a moment to pen these few words. I know we will win this war and the world will be set right again. When I return, we will truly launch our great adventure together. Until then, be patient (so hard for you!). Our time in the sun will arrive.

With all the love my heart can hold,

Lawrence

"They look so happy in the picture. The letter is so optimistic, like they were sure everything would turn out all right."

I close the frame gently. "They were wrong."

AS WE WORK, I'M STRUCK again by how little trash we're discarding. "I gotta hand it to those old gals—they sure didn't hoard. I thought we'd find closets and drawers with seventy years' worth of crap, but most everything is empty."

"Here's some junk." Donna tosses a stack of yellowed papers into the trash. "Wonder why Vareena would have kept that."

I peer into the trash bag, then dive after what Donna discarded. "Whoa! Bruce Strickler will go crazy for this!"

Donna's face collapses in contrition. "What? What did I do wrong? I thought it was just old newspaper ads."

I pull a handful of the papers out of the black Hefty bag. "They *are* old newspaper ads. That's what makes them valuable. Advertising memorabilia is a popular collectible, and we have a regular customer who's passionate about it."

"I'm sorry! I didn't know. How will I ever get the hang of all this?"

I pat Donna on the shoulder. "Don't stress. You can't be expected to know that there are people in this world who collect antique junk mail. Where did you find it? Is there more?"

Donna points me to the top drawer of a huge chest of drawers across from Vareena's bed. When I look inside, there are stacks of the ad fliers. All of them feature a slightly demonic whirling dervish zipping around kitchens and over gleaming floors while a smug looking woman sits with her feet up. SCOUR-BRITE DOES

THE DIRTY WORK OF MAKING YOUR HOME SHINE reads one headline. SCOUR-BRITE WORKS HARD SO YOU DON'T HAVE TO proclaims another. Hmm—advertising copywriting has come a long way since the 1940s.

"I think my grandmother used to clean with this stuff when I was a kid," I say. "Do they even make it any more?"

"It's probably toxic." Donna rubs lemon oil into the dry wood of the chest, bringing out a nice sheen in the wood. "Wonder why she saved them? They're not even funny or anything."

Who knows? I've long ago given up pondering why people save the things they do. "Let's put it all aside for Bruce and I'll send him an email about it tonight."

Donna finds a small box and moves the advertisements out of the drawer. "Hey, look at this little guy!" She holds up a plastic model of the whirling dervish character that stands on two feet. "He's like the Ronald McDonald of cleaning."

I stuff him in the box facedown. He's got creepy eyes.

AFTER WE CATALOG THE CONTENTS of two more bedrooms, these with no clothes or personal items, there's only one room left. Donna opens the last door on the right and stops in her tracks. "Oh, my! A nursery!"

I crowd in beside her. The room contains a crib, a rocking chair, and shelves full of toys and books. Was this Lawrence's room when he was a child? I cross to the shelves and remove a book. *Rhymes for Boys and Girls*, copyright 1945. A toy car is a replica of a late forties roadster.

Lawrence was born in 1915. This room held a baby born in the forties.

Lawrence and Vareena's baby?

Did she get pregnant in their brief weeks of marital bliss? How come none of the articles I've read mentioned that they had a child?

An heir.

Where is he now?

CHAPTER 26

DONNA AND I SPEND OUR last hour of work talking about the possibility of a Tate heir.

"If Vareena has a son, wouldn't all this go to him?" Donna pauses with a painted wooden train in her hand. "Unless she fought with him and cut him out of her will."

"He can't still be alive. None of the articles I read even mentioned him." I open the dresser drawers, but they're empty. "And there's no bedroom with a young man's possessions. He must've died as a baby. Or maybe she had a miscarriage. She fixed up the room when she found out she was pregnant and then...."

Donna's face crumples. "Stop! That's too sad. First her husband, then the baby."

I can see I'm upsetting my new assistant, so I keep quiet, but my mind continues to churn with theories. The miscarriage idea would explain why the articles don't mention a child, but the nursery is definitely decorated for a boy. There were no sonograms in the 1940s, and parents of that era didn't fight gender stereotypes by giving trains to girls. Was Vareena simply convinced she'd produce a male heir? Or had a son actually been born?

AT FIVE-THIRTY, DONNA AND I call it a day. I'm still pondering the notion of a Tate heir. The best way to satisfy my curiosity is to do the good deed I've been putting off—return the library books I found downstairs and take the ledger to the local history room. I can stop there on the way home tonight.

The library books are still in my tote bag. But the ledger? I shut my eyes trying to remember where I put it. The last time I saw it was in the van.

Crap! That's been lost too.

But wait. The picture is starting to fill in with more details. The ledger was on the front console the last time I saw it in the van. But it wasn't there on the trip to Newark.

Now I remember! Ty told me to clean out the van so Donna wouldn't toss it. I took the ledger out and put it…where?

I picture the stiff brown leather and the crumbling gold embossing of ACCOUNTS. I see it on top of something white. My dryer! I dumped a load of stuff on top of the dryer when I came into my house through the laundry room the night before the Armentrout sale.

So I can't stop at the library on my way home. I'll have to go tomorrow.

Thinking about the van makes me wonder if Sean had any success questioning Crawford. I've been so busy, I haven't even tried to text him.

When I pull out my phone, I see I've missed a text from him.

Following a lead on the van. Home late. Talk when I see you.

I feel a birthday-gift surge of excitement. Of course, I'm dying to call him right now for details. But "talk when I see you" means "I'm busy and it's complicated so wait."

So I drive home and wait.

After walking Ethel, I spend an hour emailing photos of Tate mansion antiques to dealers whom I think might be interested. One of the emails is a photo of the Scour-Brite ad memorabilia, which I send to Bruce Strickler. Not ten minutes after I hit SEND, my phone is ringing.

"Audrey, what a fabulous find!"

"Hi, Bruce. I thought you might like it." I get a kick out of Bruce. He's a retired business executive. I'm sure in his professional life, he must've been a tough negotiator, but when it comes to his collecting passion, he's as transparent with desire as a kid in the Target toy aisle.

"You say you found it at the Tate Mansion? Fascinating!"

"Yes, I'm curious about the connection. Was Edgar Tate's metal fabrication business connected to Scour-Brite in some way?"

"Doubtful. Scour-Brite was founded by Julius Crawford."

"Crawford? Any relation to Loretta Crawford Bostwick?"

"The woman who was murdered at the 1740 Club? Yes, Julius would have been her great-grandfather. Loretta inherited all the family money. She saved Heatherington, the ancestral Bostwick home, from going on the block."

"Whoa—you mean the Bostwicks are broke?"

"Well, broke is a relative term, isn't it?" Bruce laughs. "Frederic Bostwick had the pedigree, but Loretta had the big money. Frederic is a direct descendent of a Revolutionary War officer. Loretta is the heiress to the Scour-Brite fortune."

"Was," I correct. "I wonder if her son Crawford inherited it all?"

"I have no idea. All I know about is the history of where the money came from."

"Tell me about that. I'm interested."

"The original company was started by Loretta's great-grandfather, Julius Crawford. People used to clean everything with lye soap. He came up with a better product. But more important, he found a way to make women want to pay more for this green liquid in a bottle. The not-so-subtle message was that if you unleashed the dervish in your house, your cleaning would be done in record time and you'd be able to put your feet up and relax for an hour before your old man got home. Scour-Brite was one of the first consumer products promoted with mass advertising to women."

"Cleanser and floor-scrubbing soap are enough to make you a billionaire?"

"Scour-Brite is now SB Enterprises, a publicly traded company with five billion in revenue. They have their hands in all kinds of businesses, from industrial solvents to bio-medical solutions. But it all started with Julius Crawford's green soap in a bottle and his whirling dervish mascot."

"Why would Vareena Tate have saved the ads and the mascot figurine?"

"I'm sure the Tate family and the Crawford family moved in the same social circles, back in the day. I guess she must've been friends with one of the Crawfords."

"I suppose." Bruce and I settle on a price for the memorabilia, but I continue to dwell on the items. Why did Vareena keep these when she kept nothing of sentimental value except the photos and letter from her husband?

CHAPTER 27

THUMP.

My eyes open and squinch shut again. The house is quiet and dark except for my bedside lamp. The book I had been reading has slid to the floor, and Ethel is at the bedroom door with her nose pointed into the hall, her entire rear end wagging.

"Sean?"

He slips through the door, patting Ethel on the head as he makes his way to our bed.

"Why are you so late?" I reach for him groggily. The alarm clock reads 3:50. I'm pretty sure my mother-in-law never fell asleep until she was sure her cop husband had returned safely from his shift. I feel neglectful.

He sits beside me on the bed and dangles his phone before my nose. On the screen is a photo of a chipped red Jersey Devils key chain.

My sleepy brain can't process the significance.

Then I jolt up and snatch it from him. "My van keys! You found my van?"

He groans and stretches out beside me. "Not quite yet. Cops in Sister Alice's precinct arrested a junkie this morning on shoplifting charges. When they were processing him, they found these keys. By some miracle, the guy at the desk remembered your description. They called me in to help question him."

"How old is he? What did he look like?"

"Short and chubby and middle aged. Not your gunman. He found the keys in a trashcan in front of a bodega a few blocks away. And it seems like the guys who hang on that corner might know the kid with the new Jordans."

"Great! Who is he? Did you catch him?"

Sean pats my leg. "All in good time, my sweet. The citizens of Sullivan Street don't snitch unless there's something in it for them."

"I'll bribe them," I offer. "It's gotta be cheaper than buying a new van."

"Not necessary. The van can't be far from the keys. We'll search in the morning. But in the meantime, you'll be interested to know I had a conversation with your pal, Crawford."

I prod Sean to get the details coming faster. "He hired the kid?"

Sean shakes his head. "I don't think so. At first, Crawford seemed genuinely puzzled by my questions, then bored and annoyed. But when he finally understood that your van was stolen when it was full of stuff from Birdie's sale, he lit up like Times Square on New Year's."

Ethel jumps on the bed and settles between us like she wants to hear this too.

"Crawford wanted to know what was in the van. I asked why he cared, kept pressing him about what he was looking for when he came to Birdie's house." Sean scratches Ethel's head, then grimaces at the big tumbleweed of fur that lands on the duvet. "Finally, he said I was harassing him and he was going to call his lawyer. I reminded him that he was free to leave at any time. We were just having a friendly chat. And that really pissed him off. He left, but I could tell he really wanted to know what was in that van. Poor Crawford's not used to having civil servants get the best of him."

"What does it all mean? Crawford didn't hire the carjacker but he still wanted whatever he thought was in the van?"

"Two people are after the same thing. I'd say the other guy is more determined than Crawford."

"But if it's the photo they're after, maybe having it is putting George in danger. We should warn him."

Sean turns out the light and pulls up the covers. "I plan to talk to him tomorrow."

CHAPTER 28

IN THE MORNING, SEAN LEAVES me with a promise to bring home my van by nightfall.

I head out after him. The weight of my tote bag reminds me of the errand I need to do before work—drop off the library books I found at the Tate mansion.

And bring the ledger to the local history room. Sure enough, it's right there on the drier where I left it. I jump in my car and go.

As I walk into the Palmyrton Library, I can see my favorite librarian at the circulation desk. Her round, sweet face lights up when she sees me. She's worked here since I was kid, but she has the ageless demeanor of a woman who's spent her life in service to books instead of clothes and cars and other trappings of status. I still think of her as Miss Joan although she's probably only in her fifties.

"Audrey! How nice to see you." She glances at the copies of *Hamilton* and *The Nightingale* in my hands. "Those don't look like the epic fantasy novels you usually like to read."

How well she knows me. "You're right. These aren't mine. I found them at the Tate Mansion." I explain in greater detail as she checks them back in. "I thought I'd do a good deed and bring them back."

"Of course, I read about their deaths in the paper, but you're right—I wouldn't have noticed the account if you hadn't pointed it out. Thank you. I'll just close this account down. My goodness! Maybelle Simpson was a member since 1944 and never an overdue book until now!"

"Did she come in often?"

"Once a week on Tuesday morning ever since I started working here—regular as clockwork."

"What was she like? Did you talk to her?"

"Very reserved. Always pleasant, but not very chatty."

"Were the books she checked out for her or for Vareena Tate? I found such an odd mix of books in their sitting room."

"Sprawling family saga novels and romances," she holds up *The Nightingale,* "and biography and nonfiction like this," she holds up *Hamilton*. "Right?"

"Yes! Who read what?"

"I suspect Mrs. Tate read the novels. Once when Miss Simpson was checking out *Lonesome Dove* I mentioned that I had enjoyed that novel very much, and I hoped she would too. She smiled slightly and said it wasn't for her. Then she pushed her nonfiction forward and said, 'These are mine.'"

"Did Vareena Tate have a library card?"

Miss Joan taps a few keys, then shakes her head. "Maybe she did at one time, but our system deletes accounts that have been dormant for ten years or more." She looks at me with childlike wonder. "I've seen your ads for the estate sale. Is there a fabulous library in the Tate Mansion? Maybe I should come."

"Actually, there's not. All the books the ladies read are paperbacks that Maybelle—Miss Simpson—seems to have bought at the thrift shop. Edgar Tate had some shelves filled with leather bound classics that were there for show. But if you're in the market for some monumentally massive Victorian furniture, we can fix you up."

"All that money and no real library?" Miss Joan shakes her head as I walk away.

The mysteries of human nature are too much for her.

NEXT, I HEAD UPSTAIRS TO the Local History room. I don't know the librarian here, an earnest bearded man about my age wearing wire-rim glasses and sandals with socks. I pull out the ledger and explain how I came to have it. He listens with his eyes focused over my left shoulder. When I end with, "so I thought you might be interested in having it," there's no response for a full ten seconds. I feel like I'm a live TV show with a tape delay.

Finally, he says, "Fascinating." He slides the ledger toward himself and opens it like a new mother counting her baby's fingers and toes. He studies each page silently, and I feel he's forgotten I'm still here.

"I thought it was interesting to see how prices changed over the years." I speak to remind him I'm alive.

He startles and looks over my shoulder again. "Thank you very much for bringing this in. It will be invaluable to my research. Palmyrton in the Gilded Age is a special interest of mine."

"You're doing research on the Tate Mansion?" This guy could be a gold mine of info for me. "Do you know whether Vareena and Lawrence Tate had a baby? I didn't read anything about a baby in any of the recent news articles, but yesterday we discovered a room decorated as a nursery with toys dating from the 1940s."

The librarian grimaces. "Those reporters take shocking short cuts. I gave them reams of information they didn't bother to use."

I can't help smiling at the thought of a *New York Times* reporter on deadline having to wait for information from Mr. Slow Talker here. "So there *was* a baby?"

"Yes, Lawrence Tate, Jr., was born in 1943 after his father had already been killed in the war. His grandfather died the day after the baby was delivered."

Long pause. I'm dying here.

"So what happened to the baby? Lawrence Tate, Jr. isn't still alive, is he?"

"He died before his first birthday. No record of the cause of death. He's buried in the Tate family plot behind St. Stephen's Episcopal." The librarian's watery blue eyes blink behind his thick lenses. "And Vareena Tate, daughter of Portuguese immigrants, became the wealthiest widow in Palmyrton."

"How sad. I guess that's why poor Vareena became a recluse." Then I think of another question I had. "Let me show you something. The handwriting in the ledger changes in 1964. It seems like Vareena kept the books until then, and suddenly turned the responsibility over to Maybelle. Do you have any idea what could have happened in '64?"

Lo-o-o-n-g silence.

"There was quite a building boom in Palmyrton at that time. Farmland and woods turned into middle-class housing developments."

"Yes, but anything that would have affected Mrs. Tate?"

The librarian shrugs. "The Vietnam War was intensifying at that time."

That seems like a dead-end. "What about the kitchen? According to the ledger, Vareena hired an architect in 1945 and had the new kitchen built."

"Yes, indeed. I happen to have a copy of the blueprints in our architecture collection."

Having asked the question, I'm obliged to look although I'm getting restless with this visit. I glance over his shoulder at the drawings. "Yep, that's just what the kitchen looks like."

The librarian taps the drawing and shudders. "They destroyed the symmetry of the original gothic revival design. The back of the house has been bastardized."

I give him a "whattaya gonna do" shrug. Considering Vareena hardly spent a penny her whole life, I can't really begrudge her wanting a kitchen with a gas stove and a real refrigerator.

The entire time I've been talking to the librarian, there hasn't been another soul in the local history room. "So, do many people look at this stuff?"

He ponders and finally nods. "Yes, interest in the Tate Mansion has been particularly high."

Somehow, I suspect two or three visitors could fill up this guy's week, given how slow he is.

"Really? Who else has been in?"

He draws himself up straight and for the first time looks me in the eye. "The research of other patrons is strictly confidential."

I LEAVE THE LEDGER IN THE care of the socially awkward librarian, and head for the office thinking about the tragedy of Vareena's life. When her husband was killed, she and her father-in-law must have been so comforted by the fact that Vareena was pregnant with the next generation of the Tate family. The old man must've held on to life until he saw he had a grandson. And then, for little Lawrence Jr. to die as well—how cruel!

I enter the office to find Donna holding a stack of index cards and Ty sprawled across the easy chair with one wobbly leg that's awaiting the next Sister Alice run.

"Opportunity Cost," Donna says.

Ty shuts his eyes and massages his temples. "That's when like you have to give up something to get something."

Donna flips over the card and reads from the back. "The quantity of other goods that must be given up to obtain a good."

"Right. What I said."

She places that card in a small stack on the desk and reads from the last one in her hand. "Federal funds rate."

Ty chews his lower lip. "Hmmm." Opens his mouth. Shuts it again. Squints at me. "You know what it is?"

I throw up my hands. "It's been fifteen years since I took macro-economics."

"You give up?" Donna asks.

Ty grimaces. "Yeah. Hit me."

"The interest rate at which depository institutions lend reserve balances to other depository institutions overnight, on an uncollateralized basis," Donna reads from the back of the index card before placing it in a larger stack on the desk.

Ty rolls his eyes. "How many did I get right?"

Donna counts the cards in the small stack. "Four and a half, if I give you partial credit for opportunity cost."

"Auugh! I can't afford to fail this test. I gotta get at least a C+ in this class to keep my scholarship."

"Take the afternoon off. Go somewhere quiet to study," I tell Ty.

"I don't have anyplace quiet. People track me down wherever I go. School library is like party central. Marcus found me at the Palmyrton Diner. I can't even go to the town library! Do you know Kyle and Jamal rode their bikes there last week to hit me up for arcade money?"

"You can go to my house. Sean is working late and I'll go to the gym after work." I reach for my keys.

"Ethel won't give me no peace, you know that."

"Oh, right. But there's gotta be somewhere."

Ty's face lights up. "I know a place! Won't nobody find me there, and there's no distractions."

"Where?" Donna asks.

I hold up my hand. "Don't even tell us where."

Ty's phone chirps and he looks at the screen. "Renee again! That's another reason I can't get nuthin' done. Marcus. Grams. Renee. Renee. Renee. Charmaine. Kyle. Grams. Kyle. Henry. Renee. Marcus. All them blowin' up my phone. Everybody always buggin' me."

I tug gently at the phone in his hands. "Leave it with me. Go."

He hangs onto it, then reluctantly loosens his grip, looking like a new mother leaving her infant with Granny for the first time. I slide it out of his hands, and put it on my desk. "Go."

Ty stands up and looks around the office. "What about the research for pricing those oil paintings?"

"It can wait until later in the week."

"I should really—"

"Go!" Donna and I chorus.

Ty collects his index cards and econ book and heads for the door. With his hand on the knob, he looks back at me and the phone. "What if Grams really needs me? Her knee's been actin' up again."

"If Grandma Betty calls, I'll answer and help her myself. Now go."

Ty ducks his head. "Thanks, Audge."

And he's gone.

"Do you think he'll pass his test?" Donna asks.

"Yeah. Ty has a way of pulling things out of the fire." I smile, thinking of the way he recovered a large sum of our client's money that had gone missing, and talked his way out of trouble with the cops. "He's just too generous with his time. His family and friends all rely on him, and sometimes he gets overwhelmed."

As if they know I'm talking about them, Ty's contacts send his phone into a flurry of chirps. I glance at the screen. Most of the texts are from this Renee person.

"I wonder who Renee is?" I look up from my financial projections. "I've never heard him mention her."

"She's this girl he met at college. Her car was stalled in the parking lot and he jumped the battery. Now she texts him all the time. She's real pretty, but too needy, ya know? I told him he needs a girl who's more independent. Someone like you."

I smile at the compliment, but a part of me is a little miffed. Why does Donna know all about this Renee? How is it that Ty is accepting romance advice from someone he's only known for ten days?

I jam my papers in a folder. How ridiculous! Am I jealous of Donna? I should be thrilled that they get along so well. It's a pleasant change from the simmering animosity between Ty and Adrienne and even the sibling bickering between Ty and Jill.

The phone chirps again. Geez, this really is distracting and the messages aren't even for me. I set it to vibrate. I would turn the phone off altogether, except that I promised to keep tuned in to any calls from Grandma Betty.

This string of messages is all from Ty's sister.

I need to talk to you.

Where are you?

CALL ME!

I'm confident these can be ignored. Charmaine is always texting Ty frantically with pleas like, *How do I get to Rockaway Mall?* Or *Where do I go to get my driver's license renewed?* She treats Ty like her personal search engine. A little neglect will teach her how to use Google.

I return to my spreadsheet. After a ten minute pause, one more.

Dad is out. Please call me.

CHAPTER 29

CRAP!

I never expected this. How could Ty's dad show up in the precise twelve hours that Ty chooses to go off the grid?

I use Ty's phone to call Charmaine, and before I can even say hello, she floods me with a tidal wave of words. "Ty, Daddy got out yesterday and he's here at my place and he wants to see you real bad so you need to come over today, like right now, and talk to him, okay."

"Char—"

"And don't be a douche about it."

"Char—"

"I'm at work right now but I can leave at four, so go over to my place by then, okay."

"Charmaine!"

There is a shocked silence on the line. Then Charmaine's voice goes up half an octave. "Who *is* this? What you doin' with my brother's phone?"

"Charmaine, it's Audrey. Ty left his phone with me while he's studying for his economics exam." I explain Ty's seclusion, but Charmaine isn't having it.

"Look, Audrey, I need to talk to my brother. I'm not messin' with you." There's panic in her voice. This doesn't sound like a happy, long-awaited family reunion to me. "You gotta tell me where he's at."

"I truly don't know, Charmaine. I wouldn't lie to you. But he'll be back at work tomorrow at noon, right after the exam."

"Daddy won't wait that long! And he'll never believe me that Ty is studying for a test." Long pause. "You hafta tell him."

"Me? But—"

"I'll bring him over to your office at four-fifteen. I gotta go now. Thanks, Audrey."

DONNA AND I SPEND A few hours researching prices for certain obscure items at the Tate Mansion. Then I send her home early so I can await the arrival of Ty's father without Donna's bug-eyed amazement. I've heard so much evil spoken about Ty's father that I'm expecting a cross between Darth Vader and Voldemort. Instead I see a middle-aged man with a startling resemblance to Ty. Like Ty, he's tall and lean with a strong chin and high cheekbones. Like Ty, he projects an aura of physical power. But while Ty has gained strength from hard physical work and intense street basketball competitions, his father is pumped up from twenty years of lifting weights in prison. His neck is thick and his biceps strain the sleeves of his Yankees t-shirt.

"Daddy, this is Audrey Nealon, Ty's boss."

He doesn't speak, just looks me up and down and finally nods an acknowledgement. His eyes are hard and cold. Even when Ty is administering the prison death stare, his eyes never look like that. Ty's essential kindness can never be hidden, even when he's working his hardest to be fierce.

I extend my hand. "Hi…er…Mr. Griggs. Nice to meet you." His first name escapes me. Marvin? I think that's it. It's most certainly not nice to meet him, but definitely interesting. This man has cast a long shadow over Ty's life, one that he still hasn't outrun.

Mr. Griggs lets my hand dangle in the air for a moment, then gives it a hard squeeze. "Where's my son?"

I choose to ignore his suspicious tone, and answer with a cheerful smile. "He's holed up somewhere studying. He has an economics exam tomorrow."

"Where? I need to see him."

I shrug. "He purposely didn't tell any of us. He wanted to go somewhere where no one would bother him." I'm so glad I honestly don't know where Ty is because I'm a terrible liar, and Mr. Griggs looks like he could extract information from a stone. Eventually, Ty will have to have this reunion with his father, but

I'm determined that it wait until after the exam. Milton Friedman himself wouldn't be able to answer questions about economics if he had to cope with the stress of seeing his imprisoned father for the first time in eighteen years.

"He still livin' with Betty, right?"

Charmaine's eyes open wide. "You can't go over there, Daddy. Betty won't like it, and she'll get mad at me."

Griggs turns on his daughter. "Don't you tell me what I can and can't do, girl. You think I care what that old woman has to say?"

"But I rely on her to watch Lo every Wednesday. I can't afford to—"

Griggs grabs Charmaine's shoulders. "That bitch is nuthin' to my grandson. You shouldn't be leavin' him with her."

Charmaine jerks away. Like Ty, she's not easily intimidated. She faces her father with her feet spread and her hands on her hips. "She loves Lo, and Lo loves her. And it's not like he has any other grandmothers."

"I don't want her pourin' poison into his ears about me."

"She wouldn't do that," Charmaine says, but her tone is less defiant. She and I well know that Grandma Betty will spew a stream of venom about Marvin Griggs at the slightest encouragement. In Betty's mind, her daughter lost the will to fight her cancer because of the stress of her husband's imprisonment.

I speak up. "Look, I know for a fact that Ty isn't home with Betty. He can't get any studying done there—too much commotion." I hold Ty's phone up. "That's why I promised I'd take care of Betty if she called and said she needed something."

Marvin Griggs snatches his son's phone away from me and starts pressing buttons. A scowl of frustration contorts his face. I realize that he has no idea how to use a smart phone; cell phones had barely been invented when he went behind bars. But he doesn't want to admit he needs help.

He slams Ty's highly customized Samsung Galaxy back onto the desk. "I need to find my son." His voice is low and gravelly. No doubt he's had years of practice threatening other inmates without attracting the attention of guards. "Now."

I project a confidence I don't feel. "He'll be back here around noon tomorrow. You're welcome to stop back then."

Marvin's powerful hands form into fists. The rage pulsing off him is almost visible in the air. Would he actually hit me? Ty has spoken about how profoundly disorienting it was to reenter the wide world after just a year in prison. That he had forgotten how to speak in a normal tone of voice…to smile…to say please and thank you. Imagine what eighteen years of captivity would do to a man's social skills.

Marvin takes a deep breath and swallows. His right fist unfurls, and he flexes the fingers. Then he turns on his heel. "C'mon Charmaine."

Charmaine glances over her shoulder at me as she leaves with her father. Is she relieved…or scared?

WHEN THEY'RE GONE I IMMEDIATELY call Grandma Betty and tell her that Ty is studying in seclusion.

"I know. He already called me to say he wouldn't be home tonight."

Of course, Ty would never allow Grandma Betty to worry about him. He must've checked in using someone else's phone. Then I break the news that Marvin Griggs is out of jail and back in Palmyrton. This update elicits a stream of abuse that I didn't think someone as kind-hearted as Betty was capable of, even if the subject is her despised former son-in-law. When I can finally get a word in edgewise, I warn her. "Betty, I'm afraid Marvin's going to come to your place sometime this evening looking for Ty. I don't want you to be there alone. Come and stay with Sean and me until Ty can deal with his father tomorrow."

"Child, that's so nice. But I happen to be at my sister Vonda's house right now, so I'll just stay put here. Marvin don't have no idea where Vonda lives."

"Are you sure? Because I promised Ty—"

"Girl, I been takin' care of myself since long before you was born. I don't need nobody treatin' me like a helpless old lady."

No sooner do I hang up with Betty than my phone rings again. Sean.

"We got the van. They're dusting it for prints. And they found the gun. It was a toy."

"No way! It sure looked real to us."

"Don't feel bad. Plenty of cops have mistaken toy guns for real. You'll have the van back tomorrow."

"Yay!" With all the commotion today has brought, I'd forgotten about the van. I'm thrilled to have it back, but worried, too. "Is it all torn up?"

"I'm in Palmyrton," Sean says. "But the guys in Newark say it's not too bad. You're going to need two new front tires."

"What about the stuff inside? Was it still there?"

"I'll send you the pics of the interior that the Newark team sent to me," Sean says.

"Did you talk to George?" I ask.

"Couldn't connect with him. Left him a long message about the photo and the theory that someone might be after it. Gotta go, Audrey--I have actual work to do on Loretta's case. I'm sending the pics now."

A moment later, I'm studying pictures of the jumbled interior of the van. The box of kitchenware, some garden tools, and a small end table are all that were inside at the time of the theft. The box was dumped out and all the stuff scattered, but as far as I can remember, everything that we intended to give to Sister Alice looks like it's still in the van. So clearly, we didn't have whatever the thief was looking for.

What was he looking for?

I've been so certain it was the photo in the box, simply because the fact that it was hidden makes it seem valuable. But what if I'm totally wrong?

Just as in advanced mathematics or chess, the best way to get out of a seeming dead end is the approach the problem from an entirely different angle.

Who knew that we take stuff that doesn't sell to Sister Alice?

George, because this is spelled out in every contract.

Crawford? Only if George told him, and why would they be discussing that? But I can check with George.

So maybe the theft had nothing to do with the Armentrout job. What else was in my van that someone might want?

I think of the piles of clutter in the footwells and sliding across the front seats. I try to envision the interior of the van the last time I saw it.

Nothing valuable appears in my mind's eye. But something

unusual was there. I can picture it fluttering in the corner of my memory.

Except....the ledger. The ledger was on the front console for days until Ty told me to put it somewhere safer so Donna wouldn't toss it.

Anyone could have seen it there.

Who would want it?

Henry knew I took it, and he might have mentioned it to Levi or Dennis. But if they wanted it back, all they had to do was ask. It technically belongs to the Rosa Parks Center. Why try to steal it back?

Unless it contains information you want to keep secret.

CHAPTER 30

AT 11:30 THE NEXT MORNING, Ty's phone blows up. It buzzes and chirps across my desk as a hail of text messages and SnapChats roll in. I glance at the screen.

Where were you, man?

How come you missed the test?

Prof. was asking where you were.

You OK?

Shock hits me like a dodge ball in the gut. Ty missed his exam? Totally didn't even show up? Oh my God—what if he pulled an all-nighter, then slept right through the test? He'd normally use his phone as an alarm, but he didn't have it. And he wasn't home where his early-rising grandmother could wake him.

Our whole study retreat concept has backfired, big time.

This happened to Maura once when we were in college, and the professor was totally unsympathetic. She prostrated herself and begged to be allowed to make up the exam and he finally relented after she burst into tears.

Well, I know that's not happening with Ty. He'd never beg anyone for anything. Not even his life.

Eventually, Ty will wake up and realize what's happened. He'll come back to work angry and ashamed. And in another hour, no doubt Marvin Griggs will show up here. A double-whammy of catastrophe.

Oh God—I'd love to run away so I don't have to be here for all this agony. But I can't abandon Ty in his hour of need. I have to wait and offer comfort and help him with a strategy to solve this mess.

The minutes tick on. Lunch comes and goes with no sign of

either Ty or his dad.

Could he still be sleeping? No way. Ty's not a teenager. He's used to being up and working during the day. Is he just too ashamed to come to the office? A hopeful thought hits me. Maybe Ty's professor is nicer than Maura's was. Maybe Ty went straight to Palmer Community, spoke to his professor, and is taking his exam right now.

I return to work feeling more cheerful.

But another hour passes and still no Ty.

And no Marvin.

That combination is what's making me really uneasy. There's no way Marvin simply gave up on finding Ty. They must be together.

Damn that man! He made Ty miss his exam.

A wave of fury washes over me and some of Grandma Betty's choicest curses run through my mind.

I call Charmaine using Ty's phone.

"Ty? Thank God! Where are you?"

"It's still me, Audrey. You haven't heard from Ty?"

"No. Shit!"

"Where's your father?"

"I don't know. After we left your office yesterday, I went to pick up Lo at daycare. Daddy never came back to my apartment. He wasn't there this morning when I left for work. I don't know who he's with. He doesn't have any friends left in Palmyrton."

That clinches it. They're together, somewhere. But where?

I think about the moment yesterday when Ty's face lit up as he figured out where he would go. He had a "Eureka" kind of expression that wouldn't come from staying at a friend's house. And Ty hates asking anyone for a favor. Then I remember he called Grandma Betty from wherever he was to let her know he wouldn't be home. I hate the idea of calling her and getting her worried, but there's no way around it.

Just as I'm steeling myself to make the call, Betty calls me. "Charmaine just called me looking for Ty. He hasn't come into work yet? What's going on?"

"I'm trying to track him down. Can you check your phone and tell me the number he called you from yesterday?"

"I already called that number. It just rings and rings. Don't even roll over to voicemail or an answering machine."

"Read me the number."

I write down the ten numerals and stare at them. I have a better memory for numbers than faces, and I can often recognize a number I've seen just once before. It's a quirk that creeps out my friends and family.

973-555-1818

Have I dialed that number? I pull out my phone and look at the pattern the numbers make: three corners, the center, then the fourth corner and lower middle. Interesting pattern. I don't think I've dialed it.

Five-five-five is a long-time Palmyrton exchange. My grandmother's number began with five-five-five. Could Ty be hanging out with an old person? That would explain his claim that there were no distractions where he was going.

And yet the number looks familiar. I've seen it. I close my eyes and try to conjure up the image. And I see old-fashioned black typeface. A dingy beige background.

I leap up.

"The Tate Mansion! This is the number printed on the dial of the big, black phone in the office of the Tate Mansion. Ty has the key. It's the perfect place to study—absolutely no electronic distractions whatsoever."

Donna's face contorts in horror. "Stay in that creepy house all alone all night long? Geez, it's bad enough in the daytime."

"Yes, but Ty hates asking for favors. He could sleep there without inconveniencing anyone."

But if that's where he went to study, why hasn't he come back? Why did he miss his exam? Could this have something to do with Marvin? Does he know about the Tate Mansion? Could Charmaine have told him about it?

I snatch up my car keys and head for the door. "I'm going over there. You hold down the fort here."

Donna scampers after me. "No! You can't go there all alone. Call your husband."

I can just imagine that phone call. *Honey, can you come help me find out why Ty missed his econ exam?* "My husband is running a murder investigation. He can't drop everything for me and my staff."

But even as I say that, I know Donna is right. It could be risky to go to the isolated Tate Mansion all alone when I don't know what I'll find. "Call Henry and ask him to meet me there," I tell her.

And while she's busy dialing, I head out.

I PULL UP THE LONG DRIVEWAY to the Tate Mansion. My heart sinks as I see no sign of Ty's car. Was I totally wrong, or did I just miss him? I've come this far—I may as well go in.

I let myself in the back door and experience the unvarying sensation of tumbling into a time machine. I expect a woman with permed hair wearing a shirtwaist dress to be pulling a pan of biscuits from the oven while Bing Crosby plays on the radio.

But mixed with the musty smell of 1940's nostalgia is something different. Something distinctly modern. Something...fried.

I glance into the trashcan and pull out a crumpled white bag with a familiar red and yellow bird. CluckU Chicken—Ty's favorite. The take-out that I, Jill, Adrienne, and now Donna consistently vote against. He *was* here last night.

There are no crumbs on the table. Just like Ty to clean up after himself even if he was technically trespassing. So we must've crossed paths. I call Donna to report my success, but she says Ty still hasn't shown up.

"Henry says he's coming over to the mansion. He should be there any minute. You wait for him outside, you hear me?"

"Will do," I say, but even as I'm reassuring her, my eye falls on a white rectangle lying on the floor of the hallway leading to the sitting room where Maybelle and Vareena spent their time.

I pick it up. Gross National Product in Ty's scrawl. I turn it over: "the total value of goods and services produced by a country in a year."

Ty left one of his study cards here. I put it in my pocket and stick my head into the sitting room. The lamp on the table between the two chairs is still lit, shining down on rest of the study cards. Ty's thick econ textbook lies upside down and half-open on the floor, as if it tumbled off his lap.

An unsettling worm of worry crawls through my gut. I remember Ty complaining about how much that book cost him.

He would never leave it here like that.

Right above my head, I hear a noise.

Did I imagine it because I want to find Ty walking around upstairs?

But it wasn't the sound of footsteps. Just a faint rustle.

Mice?

"Ty?" I call. My voice sounds croaky and weak in this echoing hulk of a house. I summon some power. "Ty!"

With the second shout, I clearly hear the noise again. When I look up, the dangling ceiling light fixture is swaying slightly.

That's not mice. Ty is definitely upstairs.

Or someone is.

If it's Ty, why doesn't he answer me?

I venture into the foyer and stand at the foot of the big, turning staircase. "Ty? Are you up there?" I shout into the dim gallery above me.

Nothing. Just the slow, steady tick of the grandfather clock.

Who's on the second floor? Why is Ty's stuff here, but not his car? I don't like this. Not one bit.

I hear a car door slam and my heart kicks into overdrive.

Heavy footsteps tromp through the kitchen.

"Audrey? Where are you?"

Henry! I'd forgotten he was coming. I run toward his voice and we nearly collide in the back hall. I've never been so glad to see his grouchy, reliable face.

Quickly, I fill him in, ending with, "I hear someone upstairs, but whoever it is won't answer me."

His elevated eyebrows carve deeper grooves into his dark forehead. He doesn't have to speak for me to know he thinks I'm a hysterical woman with nothing better to do than disrupt his hard work. He pushes past me. "Well, come on, girl. Let's see what this nonsense is about. Ain't got all day."

Together we climb the stairs. Hearing his heavy breathing, I'm acutely aware that Henry is over sixty years old and not particularly large. Still, his presence makes me bolder.

We start with the rooms that face the back of the house, opening each door and calling for Ty. Checking each closet, even opening the two big armoires. Each room is empty, looking just as we left it prepped for the sale. Then we search the rooms on the other side of the hallway.

Nothing.

We trudge up to the third floor, to the tiny, empty rooms once used by the servants.

Still empty.

Where could he be?

"Quiet as a graveyard in here." Henry starts down the stairs. "You imagining things. Ty was here, but now he's gone. The man can handle himself. Why you actin' like he's a lost chile?"

Something is wrong. I feel it in my gut. But I'm not about to tell Henry I'm having a premonition. "Come down to Vareena's sitting room with me. That's where I heard the sound. I even saw the ceiling light move."

Henry pauses on the landing and turns to face me with his hands on his hips. "I thought you told that helper girl of yours not to talk about this place bein' haunted. Now you tellin' me you believe in ghosts."

I slip around him and hurry down the last flight of stairs. Of course the house isn't haunted! The sound I heard was real and caused by a living being. Henry needs to hear it himself.

We stand in the sparsely furnished sitting room. The only sound is the faint chirp of a bird outside the window. "Ty!" I shout.

Immediately, the rustling sound begins above our heads. I nudge Henry. He hears it too. "Ty, where are you?"

The rustle turns into a scrape and again the light fixture sways.

Henry pushes back his cap and scratches his head. "He's right above us. Which bedroom is above this room?"

"It should be Maybelle's. Her bedroom faces the backyard, just like this room does."

"We checked her room. We opened the closet and everything." He heads for the door. "Let's go outside."

I trail after him, not sure of his purpose. But at least now he believes I'm not crazy.

In the backyard, we stand side-by-side gazing at the rear of the Tate mansion.

Henry points. "Look how them windows is lined up."

The kitchen addition juts out of the back right side of the house. Beside it is the window to the little sitting room. Above that window is a blank spot on the second floor where an original window, partially covered over by the peaked roof of the one-story kitchen addition, was filled in with stone that doesn't quite match the original. That's what the librarian was complaining about when he said the addition ruined the lines of the house. After that blank space, the windows are lined up evenly, a mirror image of the left side of the house.

"You think when they built the kitchen..."

Henry jogs back toward the door. "There's some extra space where that window used to be."

Henry and I thunder up the stairs and burst into Maybelle's room. "Ty! How do we get to where you are? Make a noise."

We stand stock still, the only sound our ragged breaths. But we can't detect the rustling sound we heard below.

Henry begins tapping on the wall closest to the center of the house. "It has to be behind here." Like all the walls in the house, the bottom half is covered in walnut wainscoting. The upper half is wallpapered in a busy print of vertical lattices covered in twining green ivy.

"You know, the wallpaper in this room looks a little less faded than in the other bedrooms. They had to re-wallpaper up here after they finished the kitchen."

Henry runs his hands along the wallpaper. "There could be a seam that the pattern hides."

In the corner formed by the outside wall and the middle-facing interior wall-there is a built-in, triangular shelf that holds a vase full of dusty dried flowers. I examine the way the shelf is fitted to the wall, then run my fingers along the underside. The wood is smooth and glossy until my finger encounters a divot on the right side. I fit my finger into it. Henry staggers forward as the wall he is tapping turns smoothly inward.

CHAPTER 31

I CAN'T SEE ANYTHING IN THE dim interior, but I can smell. Musty age overlaid with the pungent scent of fresh sweat and coppery blood.

A low wattage bulb dangling from the ceiling reveals Ty crouched in a corner. A trickle of dried blood cakes his forehead. His eyes bulge in fear before he raises his forearm to protect them from the glare of Henry's flashlight.

"Good Lord, what happened to you?" Henry heads into the room ahead of me.

"Water," Ty coughs.

I sprint across the hall to get it for him. By the time I return, he has left his prison and sits on the edge of Maybelle's bed. His head hangs and his whole body shakes.

"Oh, Ty!" I fling my arms around him and pull him close. He doesn't resist. He drinks the water greedily, his eyes squinting against the bright daylight.

Gradually, the tremors subside. I realize that I've seen Ty angry, and shocked, and worried, but I've never seen him terrified.

"What day is it?" His voice is raw.

"Thursday. Two-thirty."

He massages his temples. "I thought I was in there a lot longer. It felt like days. I thought no one would come until the sale. I didn't think I could last that long."

"Audrey knew somethin' was wrong and she came lookin' for you." Henry stands a few feet away, letting me take the lead in comforting Ty. "What happened to you? How did you get stuck in there?"

Ty finally lifts his head and looks around, getting a grip on where he is and how he got there.

"Take your time." I examine the top of his head. "Where is that blood coming from? Did someone hit you?"

Ty rubs the crown on his head. "Yeah. I blacked out for a while."

"My God—you must have a concussion. We should get you right to the hospital."

Ty waves me off. "No hospital. I'm okay now."

Henry has gone back into the secret room and returned to the bedroom. "What'd he hit you with? I don't see anything."

"I don't know. I was studying downstairs and I must've dozed off in the chair. A noise woke me up, and I could hear someone walking around upstairs, not even trying to be quiet. So I headed up—"

"Why didn't you call the police?"

Ty scowls at me. "How was I goin' to explain to them what I was doin' here?"

"Well, you should have just slipped out the back door and called anonymously. It's not on you to protect this place from burglars."

"You had my phone, remember? If I called from the landline, whoever was here might've heard me."

"Let the boy talk," Henry scolds. "You wanna hear what happened or not?"

That's normally the kind of response I'd get from Ty, and it worries me that he still seems too rattled to defend himself. "Go on. Just tell us what happened."

"So I started upstairs. I wasn't even nervous. Somehow in my head, I expected it to be that Crawford dude."

"Crawford Bostwick? Why?"

"Everyone knows the house is empty. Crawford heard us talking about what the house was like. And he needs a place to live, right? He wanted to crash at Miz Armentrout's house."

"But—"

Henry glares at me and I stop questioning Ty's judgment. After all, I've made some questionable choices that have landed me in hot water in the past.

"So I went up the stairs real quiet, and the person was banging around like he was looking for something. The light was on in Maybelle's room. So I just peaked around the edge of the door and right away saw how that wall opened up. So that blew me away, 'cause I worked on this room and never had an idea that door was there. I guess I got kinda excited to check it out, and I musta made some noise."

Ty gingerly touches the top of his head. "When I got close to the opening, this arm shot out and—wham!—slammed me over the head with something. Knocked me right out."

Ty swallows hard and takes a couple of deep breaths. His dark skin takes on a grayish cast.

"Do you feel sick?"

Henry grabs a little wastepaper can and offers it to Ty. He holds it in front of himself for a moment, gulping until the wave of nausea passes.

"I'm a'ight. I've never been unconscious before. I came to and I was locked in the room. I tried and tried to figure out how to open the wall from the other side, but I couldn't. I got kinda crazy—" His upper lip trembles and he can't continue.

Now I feel sick. What could be worse than being accidentally locked up when prison was the worst experience of your life? A shiver passes through me.

What if we had never found him at all?

Ty sits silently for a long while. I reach for his hand. He holds mine tightly and doesn't let go.

"It felt like I was in there for a whole day at least. It was so quiet and dim, I couldn't keep track of time. I paced back and forth and tried to do some exercises just to keep busy. Lotta thoughts went through my head..." He stops, gazing into space, then gives himself a little shake.

"You must've moved right when I was finding your book and cards in the sitting room. I heard something and I called for you."

"When I heard your voice callin' me, at first I thought it was a dream. I got so excited and I stomped as hard as I could. But then you didn't come." He turns and his big brown eyes well with tears. "That was the worst moment. I thought you gave up and left. It was like one of those shipwreck movies when the rescue plane flies over and they're yelling and screaming and thinkin' they're saved and then the plane doesn't see them and flies away. That's worse than no plane coming at all."

"Oh, Ty." I pull his head onto my shoulder. "I would have torn this house down to find you."

Henry coughs uncomfortably. Ty squirms out of my embrace.

"We came up to this bedroom and called you. How come you didn't answer?"

"I didn't hear you on the other side of the sliding wall. I only heard the sound coming up through the floor."

Henry goes to examine the wall. "It's insulated, like they built it to be soundproof."

"Luckily, we didn't have to tear the house down." I strive to lighten the mood and explain how Henry figured out the hidden space in the house.

"What's in that room, anyway?" Henry edges away from our emotional collapse and enters the secret room shining the flashlight on his phone.

"I could barely see in there." Ty eases himself up from the bed and sways, then regains his balance. He seems torn between curiosity and reluctance to re-enter his prison. "There's a buncha framed photos is all I could make out."

"Yeah, lotsa pictures, family photos," Henry calls back to us. "Weddings, graduations, baptisms, army enlistment—stuff like that."

Now curiosity gets the best of me and I step away from Ty's side. "We were talking about how odd it was that there were no photos anywhere in this house. Why would Vareena keep them all hidden in a secret room?"

Henry steps further into the tiny room and gestures for me to enter. "These pictures ain't of Vareena's people. They're Maybelle's."

"These folks all black."

CHAPTER 32

I CROWD IN NEXT TO HIM. The room is barely six by six feet. The three walls that don't move are lined with large framed photos, not snapshots, but studio photos of the big moments in people's lives. Quite a few are graduation photos: young African American men and women in black gowns and mortarboards. Three show young men in uniform: two Army, one Navy. There are several wedding photos and two award ceremonies.

I squint at each picture looking at the serious, proud faces. "From the hairstyles and the clothes and the way the photos have faded, these all seem to have been taken in the fifties and sixties."

Henry nods. "Yep. My folks never even had a camera till those little instamatics came out in the seventies. Before that, you mostly just had these studio portraits on special occasions."

"I wonder why they stop? Why wouldn't her family keep sending them, especially once snapshots were so easy to take?"

"Next generation, I guess. The older she got, the less people in the family remembered her."

"What are you look—" Ty's voice is cut off by a rattle and a thump.

Henry and I rush out of the room to find Ty slumped against Maybelle's bed.

"I got a little dizzy when I went to stand up."

I pull out my phone. "No more delays. We need to call for the EMTs and report this attack to the police."

Ty grabs my hand. If he's sick, you certainly wouldn't know it from the strength of his grip. "No! I'm a'ight—just hungry and thirsty. Leave the cops outta this."

I jerk my arm away. "You were attacked. You could have died.

A crime has been committed and we have to report it. You're not going to get in trouble for being here. The Parks Center has given us access to the house. No one from the Center is going to object to your studying here."

Ty keeps shaking his head. "I didn't see who hit me. Got no clue if he was tall, short, white, black. No clue if it was even a man. What the cops gonna do?"

I guess I should no longer be surprised by Ty's abiding distrust of law enforcement. He and Sean have achieved mutual respect and even a bit of camaraderie, but Ty clearly considers my husband to be the exception to the rule that no cop can be counted upon for help. "Your car is gone." I'm clutching at straws. "The intruder stole it. We have to report that."

Ty shakes his head. "I drove my car over the grass and parked it behind the garage. That's probably why whoever broke in had no clue I was here until I stuck my head in this room."

I plant myself in front of him and demand eye contact. "Ty, I am the wife of a Palmyrton police detective. I can't just not report a crime."

"Why? Women all the time choose not to report being attacked. It's not a crime to not call the cops. I'm the victim. I get to decide."

Ah, now he's given me an opening. "You're not the only victim. The intruder obviously broke into this house to steal something that belongs to the owner, the Rosa Parks Center. We have to let Levi know that."

Ty pushes past me in disgust. "Fine. Call Levi. I'm outta here."

"You can't drive if you're dizzy." I follow Ty down the broad staircase, trailed by Henry, even as I'm calling Levi on my cell.

Of course, I get his voicemail. No one is ever available when you really need them. I leave a garbled, breathless message telling him to call me ASAP, and return my attention to Ty.

"Levi didn't answer. I'm going to call 911 right now."

Ty's hand closes over my phone. "What's the big rush? Whoever hit me has been gone for hours. Few more minutes not gonna make any difference. Just wait 'til Levi calls back."

I'm tired of arguing. Levi will talk some sense into Ty, I'm sure.

We've made it into the kitchen where he spies a box of granola bars we'd all been snacking on earlier in the week. Ty devours two and gulps down another long drink.

Food and water seem to restore his common sense. "How did the guy who whacked me get in? I locked the back door behind me."

While we're waiting for Levi to call back, Henry, Ty and I walk through the first floor of the house. We can't find evidence of a break-in. The massive front door is bolted tight from inside and the two sets of French doors leading to the veranda are also bolted.

"These windows are big enough for a man to fit through, easy," Henry says as he tries to raise one of the big double-hung windows in the back parlor. But the window doesn't budge. He peers at it closely, then moves to the window beside it and repeats the process. "Here's something we never noticed. These big windows are nailed shut."

"That makes sense. They never used these rooms, so they didn't need fresh air. And they were vulnerable living here all alone."

"Maybe the turd broke in through the basement," Ty says.

But Henry shakes his head. "Me and my guys looked around down there. It's an ol' time cellar with a dirt floor. There's a trap door where the coal used to get delivered, but that's been boarded up, and a couple of tiny little windows even a kid couldn't fit through."

While we've been looking for the entry point, I've been keeping an eye out for things that might have been stolen. I've been promoting this sale for two weeks—social media, fliers, ads, emails to my mailing list, mentioning some of the most interesting items for sale. I wanted a huge turnout. In short, the immediate world knew about it. So it's possible that someone wanted to rip off the sale before it even began.

The ultimate early bird.

But as far as we can tell, everything is just the way we left it two days ago, priced and ready for the sale. The most valuable things in the house are quite large: the statue of Aphrodite, the grandfather clock, the antique sideboard and mirrored hall tree. They're all still here. Vareena had no jewelry other than her wedding and engagement rings, which are still in her dresser drawer.

And of course, there were no electronics. In short, nothing that a typical break and enter thief would want.

Which leads me to an inescapable conclusion: this wasn't a typical B&E job.

The intruder came with the specific intent of going to that secret room.

CHAPTER 33

FINALLY, MY PHONE CHIRPS.

A text from Levi: *I got your message. I'm on my way to meet you at the house.*

Silently, the three of us sit down in the kitchen to wait for Levi. My brain stews with conflicting ideas. Ty and Henry seem equally preoccupied.

What was the intruder looking for in that room? What did he take from there?

Most important--who could possibly have known about the room?

Not Henry, unless he's a world-class actor. Yes, he got the idea that there could be a hidden space on the second floor, but he was genuinely stunned when that wall started to move.

Wasn't he?

Could he have known before he arrived at the house that Ty was in there and went through an elaborate ruse to set him free?

I steal a furtive glance at my colleague as he paces around the kitchen. His brow is furrowed and occasionally he gives a little shake of his head. No way. Henry is a kind, honest man, and I think he's as perplexed as I am.

Of course, I've been wrong about people before. Why does he seem so restless? Maybe he suspects his two helpers.

I don't know them from Adam. Could one of them have discovered the room sneaking down to the second floor when he was supposed to be on the third floor in the servants' rooms, and then made a plan to come back and empty it of valuables?

What about *my* helper? I really don't know Donna that well, do I? She was occasionally alone in the room when I stepped out to go to the bathroom or call Sean. Could she have helped set this up?

But she and Ty are tight. And whoever left Ty in that secret room was quite willing to risk him dying.

Even if any of them had the time alone, I think it's highly unlikely that anyone could trip that door by accident. Even if someone found the button under the shelf, he would have to lean pretty hard on the wall to make the door open.

Who would be familiar enough with this house to know about that room and how to open it?

Someone from Maybelle and Vareena's past.

A SHARP RAP AT THE BACK door jolts us all back to the here and now.

Levi comes into the kitchen and surveys our grim faces. "What's happened? Has something very valuable been stolen?"

I rise to greet him. "No, we can't see that anything's been stolen. That's what makes this break-in so weird."

We fill Levi in on the details, occasionally tripping over one another with corrections and clarifications.

As I suspected, Levi is not at all concerned that Ty intended to use the house as his study hideout. He pats Ty on the back. "Don't worry about that, son. I'm just glad you weren't seriously hurt."

"I appreciate that, Levi. But I'm still not crazy about getting the cops involved in my part of the story." Ty meets Levi's gaze and some acknowledgement passes between them. "Just report the house was broken into and we found the secret room open. Leave me out of it."

This approach has occurred to me, but I've already rejected it. Telling the police partial truths always leads to trouble. They ask questions…find evidence… and your lie is revealed. Then you have even more explaining to do.

Been there, done that.

Before I can protest, Levi is shaking his head. "The Lord detests lying lips, but he delights in people who are trustworthy. Proverbs 12:22."

"You say the room is filled only with old photographs?"

"That's what's left in it now. Maybe the person who broke in took something valuable with him."

Levi frowns. "And you think these photos are Maybelle's relatives?" Levi asks. "Show it to me."

So we all troop back upstairs. I too want to see the photos again. I'm sure they hold the answer to the break in.

LEVI STARES AT EACH PHOTO intently. Sometimes he nods or makes a little cluck of approval. He picks up one graduation photo and squints at it, adjusting his glasses and waving Henry closer with the flashlight. He sighs and returns it to its spot on the wall with what seems to me is reverence.

"Do you recognize these people, Levi?"

"I recognize their dreams. I recognize their courage." He turns to face us. "I would have been a child when these photos were taken. This was the generation that preceded mine. The generation that opened so many doors for our people."

He gestures to the photo he had studied so intently. "That young man is holding a diploma from the University of Maryland. Do you realize how hard it was for a black man to gain admittance and earn a degree there in the early sixties? And this one—" He picks up a class photo that shows a young teacher and her entire third grade class. "A black woman teaching a class that contained both black and white students. Do you understand how extraordinary she must have been?"

I'm embarrassed that I hadn't thought of that at all. To me, they were simply photos of average people at familiar milestones in their lives.

"Why do you think Maybelle kept them hidden in here, Levi? Why wouldn't she have kept them out in her room to enjoy all the time?"

"Maybe Miz Tate didn't like it that her maid had such uppity relations," Henry offers.

Could that be it? Maybelle had to hide the fact that her relatives weren't maids and waiters and janitors? But surely the room was created when the kitchen addition was built, and Vareena was still managing the accounts then. If Vareena was aware of the secret room, why is it filled with only Maybelle's photos?

Could Maybelle have had the secret room built in the Sixties when she took over the accounts? What power did Vareena have over her? Why did Maybelle stay a servant all those years? Surely she could have gotten some assistance from the teachers and doctors and scholars in this room.

"Does the executor of the estate have any idea how to get in touch with Maybelle's family?"

"The law firm handling the estate says she has no family. Neither of them had any family. That's why Vareena left the money to us. There was a small bequest to Maybelle to take care of her after Vareena died. But Maybelle died just two days later, so she never collected it."

"But wouldn't Maybelle's relatives be entitled to that bequest?"

Levi shakes his head. "Vareena drew it up so that the money was in trust for Maybelle's use as long as she lived. After she died, the balance was to go to the Parks Center."

"When was the will written, Levi?" I've always been curious about this. "When did Vareena decide to leave her money to the Parks Center?"

"Vareena's will was drawn up by one of the leading law firms in Palmyrton. Naturally, everyone on the Board wanted to know why she selected us as the recipient of her estate. But the partner acting as executor said that the terms of her will specifically forbid him from revealing anything about when or why her decision was made. He simply assured us that the firm was confident she was in sound mind when she made the decision."

Levi turns his back on us, and moves to unhook a picture from the wall. "Let's get these photos packed up. They shouldn't be discarded."

"Wait," I say. "The police will want to see all this. We should call now—"

"I don't think that will be necessary." Levi sets down the first photo and unhooks another. "Since nothing was stolen and Ty doesn't want to report the assault, I think there's no need to call the police. After all, we want the sale to begin tomorrow after all the promotion you've done. The police might interfere with that."

"Right, Audge." Ty jumps to agree with this rationale. "You know they'll mess us up. We can't afford for the cops to shut us down as a crime scene."

What's gotten into Levi? When he arrived, he was preaching the evils of lying. Now, he's on board with a cover-up. "Are you two thinking straight? My husband is a detective with the Palmyrton police force. I can't lie to him."

"I'm not asking you to lie. It's not illegal for a victim to decline to report a crime." Levi looks at me with the calm self-assurance of a longtime pastor. He's wearing a suit and tie. His voice is deep and steady. He's the picture of law-abiding respect for authority. "Feel free to tell Sean tonight over dinner. But we're not calling 911."

"Fine," I say, pulling out my phone. "But I'm taking some pictures to record the crime scene."

I take several shots of the sliding wall and then step further into the room to take shots of the pictures hanging on the walls. But Levi has been removing them and only a few are left. Only lighter rectangles on the walls mark where they have hung.

Levi picks up a stack of the framed pictures. "I'll take these with me...show them around to some of the older folks at church. Who knows? Even though Maybelle didn't attend my church, maybe someone will recognize one of them."

"Do you know if Maybelle was originally from Palmyrton?" I ask Levi as I return with a box to pack up the photos.

"I doubt she was since she started working here during the war. There wasn't much of an African American community in this town then. She probably came out from Newark looking for work in one of these big houses. Or maybe she came up from the South. Lots of people left the farms and came to the city searching for a better life."

If she came from down South, that might explain how she drifted out of touch with her family. I suppose living in the Tate Mansion was more comfortable than living in some sharecropper's shack. A better life, but a lonelier one. Levi's mention of his church prompts another thought. "If Maybelle didn't go to Mt. Zion AME, maybe she went to the Baptist church. Ty's Grandma Betty is a deaconess there. She could show these pictures around if you don't have any luck."

"Sure. She knows everybody," Ty chimes in.

"Thank you for that offer," Levi says, but he doesn't seem all that enthusiastic. He picks up the last photo and checks around the room to see if he's missed anything. Then he passes it to me for packing in the box.

It's the photo of the teacher with her class. Printed along the bottom in faded letters are the words "Ebenezer Foight Elementary School, 1964." Two kids in the front row hold a felt banner that says GRADE 3.

I place the picture in the box and close it up. Ty lifts it and we all stand looking at each other and at the empty secret room.

"Let's close the room up and be on our way." Levi heads down the stairs and Ty follows him with the box. I swing the secret door in place and trail behind with Henry.

"Don't you think his reaction is a little weird?" I murmur under my breath as I let Levi and Ty get further ahead of us. "Why won't he call the cops? And why does he want those photos?"

"Hmm. I think he's afraid someone's after the inheritance."

"But who? Those pictures are Maybelle's relatives. Vareena had no family."

Henry snorts. "Everybody's got family. That old lady didn't hatch from a rock. Just gotta look for the connections."

Outside, Ty is pulling out of his hidden parking space. When the car is next to me, he leans out the window and extends his hand. "You got my phone?"

In all the excitement, I forgot that I still had it. I dig it out of my bag, but then I remember the news that Ty will see as soon as he glances at the texts. I hold the phone back as I speak. "Ty, something happened yesterday while you were gone."

His eyes narrow.

"Your dad was released from prison." The words spurt out of me like shaken soda. "He was with Charmaine. They came looking for you. But now Charmaine says she doesn't know where he is."

Ty fixes me with a steady dark glare. He rolls his fingers and I place the phone in his hand. "I'll see you here in the mornin'."

And he's gone.

I TEXT DONNA AND TELL HER Ty is fine and to meet us at the Tate Mansion at 7 AM tomorrow for the sale. When she responds with questions, I mute my phone. Let Ty tell her what he chooses. On the drive home, I mull over all that's happened. And the more I think, the more worried I get. First of all, there's no way Ty is just going to walk away from this assault. *You hurt me. You scared the shit out of me. You coulda killed me. But hey, no problem. I'm just gonna turn the other cheek and forget about it.*

Would Ty ever say that?

No.

So that means he's got some idea of who the assailant is, and he's going to go after him by himself.

And that can't end well.

And what about Levi? Does he have some idea of who those people in the photos are? Could one of them have known about the room and been responsible for the attack? Is Levi protecting someone?

And the one person who might help me figure this out is the one person I dread telling: Sean. I can hear him already. *How could you have compromised the crime scene by tramping through that room? All the forensic evidence is destroyed. How could you have let Levi walk off with those photos? They're evidence.*

I know all that. I do. But what could I have done to stop them?

You could've called 911 the moment you got to the house and suspected Ty was there.

Yeah, right. And how would that call have gone down? *Hi, this is Audrey Nealon. I'm sure something terrible has happened to my assistant because he missed his econ exam. Can you come over to the Tate Mansion and help me look for him?*

You could have called the moment you found Ty bleeding and knew a crime had been committed.

I could have. But I hesitated because of the sale. Because of all the work we've put into it. Because of the money it will bring in, not just for me, but also for the Parks Center and my dad's program and the kids it will help. I hesitated, and once Ty saw that moment of weakness, I was doomed.

This is what I must confess to Sean.

But when I pull into the garage, his car isn't there. The house is dark. Ethel whines patiently next to her empty dish. But he told me just a few hours ago that he was heading home to cook dinner for us.

While I'm fixing Ethel her dinner, I get a text from Ty.

Yo—send me that pic you took of the room.

I forward it with a “why?”, but of course I get no answer. What’s with the men in my life?

Ethel is dancing on her hind legs as I check the fridge for some leftovers to dress up her dog food. As I set her dish down, I spot a piece of paper on the counter.

Audrey,

I’m sorry about dinner. I got called in on another security job. I might have to spend the night. Good luck with the sale tomorrow.

Love,

Sean

I stand in the kitchen holding the sheet of paper. Why did he leave me a note instead of calling or texting? There’s only one answer—because he didn’t want me to ask him questions. He was supposed to be done with this moonlighting and now he’s taken another shift. Sean is avoiding me, so I can avoid him with a clear conscience. Maybe by the time the sale ends tomorrow, I’ll have a better justification for my actions.

Maybe.

CHAPTER 34

WHEN I DRIVE UP SILVER Lane at 6:55 AM, cars are already parked on the shoulder all the way from the intersection to the front gates of the mansion. I wave at my regulars as I pass. First order of business: send Donna out with the numbers that will admit the early birds in the order they arrived even if they leave the line to go for coffee.

When I enter the house through the back door, I follow the sound of voices to the foyer. Ty and two of Henry's men are moving some tables to create a payment area and block shoppers' access to the back hall. Ty is his usual self—relaxed, joking with the guys, lifting and hauling with no complaint. Donna pops in from the parlor, her ever-present microfiber cloth in hand.

"I'm so excited! Everything is good to go. Can we open the doors?"

"No!" Ty and I chorus.

"Never open early. It sets a bad precedent," I explain.

"Yeah, then next sale, when we happen to be running behind, they'll be clawin' and scratchin' to get in early. Jus' chill."

I send a crestfallen Donna out to distribute the numbers and wait for Henry's men to return to the garage. "What's happening," I say to Ty in a low voice. "Did you meet up with your father?"

He shakes his head. "I talked to Charmaine. Everything cool."

"What about—"

Ty turns his back on me. "Don' worry about it."

O-*kay*. I guess we're not going there. "And your exam....?"

His face lights up. "I went straight out to campus to talk to my professor after I left you yesterday."

"What did you tell him?"

"The truth."

Ty laughs at my dropped jaw. "Well, not the whole truth. I told him about my job, and how I was studying in the mansion… of course, he knew about the place after all the news articles. So then I showed him the picture of the hidden room and told him I accidentally got trapped in there until you found me the next day. I left out the part about being hit on the head."

"So that's why you asked me to send you the picture of the room! What did he say?"

"That it was the craziest excuse he ever heard, and that he didn't think I was creative enough to make it up, so it must be true. And he said I could take the exam on Monday."

I fling my arms around Ty "See, honesty is the best policy."

"Yeah? What did Sean say when you told him about me and the room?"

Finally, we come to the most pressing matter. "When I got home last night, Sean wasn't there. He had to spend the night at his moonlighting job."

Ty continues to busy himself with the cash box and the receipt book. "So?"

"So I haven't told him yet about what happened in the secret room."

"Mmmm."

"Ty." I scoot around so he has to meet my eye. I clutch his wrist and don't let go. "It's not like you to brush off something this big. I thought about it all night long. You have some idea of who attacked you, don't you?"

Ty takes a pained breath, tries to squirm away without being rough. "There's been some guys comin' around."

"Guys?"

"Old gangsters who knew my pops back in the day. Guys who knew him inside. Word on the street was he was gettin' out soon."

"And how did these *guys* find you?"

Ty stands silently.

A light bulb goes off in my mind. "Charmaine did this! She took your father's messages to his crew. And then they came looking for you to help them with their schemes? They think you're one of them because—"

Ty interrupts my rant. "I set them straight. I told them I didn't want no part of what they had to offer."

"When was all this?"

"End of last week."

"And you think these men came here on Thursday night? How would they have known where to find you? And how would they know about the secret room? Could this be related to the carjacking? "

"They know who I work for, and signs for this sale have been up all over town for the past week. But the room—" Ty shakes his head. "I can't figure out how they discovered it before we did."

"And these thugs attacked you out of revenge? Because they were mad you wouldn't go along with them? Then why didn't you want me to call the police?"

Now Ty gives his arm a sharp shake and breaks free. "You don't have no idea what kinda people you're messin' with here! Callin' the cops would bring a whole world a trouble down on us."

"You know what—I don't care what kind of trouble I bring down on your father and Charmaine."

"I'm not trying to protect my father. I'm trying to protect *you*."

DONNA CHOOSES THAT MOMENT TO reenter the house, so our discussion is tabled. Together we focus on our final preparations. But I'm distracted. Who is trying to harm me, my business, my staff?

At 7:58, I lift the heavy velvet drapes in the dining room and peek out. A huge line snakes down the driveway.

A thrill of excitement flutters in my chest, pushing away the wad of worry. This may be our biggest sale ever.

"Take your places, everyone." I nod to Henry's helper. "Let them in fifty at a time. No more."

The heavy door swings open. We're off!

THE FIRST TEN PEOPLE THROUGH the doors are regulars. I watch as nimble Jonathan Streit dodges past lumbering Donald Porter to lay claim to the Rococo Revival étagère in the parlor. But sometimes slow and steady wins the race because

Donald has snagged all the oil paintings in the foyer, not even bothering to haggle on the price.

The morning continues at a lightening pace. Experienced antiques dealers act decisively. They know if they can make a profit reselling a piece at the price I'm asking, or if the furniture will languish in their showroom. They write a check immediately, or they walk away without a backward glance.

People buying for their own use are different creatures entirely. They fall upon a table or a cabinet gushing and squealing, and then ask me if I'll drop the price. Note to shoppers: not a good negotiating strategy. Or they circle the piece, caressing, measuring, discussing. They walk away. They come back. They walk away again. They argue with each other, sometimes to the point of tears. In the end, I get the money and they walk out with their purchase. Whether they're elated or disgruntled matters not to me.

Fully one-third of the people in the line are sightseers eager for a glimpse inside the mysterious Tate Mansion. That's fine—although they clog the rooms and delay the entry of buyers, they also create a sense of urgency that fuels sales. The classic Manhattan conundrum: if this many people are lined up for it, it must be worth the wait. And the corollary: if there's no line and you can stroll right in, why would you want to go?

I've been worried that some of the furniture in the mansion is too massive to be sold to private homeowners. So I'm relieved when Reggie and Chris arrive in a swoosh of powerful aftershave and hair product.

"Dah-ling, this place is to die for!" Reggie—or is it Chris?—bestows double air-kisses. One is tall and dark, the other short and fair, but between them they have just one personality.

Gush-o-rama.

"Squee! Look at this breakfront! Wouldn't this be fabulous in the tasting room in that vineyard in Sonoma?"

"Or the farm-to-table in Vermont…"

Either way, they're taking it. Reggie and Chris own a huge warehouse in Queens where they stock decorative items for restaurants, hotels, and movie sets. If I have something truly bizarre to sell—a stuffed rhino head, a rodeo rider's saddle, a 20-foot long banquet table—they're the guys most likely to buy.

Of course, they don't always maintain the integrity of the piece—I can hear one of them in the parlor saying, "We could rip the drawers out and replace them with shelves...paint it gray--" –but that's not my business. I'm here to sell, not preserve.

Just before noon, a familiar voice causes me to pause in my transactions.

"Well," he drawls. "This sure is a gloomy old pile, isn't it?"

I look up to see Crawford Bostwick standing in the foyer, hands thrust into the pockets of his faded Nantucket red Bermuda shorts, blond hair held back by the sunglasses pushed up on his head.

"Hello, Crawford. What brings you here?" *Looking for a new place to crash? Or something small to steal?* I want to say.

"Oh, I have an interest in the stately homes of Palmer County. After all, I live in one. Or used to." He spins around, looking up. "Gothic Revival...so grim, so dour. Why not revive something fun?"

He prowls around the foyer, peering at the few small paintings that haven't been purchased. What's he up to?

"By the way, Crawford—we found something here related to your family. Your mother's side of the family."

Crawford's hand freezes as he was about to touch an ornate, carved bird on the case of the grandfather clock. "Oh?"

"Vareena Tate seems to have saved some advertisements of your great-great-grandfather's product, Scour-Brite. Any idea why?"

Crawford's shoulders relax. "Really? Maybe the other lady—Mary Ellen?... Annabelle?—used it to clean this place. Where are all the things that belonged to Vareena Tate?"

"Miss? Who should I make the check out to?"

I snap back to taking care of the customers checking out. When I look up again, Crawford is gone.

I text Donna, who's working in the dining room where we've gathered all the smallest, easily stolen items, and Ty, who's upstairs. *Crawford Bostwick is here. Keep your eye on him.*

A few minutes later, Donna texts back that she hasn't seen him, but will watch out.

I get busy again, and a half-hour passes. Then I hear a commotion from upstairs. A few moments later, Crawford Bostwick is trotting down the grand staircase. He pauses by my checkout table. "That *thug* who works for you is out of control."

Before I can respond, Crawford sails out the front door.

Good riddance.

"What do you think of this sale compared to the one at Birdie's house?" I ask Donna as we finally get a lull around 1:00 PM. She has moved the remaining small items from the dining room to the foyer, consolidating our area of operation. Henry's men have been keeping an eye on the kitchen and the back of the house.

Donna drops in a chair behind the checkout desk. "It's like Black Friday at Wal-Mart, but with antiques. Is every sale as busy as these first two have been?"

"No. Sometimes we could sit around playing canasta. Those are the sales with nothing but standard old-folks clutter. I want to limit them to on-line sales only, but I just haven't been able to devote the time to developing our on-line presence. I'm hoping you'll help me with that."

Donna's eyes light up. "Oh, I'd love that. I already have so many ideas." She chatters to me happily about creating a cyber-store and improving our SEO as we complete transactions for a few more buyers.

Ty appears on the landing above us. "Slowin' down up here. How about calling Bangkok Palace for a delivery?"

"Pad Thai and basil chicken?"

Donna sighs. "Perfect!"

When Ty comes down to eat, I ask him what happened with Crawford.

"I was following him from room to room. He didn't like it. When we were alone, I asked him if he was in here last night. He told me I was crazy. Then some real customers came in and I had to lay off."

"Do you think he was lying?' I ask.

Ty shrugs. "He's got that 'who, me?' act down pretty good."

I frown. "He's had plenty of practice, I think."

As we're polishing off the last of our rice noodles, Ty spies a horde trooping up the driveway and tosses down his almost empty Pad Thai container. "Ima head back upstairs and close off two of the bedrooms. Move what's left into the three biggest rooms."

Donna springs up. "I'll help you."

Ty pushes down on her shoulders. "Chill. I'll call when I need you."

The pace of the sale picks up again. It's the late afternoon mini-rush of casual buyers—people with a real life who don't have the time to camp out in line. Most of the best stuff is already gone, but there are some surprisingly good antiques still available. I've given up predicting what will sell immediately and what will be passed over at any sale. It's like trying to accurately guess if the Mets can hang onto an eight-run lead.

At four, we begin herding the stragglers out the door. Ty comes downstairs to report that everyone's gone. But he looks worried.

"What's wrong?" I ask.

Ty reaches into his shirt pocket and pulls out a pair of sunglasses. Oversize horn rims.

"Ooo—Vaurnet!" Donna squeals. "Since when are you into designer shades?"

"Not mine. I found 'em. In Maybelle's room."

"I bet the customer who dropped them will come back tomorrow asking for them. Vaurnets are like five hundred bucks." Donna shakes her head. "I lose sunglasses all the time. I could never trust myself with something so expensive."

"Well, if he comes back, I'll be ready for him. You wanna know where I found these?" Ty continues even without encouragement. "Right by that little corner shelf in Maybelle's room that hides the lever to open the room."

"That could just be a coincidence," Donna says. "Who would try to open the room during the sale?"

I put the sunglasses on top of Donna's head, using them to hold back her hair. Now I know where I've seen these glasses.

"Crawford Bostwick. He was wearing sunglasses when he came in."

CHAPTER 35

"CRAWFORD BOSTWICK KNEW ABOUT THE secret room," Ty thumps the ornate newel post with his fist. "I was right when I thought it might be him sneaking around here."

"Hold up. Crawford knows about the room now. Maybe he just found out about it."

Ty juts his chin in my direction. "From who? My sister? Henry?"

"Let's make a list of everyone who definitely knows about the room." I start taking dictation as Ty and Donna call out names. "Henry…Levi…me…you…Donna… Charmaine…Grams…my professor…" The list grows longer as we add people that those people were likely to have told—spouses, friends, colleagues. Pretty soon we have a list of well over twenty names and growing.

"Okay, so it's a lotta people. But none of 'em rich. No one on that list is parta Crawford Bostwick's crew," Ty says.

"Just because they're not his drinking buddies…or polo buddies…whatever people like him have, doesn't mean there aren't connections. Remember the rule of six degrees of separation," I insist. "What do you, me, Henry, and Levi have in common, Ty?"

"The Rosa Parks Center."

"And whose mother was on the Board of the Rosa Parks Center and died at a party raising money for the Rosa Parks Center?"

Ty scratches his head. "Yeah, but Crawford never showed any interest in the place. Why would Levi be talkin' to Loretta's son now that Loretta's dead?"

"I think the Parks Center still gets money from the Scour Brite Enterprises charitable foundation. That money comes from

Loretta's side of the family—the Crawfords. The connection is still there."

"But if Crawford found out about the room from someone connected to us, then he'd know it was empty now. Why come here and try to open it up again?"

Donna's head has been swiveling back and forth as she listens to the volley of Ty's and my conversation. Now the ball is in my court and she squints at me. "Yeah, why?"

I don't have an answer.

WITH DAY ONE OF THE Tate sale over, I send Ty and Donna home with orders to meet back here at 7AM tomorrow. Day Two will be less busy, but we still have plenty to sell.

Now, Henry and I sit in the kitchen going over the proceeds. I count all the cash and tally the checks both from today's business and the things I've sold in advance to specialized dealers, then turn it over to him to double-check my work.

"$275,000." Henry sways in the hard, wooden kitchen chair. "My, my."

That's about as excited as Henry ever gets.

A moment passes and he meets my gaze over the mound of checks and cash on the table between us. "I do believe I made a good decision partnering up with you, Audrey Nealon."

I smile. "Thank you for giving me the opportunity, Henry. I enjoy working with you. And I think this sale is turning out great for all concerned."

"Yeah. Maybe now Dennis will leave me in peace. These profits prove I know what I'm doin'."

"Dennis has been giving you a hard time about working with me?"

"He wants updates on what we're finding in here and how you know what it's worth. I told him you and Ty are all studied up on antiques and art and even old bowls and pans. That just makes him ask more and more questions." Henry leans back and shuts his eyes. "That chile thinks he's got all the answers."

"Answers to what?"

"How the world should work. Who should be in charge of who. I told him when he gets everyone operatin' according to his plan he should let me know."

"Have you known Dennis a long time?"

Henry straightens up and starts organizing the money for the bank deposit. "Since he was a kid and Levi started lookin' out for him. Dennis had some problems at home after his father left, but Levi could tell he was smart. Made sure the kid stayed in school." Levi shakes his head. "You ask me, Dennis could use a little less time with the books and a little more time with a hammer. His father was one fine carpenter, but him and his wife fought like cats and dogs, even after they divorced. So he moved down to Florida. Dennis took it hard."

We turn off the lights and prepare to leave for the bank together. I want to pump Henry for more information about Dennis, like whether he knew I had the ledger, but I don't want to be too obvious. Despite Henry's grumbling, I suspect he's fond of Dennis. I don't want him reporting back to Dennis that I had so many questions. "By the way, Henry—did you happen to tell Dennis about the secret room and the photos?"

"Yeah. First time I ever told him something that left him speechless."

"So you didn't get the impression he already knew about the room?"

"Nah. How would he know about it? The only time he was ever here was when the Board members took that tour of the place."

So Dennis says.

"But he was real curious about those pictures. I told him Levi took them if he wanted to see them."

Henry's phone chirps and he scowls at the text that's come in.

"Audrey, could you do me a big favor? After we go to the bank, Levi asked me to stop by his house with a tally on the results of the first day of the sale. But my wife's naggin' me to get home in time for our grandson's birthday party."

I reach for the tally. "Sure, I'll take it. Give me his address and let him know I'm coming."

CHAPTER 36

LEVI'S HOUSE IS ON A peaceful residential street of homes built in the twenties and thirties. When I get out of my car in front of his brick colonial, the loudest sounds are from his neighbors: a lawn sprinkler on one side and a badminton game on the other.

When I get to the porch, the front door is open and through the screen door I see Levi's signature straw hat on a table in the small foyer. I ring the bell and wait.

Nothing.

I shout his name through the screen door and wait.

Nothing.

He was expecting me, and he must be home if the doors are wide open. Maybe he stepped out into his back yard.

I follow a flagstone walk around to the back, but there's no sign of Levi. I peek through the garage window and see his car.

I try knocking at the back door, which is also wide open.

Nothing.

Now I'm starting to feel uneasy. Could he have fallen, or had a sudden heart attack or stroke? He's not young, but he's always seemed healthy to me.

I let myself into the kitchen. A half-finished mug of tea sits on the table. "Levi? It's Audrey. Are you here?"

I don't want to prowl through his whole house. I pull out my phone and call him. The line rings and rings, but I don't hear it here in the house. Eventually, it rolls over to his voicemail.

With my ears tuned for the sound of the phone, I now hear another faint noise.

Whining. Scratching.

I follow it to a door in the hallway leading to the foyer. I open it and a small dog shoots out of the powder room. He runs around me in gratitude for being released. Then he sits and cocks his head as if it's dawned on him that I'm not his master.

"Where's Levi, buddy?"

He flattens himself on the floor and whines.

Now there's a knot of anxiety in my gut. If something bad happened to Levi, is it related to the assault on Ty?

The dog jumps up and sniffs the air. Then he trots down the hall with great purpose. I follow him as he heads into what looks to be the den.

He starts barking high and sharp. A mixture of smells, all unpleasant, reaches my less sensitive nose.

I step into the room. Levi lies sprawled back in an easy chair.

A small gun lies on the floor beneath his dangling hand.

Blood and brains splatter across the wall behind him.

"AND THE BACK DOOR WAS open?"

The police are questioning me in the backyard. The EMTs have already carried Levi's body out of the house. The Crime Scene team has taken over. The neighbors stand at a distance, all agog.

I go over my story for what feels like the fourth time, answering every question put to me but not volunteering anything extra, when Sean finally arrives. He speaks to the detective in charge out of my hearing before coming over to me.

He sits down beside me and puts his arm around me. "You okay?"

I nod, suddenly feeling shakier now that my comforter has arrived. "I'm stunned. The sale went great. Levi wanted to see the tally of results, so I brought it over. Why would he kill himself now?" I look directly at my husband. "Did Levi commit suicide, or did someone kill him and just try to make it look like suicide?"

"We'll know for certain when they test his hands for gunshot residue. But he left a note."

"He did?" Of course, I'd run straight out of the house as soon as I made the gruesome discovery. "What did it say?"

"Asked God for forgiveness and asked people to pray for his

soul. Oh, and he said please don't send Tigger to the shelter."

I glance around for the little dog.

"Don't worry. The neighbor took him."

I take a deep breath. "There's something I have to tell you."

Sean listens quietly and patiently as the story of the secret room spills out of me. I tell him everything, from Henry and I finding Ty through to Crawford's visit and Dennis's knowledge of the room and photos. Sean's expression never changes. I'm finding his lack of agitation a little unnerving. "So I couldn't persuade either one of them to call 9-1-1. But I planned to tell you last night at dinner. But then you didn't come home, and I knew you were distracted with the moonlighting, and then today was the sale—totally crazy…so…. Are you mad?" I finish in a tiny voice.

Sean sits still.

Very still.

"Sean?"

He twitches. "No. No, I'm not mad." He stands up. "We need to search the house for those photos."

CHAPTER 37

EVENTUALLY, THE POLICE SAY I can leave, but Sean stays at the scene. After what happened to Levi, I'm paranoid about the safety of everyone I love. When I get home, I call to check on Ty and Donna, and then on my dad and Natalie. Amazingly, Dad already knows the news. A neighbor called a member of Levi's church, who called the Parks Center and now everyone there is buzzing.

"Why do you think Levi would kill himself now, Dad, just when the sale is going so well and the Parks Center will be getting the money it needs?"

"I don't know," Dad answers. "I've noticed a lot of closed-door meetings recently, some including Levi, some that take place when the other Board members know he won't be around. I even spotted Dennis and Jared having coffee at Caffeine Planet."

Now what could that be about? Like any daughter who doesn't want to worry her parent, I haven't told Dad about the carjacking or the attack on Ty. "What do you know about Dennis's childhood, Dad? Henry says Levi took Dennis under his wing when Dennis's parents divorced and his dad moved away. But Dennis doesn't seem to regard Levi as a father or grandfather figure—he always seems irritated with him."

"Ah, young people are often irritated with their elders. Dennis was very close to his grandfather, went along with him on carpentry jobs. His grandfather died about a year after his dad moved. It was that double-whammy that sent Dennis off-course for a while. Dennis credits the Parks Center for turning him around, not Levi specifically."

"Was Dennis at the Parks Center when the news broke? How

did he react to Levi's death?"

"No, Dennis wasn't there. No one has been able to reach him."

I hang up with my father and start making myself some dinner. After days of eating take-out, I feel the need for something healthy. Luckily, Sean has our fridge well stocked, so I get busy making a big salad.

As I chop peppers and tear lettuce, I think about the photos from the secret room. Who were those people? With my hands occupied with mindless work, I let my brain relax. Soon an image appears: The class picture from the Ebenezer Foight School, 1964. How many Ebenezer Foight schools can there be?

I put aside my salad ingredients and sit in front of my laptop at the kitchen table. Google soon informs me there's only one Ebenezer Foight School, and it's in a small town down near the shore. Bad news—it closed seven years ago. I scroll down the search results. Good news—there's a Facebook group for Friends of Ebenezer Foight School--alumni, teachers, and staff.

Ah, social media. Where would we be without you?

The pictures posted in the group are snapshots and class photos through the years. Science Fair--1973, Spring Concert—1969, Mrs. Green's Kindergarten—1982. Under each picture there are comments: "I'm in the second row with the goofy grin. Anybody know who that kid is beside me?" "Julie McNamara had a solo in this concert. I heard she later was a finalist on *America's Got Talent*. Does anyone know if that's true?

I keep scrolling back through years of postings. I suppose it would be asking too much that a copy of the very photo from the secret room would be posted here. But among the photos, there are pleas: "Trying to reach Kevin Hartney, who was in sixth grade in 1971—anyone have contact info?" "Does anyone know what happened to Miss Pimms, who taught fourth grade back in the Sixties?" And remarkably, tons of people answer these queries.

So I try it. "Does anyone remember a young African American woman who taught third grade in 1964? My aunt had her, but she can't remember her name."

I post the message and return to my salad prep.

Sean arrives home just as I finish.

"Make your special vinaigrette." I push the olive oil and

balsamic towards him. "And tell me what happened when you searched Levi's house."

Sean pours ingredients into a bowl without measuring. "No trace of those photos from the secret room anywhere in the house. And he never showed them to members of his church like he told you he would."

"Why was Levi trying to keep them secret?"

Sean whisks furiously. "I think there's some connection between the Tate bequest to the Parks Center, Loretta's death, and Crawford's rape case. Yesterday the Manhattan District Attorney filed charges against Crawford on third-degree rape, which is sex with someone too young to give consent. "

"Like your fifteen-year-old student. The parents and the girl finally cooperated?"

Sean pours the dressing on the salad and tosses. "Yeah, because what happened is now wide open in the Bumford-Stanley community."

"Wait—I saw Crawford at the sale this morning."

"Out on bail. But the judge made him surrender his passport. Rich young rapists are considered a flight risk." Sean sets the salad on the table, and we sit down to eat.

"I'm surprised the Bostwick family lawyer couldn't get around that."

"The Bostwick family lawyer probably could have. Unfortunately for Crawford, he was represented by some jailhouse shyster who showed him how to use his Mercedes convertible to post bond. Papa Frederic is playing hardball. No money for the boy."

"Good. Serves him right. So what's the connection to Levi?"

Sean sits staring at his arugula and sun-dried tomatoes.

I wait. Nothing.

"Sean, why did you tell me there's a connection?" He flings his head back. "Because I need someone who will just listen to me!"

"That's what wives are for. Go."

"The chief of police is getting ready to back-burner the investigation into Loretta's death. The medical examiner says he doesn't have enough evidence to rule whether the mode of death is homicide or suicide. He's sticking to his guns that it's not an accidental fall though. Frederic Bostwick accepts that the ME will never rule the death an accident, and he's willing to let it stand as a suspicious death. He just wants the family name out of the headlines."

"So since it's not an ongoing investigation anymore, you're willing to confide in me."

"I need someone to bounce ideas off. At the office, everyone says, 'Let it go, Coughlin.' Even Holzer is tired of listening to me."

Sean's long-suffering partner has the patience of a saint, so that's saying a lot. "Okay, let me play devil's advocate. Why are you convinced it's murder if the ME isn't?"

"First, I explored the possibility of suicide. I did a suicide profile. Had she ever had suicidal thoughts? Had she ever made a previous attempt? Did she leave a note? All no."

"But people commit suicide unexpectedly all the time. No one expected Levi to kill himself." I pause. "But it's weird they would both kill themselves within a couple of weeks."

Sean nods. "Exactly. I didn't abandon suicide, but it was time to explore the possibility of murder. The biggest piece of forensic evidence pointing to murder is the bruises on her arms. The bruises on the right arm blended in with bruises caused by the fall. But everyone agrees the bruises on her left arm were made by someone grabbing her arm. But Loretta suffered from some weird blood disorder, which caused her skin to bruise very easily."

"So someone could have just reached out to keep her from stumbling on a curb and caused those bruises."

"Or someone could have grabbed her and tossed her over the railing."

Sean stabs his salad with his fork. "When I first talked to friends about Loretta's state of mind, no one was willing to mention how anxious she was about the trouble Crawford was in. None of her high society friends wanted to be the first breach in the wall of silence. But once I did a second round of interviews and made it clear I already knew about Crawford, the floodgates opened up."

Sean waves his loaded fork and some lettuce hits the floor. Ethel sniffs and walks away in disappointment. "People told me Frederic was tired of Crawford dragging the Bostwick family name through the dirt. The drunk driving, the cheating in college, the rehab. Frederic said his son was a bad seed and should be cut off without a cent.

"Then the scandal with the girl broke. The thought that his son might now be labeled a sex offender for life was driving Frederic around the bend, and the two of them argued constantly. Loretta confided in some of her friends that she was afraid her husband might actually hurt Crawford, and she tried to keep them physically separated while she figured out what to do."

"That explains why Crawford was looking for a place to stay," I say. "With his mother gone, things must've been really tense with the old man. And now, Frederic won't even give him money for a decent lawyer. So far, this sounds like a motive for Crawford to kill his father, not his mother."

"You been talking to my boss? That's what he says." Sean massages his temples. "I'm sure Loretta's death has something to do with Crawford needing money to bail him out of his scandals, but I can't connect all the dots."

"Why kill Loretta? She was the one with all the money. Couldn't she simply have written a check for whatever Crawford needed?"

Sean points his fork at me. "That's where it gets complicated. I found out Loretta's father decided the best way to preserve the family fortune was to protect it from rogue relatives. Apparently, his younger brother was a black sheep, like Crawford. Loretta's father took the Scour-Brite business public—turned it into SB Enterprises so it would be governed by a board of directors. The family were majority shareholders, but they couldn't skim money out of the company. Then he put a wad of money in a family charitable foundation—"

"The one that gives money to the Rosa Parks Center," I interrupt.

Sean nods. "--and he tied up the rest of the cash in a bunch of complex trust funds."

"So Loretta, Frederic, and Crawford have never had unlimited access to the Scour-Brite Enterprises fortune?"

"Correct. But they still had plenty of cash to keep that giant house running and live the lush life."

"So Loretta couldn't skim some bucks off her allowance to rescue Crawford? Was she afraid of her husband? Is he actually a violent person?"

Sean offers a rueful smile. "All men are violent, Audrey. Some are just more easily triggered than others."

"So you think Frederic abused Loretta?"

"Define abuse. I think he's a demanding person used to getting his own way. Does he hit women? Maybe not. But there are other ways to make your wife miserable." Sean lines up the salt and pepper shakers with the sugar bowl. "Remember, Loretta wasn't a rebel. She wanted to keep peace with her husband. She wanted to make her son happy and comfortable. It was hard to do both."

"So she had to resort to scheming?"

"My mother once told my dad that we weren't having meat for dinner for a week because of a salmonella outbreak. Then she used the money she saved to buy Deirdre the Lord and Taylor prom dress she had her heart set on." Sean lifts his hands skywards. "It's what mothers do."

"You're seriously telling me that Loretta Bostwick, one of the richest women in New Jersey, was scrounging for money like an Irish housewife, and that somehow got her killed?"

Sean raises his eyebrows to give me the full effect of his baby blues. "That's what I think. So now you know why no one at the office is willing to listen to me anymore."

CHAPTER 38

DAY TWO OF THE TATE sale feels subdued.

The crowd outside is smaller although still substantial. But inside, we workers have been thrown off our game by Levi's suicide. We mark down prices and rearrange the items left, but it feels like we're wading through molasses as we work.

Henry, in particular, looks shell-shocked. "I can't believe he killed himself. A man his age oughta know there's no trouble that can't be got through with the help of the Lord."

Ty also looks worried. "I wanna know what's up with Dennis," Ty mutters to me when we're alone in the back parlor. "I've been texting him and he won't answer."

"You think he has those photos? It's weird that the photos and Dennis are both MIA."

Ty doesn't answer, but he has a strange look in his eyes as he helps me move two tables into the front parlor. I keep pressing him. "Ty, is it possible Dennis is the person who hit you and locked you in the secret room?"

Ty flinches like a kid burned while playing with matches. "Why would he do me like that? I mean, we're not close friends, but we've known each other a while. And he's the one always goin' on about black men needing to back each other up."

"So we were totally wrong to suspect your father?"

"Guess so. He's livin' in a halfway house in Dover, tryin' to stay away from his old crew. Charmaine says he got a job in a warehouse."

I SET UP SOME PORTABLE LIGHTS so customers can see the items still for sale. "That's a relief." But Ty still looks worried.

He drags a chair out of a dark corner. "And then there's the van."

"The van?" I've finally gotten the van back from the Newark police, who didn't find any useful prints inside. "You think Dennis had something to do with the carjacking?"

Ty shrugs. "I don't wanna believe it. But I keep thinkin' about the smack he was talkin' that day. It was like he was trying to get me pissed off to like, distract me."

"Distract you from what?"

Ty looks me in the eye. "I think he was trying to see inside the van."

"Inside? But the cargo area doesn't have windows."

"The front seat. What was in the front?"

My eyes open wide. "The ledger! The ledger that I moved inside my house that night."

"But he musta thought we still had it in the van." Ty shakes himself as if a bug landed on him. "I can't believe Dennis, of all people, would use a kid from the 'hood like that. What if Dennis's scheme got that kid arrested?"

I gaze around the half-empty front parlor. "There's something about this house, something about the inheritance, that's causing Dennis to take enormous risks. And whatever it is, I think Crawford Bostwick might be after it too. Why else would he come here?"

Ty marches toward the front hall. "Let's open the doors and get this sale over with. I've had enough of this house."

The sale passes in a blur. Bargain hunters snap up the remaining antiques. Curious souvenir-seekers buy a surprising quantity of small odds and ends. Henry's men load his truck with junk for the dump: the sad, worn out chairs where Maybelle and Vareena spent their days reading, the old radio, the thin aluminum pots.

The Tate sale is over.

I should be elated, but I'm gripped by a strange uneasiness. Has all our work been for nothing? Is the Parks Center in danger of losing this inheritance? Is there some information in that ledger or in the secret room that's going to upend the windfall that should save the Center? Is my dad going to lose the funding for his dream project?

I sit in my car after the others have left and gaze up at the empty Tate Mansion. Are Vareena and Maybelle's secrets now lost to me?

On the drive home, a deer bounds across the road ten feet from my car. I slam on my brakes, and when I do, I see something gold-colored peeking up between the passenger door and the seat.

Birdie's trophy.

My Honda is almost as messy as the van. It must've slid up from the back when I braked.

I guess I could drop it off on George's front porch tomorrow.

Or....

I cradle the trophy in my hands. I could take it over to Birdie at the nursing home after I detour to my office and pick up the family tree I saved. And while I'm there, ask her about the erased box on the family tree and the photo she buried in the box.

The photo that Loretta gave her.

There's a link here, and I'm going to figure it out.

BIRDIE ARMENTROUT RESIDES IN "VISTAS Memory Community" of an upscale assisted living complex called The Palisades. That's a lovely name for a locked down ward with security to rival Guantanamo Bay. I announce myself through a speakerphone and stand in front of a security camera. After a few moments, a middle-aged attendant comes to let me in, securely locking the door behind my back. In the main part ofThe Palisades, the carpets are plush and the furniture elegant. Here, the floors are easily mopped wood-pattern laminate, and all the furniture is covered in Pleather. An old gentleman wanders by, his eyes fixed on something only he can see. A woman sits on a sofa calling out softly, pleasantly, "Son of a bitch. You go to hell."

"She's the wife of a Methodist minister," the aid explains. "Alzheimer's causes a lack of inhibitions."

I shiver and follow my escort to the main desk. When I ask for Birdie, the woman sighs. "I'm afraid she's not having a good day today, but you can try. Are you her niece?"

"No, I'm an old family friend," I lie smoothly. "Her brother

George told me she probably wouldn't recognize me, but he says she enjoys visitors anyway. And I found something she might enjoy." I hold up the trophy.

"Yes, some days she does enjoy visitors. But often she doesn't recognize her friends and relatives. Last week she complained that there was a strange man bothering her and asked us to get rid of him. Naturally, that upset her nephew."

George's sons live in Boston and Denver. Was one of them visiting? I saw a picture of them at Birdie's place. They look like younger versions of their dad, short and mournful.

"A short guy with dark hair?" I ask.

"No, tall." The supervisor purses her lips as she ponders. "He had kind of an unusual name. He played the piano beautifully. The other residents enjoyed his visit even if Birdie didn't."

Crawford Bostwick! I don't see him as an angel of mercy, visiting the infirm. He must've been digging for information on that photo, just like me.

"Oh, I'll leave if she doesn't want to see me," I reassure the supervisor.

"On the other hand, her garden club friend came to visit and Birdie looked straight at her and said, 'Hello, Louise. How are your clematis?' So you never know." She points me down the hall. "Birdie's in the Solarium. It's her favorite spot."

The first time I toured the house with George, there were still plenty of photos of Birdie, so I'm fairly confident I'll recognize her. When I enter the solarium, I see several very old, frail people and one healthy woman in her mid-sixties. She's hovering over a huge geranium in the window, carefully plucking off yellow leaves and spent blooms. She's thinner than in her pictures, but unmistakably Birdie.

I approach her cautiously. "That's a beautiful flower. Is it a geranium?"

"Yes." Birdie barely acknowledges me as she continues her work.

"I didn't know they could grow so big indoors. I thought they had to be outside."

She pauses and peers at me as if I'm not too bright. "Full sun. Not too much fertilizer. Careful pruning."

"Ah—that's the secret." I stay by her side as she moves to the next plant. "What's this one called?"

"Oxalis. Cut it back to encourage new growth from the tubers."

We continue in this manner all around the solarium. Birdie tends each plant, remembering their names, sometimes even giving them in Latin. Another resident says hello to her and Birdie nods. Then she stage-whispers to me, "I don't know when she joined the garden club. Too many new members!"

"Yes, I agree." Birdie seems to have accepted me as a garden club member in good standing. So far, so good.

We reach a tree-like plant in a large pot. Birdie sticks her finger in the dirt and determines it needs water, but when she tilts her watering can, nothing comes out. She holds the empty can looking perplexed. Her hand tightens on the handle and her face grows agitated. Clearly, she can't remember how to get more water.

"Can I refill that for you?" I touch the can gently.

She releases it and stands lost amid the plants as I hurry to a small sink in the corner and refill the can. When I return it to her, Birdie's hand trembles under the new weight. But she seems relieved when the water flows onto the soil in the big pot.

Crisis averted.

"Have you done any more work on your family tree?" I ask casually as we trim some dead fronds off a hanging fern.

"Oh, yes. I work on it every day."

This seems unlikely, but I consider it a good sign that she remembers the family tree. "I think your family is related to Julius Crawford—is that right?"

"Yes. Is he a friend of yours?"

Julius died eighty years before I was born, but I'll play along. "I've never met him, but I've heard a lot about him. He invented Scour-Brite, right?"

"Oh, yes. He's clever. Very clever."

"And does Julius have children?"

She gives the fern some water. "Three."

Every biography of Julius Crawford says he had two sons. Who is this third child? Will Birdie remember?

Birdie hums under her breath and speaks to the fern. "What's causing these brown tips, hmm? Too much heat for you?" Her brow furrows as she takes stock of the fern's location.

I want to bring her attention back to the family tree, but I don't want to upset her or put ideas in her head. Can I get her to sit down so I can show her the erasure on the old pencil-drawn copy of the family tree?

Birdie reaches up to try to remove the heavy hanging pot from its hook, swaying with the effort.

"Whoa." I put out my hand to restrain her. "Maybe we'd better not move that."

She pushes my hand away. "Yes! It has to come down. It's too close to the heat vent."

I glance around for an aide. What will be worse—Birdie bringing a fern pot down on her head or Birdie pitching a fit? The nearest staff person is halfway down the hall. "Okay, let me do it. I'm taller than you."

Birdie sizes me up and steps back. With her hands on her hips, she commands, "Put it on that table."

The table in question has an abandoned game of solitaire spread across it. I'm pretty sure no one wants a big, shaggy fern there, but I figure I can apologize to the staff later. The damn pot must weight forty pounds, but I manage to reposition it to Birdie's satisfaction.

"Much better," she says.

I sit down on a nearby loveseat and pat the cushion next to me. "The fern does look better there. Come and sit down. I'd like to show you something."

I guess I've earned Birdie's trust because she sits next to me without hesitation. I pull the folder from my tote bag and unfold the family tree across both our laps.

Birdie's eyes light up. "There's my great-great-great grandfather Lucius Armentrout. " She points to a box on the tree. Any worry that she might question why I have her family tree is vanquished. "And there's Barton Armentrout--he was a real scoundrel."

So far, she's gotten everything right. The drawing must be tapping into the same deep well of memory that contains her horticultural knowledge. I nudge her along. "And who are these folks here?"

"Those are our third cousins once and twice removed—Loretta Bostwick and her son, Crawford. The Armentrouts are related to the Bostwicks through Loretta's paternal line." She taps a branch of the tree.

I trace the line back. "So Loretta is the great-granddaughter of Julius Crawford. Her grandfather was Julius's younger son. And who is this line to this empty box beside the two sons of Julius where you erased a name?

Birdie giggles and covers her smile with her hand. She leans closer and whispers in my ear. "It's a family scandal. Very naughty."

"Oh? What happened?"

Birdie leans back and folds her hands primly. "It's a secret."

"A secret that you figured out?"

She nods, pleased with herself.

"Will you tell me if I guess right?"

Birdie giggles again, enjoying herself.

I whisper back to her, "I think Julius had another child. And maybe his wife wasn't the mother."

She nods and claps her hands.

"How did you discover that?" I ask her.

"Not me. Loretta. She found a picture at her grandfather's house...well, it's her father's house now. And she remembered some things her grandfather told her when he got old."

"And she showed the picture to you?"

Birdie nods. "She wasn't sure what it meant...the adoption... the payments. I told her it was very common in those days. It upset her...." Birdie gestures as if shooing a bug off her roses. "Too sensitive."

"The baby was adopted? By whom?" I reach for my phone so I can show her the photo of the photo and see what she says.

Birdie taps the screen, totally accepting of the fact that I have this picture. "This man worked for Julius. He was Portuguese."

Portuguese? Soares. Vareena Tate's maiden name was Soares. "Was the baby—"

"What in the world?" An aide comes bustling into the solarium. "Birdie, did you move that fern? Didn't I tell you to leave it be?" She heaves the fern pot off the table.

Birdie leaps up to intervene. A tussle ensues. More aides arrive. My visit has ended.

I leave the garden club trophy on the table and slip away.

BACK IN MY CAR, I study the family tree. Loretta's grandfather was Vareena Tate's father. So that makes them some kind of cousins, I guess. How long had Loretta known this, and why was she determined to keep it secret? A one hundred- year-old out of wedlock birth just doesn't seem that scandalous nowadays. Was she worried that her husband would be upset?

Then Sean's theory that Loretta needed a source of cash to help Crawford pops into my head. Was she planning to lay a claim to the Tate estate? Challenging the will would be a long and messy process. Maybe she and Crawford were planning to strike a quiet deal—they'd go away for a cut of the money.

No, that can't be right. Loretta died before anyone knew the Parks Center had inherited the money. Unlesss....

This is making my head hurt!

Maybe Sean can make some sense of it. I decide to violate my usual rule about calling him at work.

"Coughlin," he barks after the first ring.

"Hey, it's me."

"What's wrong? You okay?"

"I'm fine. It can wait. You sound stressed."

Sean lowers his voice. "Shit's been hittin' the fan here all day. Another girl came forward to accuse Crawford of sexual assault, this time in Palmyrton. Our sex crimes unit went to interrogate Crawford, who was crashing in the empty guest cottage of one of his friends. When our team got there, they found Crawford had cleared out. We got a subpoena to search his email account and found a boarding pass for a one-way ticket to Phnom Penh.

"As in...Cambodia?"

"Yep. Where the U.S. has no extradition treaty. He flew with a forged passport. They want to arrest Frederic for aiding and abetting a felon, but they have to find a paper trail."

Meeting...My office...Now! I hear in the background.

"Gotta go. Don't wait up."

CHAPTER 39

IF SEAN WON'T BE HOME until late, I might as well go to the office and work on all the accounting associated with the Tate job. There's nothing like a little math to help me get my thoughts in order. Maybe the symmetry imposed by Excel will help me see some pattern in the relationships between Vareena, Loretta, Crawford, and Levi.

After I've been poring over spreadsheets for an hour, my phone rings. Dad.

"Audrey, I hate to bother you, but I need a favor if at all possible."

"Sure, how can I help?"

"I accidentally left my pills at the Parks Center, and Natalie is away on her yoga retreat. I told her I wouldn't need the car, but .... If you're busy, I can just skip the pills for one—"

"Absolutely not! I'll go there and get them. Where did you leave them?"

"I think the bottle rolled under the desk in my classroom. I took a pill at noon, and put the bottle back in my fanny pack. Later, I was helping Shayna with her science project, and I dumped out my pack to get my pocket knife and some things fell on the floor." Dad sighs. "I'm usually not so careless, but it's the only explanation for why the pills aren't in my pack now."

"No worries—I'll go get them. When do you have to take the pills?"

"As long as I have them by bedtime. No rush."

I glance at my watch: 7:30. "I'll just finish a few things here and head out."

A few things turns into a frustrating accounting quagmire. Before I realize it, the clock has moved to 8:15. Naturally, because

I'm in a rush, I get caught in a slow-moving detour caused by a downed power line. I arrive at the Parks Center at ten after nine. The building is dark.

Shit!

But as I walk toward the front door, I see a faint glow of light within. I press my face against the glass door, and dimly make out Mr. Vargas mopping the foyer floor. He's all the way at the back, ready to mop himself out of the room.

I pound on the glass door. He lifts his head from his task and waggles his right hand in a no-no gesture.

I pound some more.

I see his mouth move. "We're closed," he's probably saying.

I wave for him to come to the front door. With disgust, he throws down his mop and tromps across his clean floor.

I shout to him through the glass. "My dad, Mr. Roger, left his medication in his classroom. I just need to run down and get it. I'll be in and out in a minute."

He shakes his head and cups his hand around his ear. He can't hear me, so he unlocks the door and opens it a crack. I repeat my request.

"No, no, Mees—no come in building when empty. No allow."

Clearly, Mr. Vargas doesn't understand what I want. But now the door is open, and I push my way through. I know I'm being obnoxious and taking advantage of an old man just trying to do his job, but I really need those pills.

"Gracias, Mr. Vargas. I'll be back in uno minuto." I tear past him so I don't have to listen to his grumbling.

A dim emergency light barely illuminates the stairwell, but once I'm in the downstairs hall, it's pitch black. I feel for a light switch, but can't find it. Oh, well—Dad's classroom is the second on the left. I feel my way along the left wall until I come to the second door. I enter and turn on the lights there. No pill bottle on the desk—that would be too easy. I get down on my knees and start searching the floor. As I'm scrambling around under the desk, I hear a voice in the room next door. Is that Mr. Vargas looking for me?

No, it's definitely two voices having a conversation. So everyone hasn't left after all. Does Mr. Vargas know people are still in the building?

I pause in my search and listen.

"You people are bleeding me dry. I'm here to put a stop to it."

Who is that? A man…foreceful…white, I think. Jared?

"Ha! You're not dealing from a position of strength, my man. When you know what I know, you're going to change your tune."

That's definitely Dennis. What's he up to? Who is he talking to?

"Talk. I don't have all night."

Where have I heard that tone of condescension before?

"Okay, Fred—here's the deal," Dennis says.

Frederic Bostwick! Why is here at night talking to Dennis? And if the SBE Foundation is still donating money to the Parks Center, why is Dennis being so rude?

"Jared has had the auditors in here to go over the books. Turns out Levi was giving money to your wife. She'd make a donation, and he'd kick part of it back to her."

"Don't be absurd!"

Sean was right. Loretta has been scrounging for money.

"Yeah, it didn't make sense to the rest of the Board, but it made sense to me. Because I know something they don't. And that's why you and I are here tonight," Dennis says.

While I've been eavesdropping, I've been sliding my hands along the floor, looking for Dad's pills. I finally find them in a dusty corner under the desk and put them in my pocket. But what I'm hearing is too intriguing to miss. I settle in under the desk and keep listening.

"You see, I was at the fundraiser not as a guest, but working for the caterer. I was in the back hall by the kitchen when I overheard Levi and Loretta arguing. Your wife told Levi she had checks and pledges from her rich friends that totaled over two hundred grand. But she said the Parks Center would only be getting half of that."

"Preposterous! Loretta was committed to her charity work. She talked about it all the time."

"Oh, she was committed, all right." Dennis's tone goes beyond sarcastic all the way to snide. "You know, she begged Jared to get put on the Board. She was committed to using the Parks Center to get money to save her darling boy, Crawford and keep you in the dark, Daddy."

"What do you mean?" For the first time in their conversation, Frederic sounds concerned.

"I heard your boy took off for Cambodia today, ahead of a second charge of child rape. Nice kid you got there," Dennis says.

"I no longer have a son." Frederic's voice could freeze water. "Crawford is dead to me. I've cut him off totally."

"Yeah, I feel you, man. But you know moms. They got soft hearts. So your wife was all about helping Crawford out of his jam. See, she knew all along there were other girls, not just the chick in New York. She knew Crawford needed an escape plan if all the shit hit the fan. You know Crawford left the country on a false passport. You got any idea how much that costs these days, what with terrorism and all?"

"Of course not, I—"

"Well, let me tell you Fred, it doesn't come cheap. And the kind of dudes who fix you up, they don't take American Express, know what I'm sayin'? And then Crawford, he didn't want to go to Cambodia and live like a peasant. He wanted the same life he had here. And he knew mommy would get it for him."

Frederic groans, as if this is painfully plausible. But how does Dennis know all this? Were he and Crawford in cahoots?

"So Loretta needed some serious cash, and she knew you weren't going to go along with her plan. That's why she made a deal with Levi to get some of her donations back in the short term, in return for giving more in the future. But then Levi got all jammed up with the new Board members looking over his shoulder, wanting to know why there was no cash to fix the plumbing and the roof and all. So on the night of the party, Levi and your wife were fighting about money. And I saw them take the discussion upstairs. They both went up. And we know how Loretta came down."

"What! Are you telling me that man killed her? You knew this and never told the police?"

I hear chairs scraping, as if Frederic has jumped up or lunged forward.

"Easy man. I didn't see anything with my own eyes. But I let Levi know I saw him go up there. He claims they argued and Loretta got all hysterical and threatened to jump, and he grabbed her, but she fell."

"And you believe that?" Frederic's voice rises in anger.

Dennis responds with an unpleasant laugh. "Let's just say I chose to believe it. Levi is, was, an old friend even though he was weak and foolish in his old age. And honestly, Fred, I don't give a rat's ass about your wife and your son and your one-percenter problems. What I want is to get the money the Rosa Parks Center deserves. And I finally see the way to do it with no strings attached."

"By blackmailing me? Well, I can tell you right now, that won't work." Frederic's voice has regained its arrogance. "Everyone already knows the worst about Crawford. What Loretta did to help him is nothing by comparison."

"Heh, heh. You'd don't know the half of it, Fred. The best is yet to come."

What does Dennis know? What is he planning? My legs are cramped from crouching here so long. Should I get up and intervene? Or just let this play out?

"I've had enough of your idle threats. I'm leaving."

Again there's a scuffle, as if Dennis is pulling him back forcefully.

"Did you know your wife and Vareena Tate were related?" Dennis asks.

So, Dennis has figured out that Julius Crawford was Vareena's biological father. But my goodness, it was all so long ago. Will Frederic really care?

"Of course, they're not. The Tate family has all died off. There's no connection, but what if there were?"

"Vareena Tate is the illegitimate daughter of Julius Crawford. He arranged for her to be adopted. Your friend Birdie Armentrout figured it out and told Loretta."

"Loretta never mentioned any of this. Why would she keep it a secret from me?"

"You know much about genetics, Fred? Like how certain qualities run in families? For instance, I'm real handy, good at fixing things. So was my dad. So was my granddad."

"Your point?"

"You know what quality runs in your wife's family? The rapist gene. Julius Crawford raped his housemaid. Then he took that baby away from her momma and gave her to some folks who worked in his factory to raise. And that baby girl grew up to be

Vareena Tate."

I gasp, but there's enough movement in the other room that I'm sure they don't notice. I imagine Dennis standing over Frederic, going in for the kill. "Get out your checkbook, man. You're going to donate a million dollars to the Parks Center, or the whole world's going to know Crawford comes from a long line of rapists. And one more thing--"

Dennis lowers his voice. I strain, but I can't hear what he says.

All I can hear is a moan from Frederic.

CHAPTER 40

POP!

The sound is so sharp that I startle and crack my head against the desk.

"Augh!" Someone stumbles and falls.

Was that sound a gunshot?

Pop! again. Frederic came here with a gun? He's shot Dennis? I burrow into my hiding place and dig for my phone.

"Mees? Mees? You still down here?"

Oh, dear Lord--Mr. Vargas! I forgot all about him. Now he's going to walk right into a crazy man with a gun, and it's all my fault.

"You gotta leave, Mees. I gotta lock up now."

I can't hide any longer. I spring out from under the desk just as Frederic passes in the hall, lifting his arm to fire again.

I need a weapon. The classroom offers nothing. I pick up a plastic and metal desk chair and charge Frederic, screaming like a banshee.

The gun goes off. Plaster showers onto my head.

I'm not in pain. The bullet hit the ceiling.

"Mees? What you--?"

"Run! Run upstairs, Mr. Vargas, and call 9-1-1."

Frederic Bostwick turns toward me. He's still got the gun in his hand. His eyes are glazed.

"Mr. Bostwick, please. Drop the gun."

"Who are you?" he pants.

I put my hands up. "I'm a volunteer here. Just someone who helps the kids."

Frederic keeps the gun aimed at my chest. His eyes dart back and forth, his tongue licks his parched lips. He's panicked. He's already shot Dennis and taken aim at a harmless old janitor. Will he hesitate to kill me?

I can't fight my way out of this. My only defense is words. "You know you don't want to hurt me. You met me once at the dog park. My dog Ethel played with Rex and Cleo."

Frederic's eyes never blink. But I sense that he remembers.

"You're an honorable man, Mr. Bostwick. Do the right thing."

Hearing his family name seems to bring the light of sanity back to his eyes. His hand trembles and the gun slips from his fingertips. I kick it far down the hall.

In the distance, I hear sirens.

CHAPTER 41

TO SAY THAT SEAN IS distressed to find me being interrogated by the police two days in a row would be a monumental understatement. But I remind him that he was the one who didn't have time to talk when I texted him, and that I hadn't gone to the Parks Center to investigate, but to do a good deed for my father.

It's past midnight by the time I finish my statement to the police, deliver the pills to my father, and arrive home with Sean.

We're both too keyed up to sleep, so we sit at the kitchen table eating stale pretzels, drinking cold beer, and trying to make sense of what just happened.

"Do you think Levi really did kill Loretta?"

Sean carefully breaks a pretzel in two before answering. "We'll never know for sure. But I suspect he killed himself because of the guilt. With his financial pressures building, he must've feared his arrangement with Loretta would come out and the argument at the fundraiser would be revealed. Dennis was probably threatening him."

"When will you be able to question Dennis?"

Sean scowls. "I'd like to pull him out of that hospital right now. He's lucky Frederic Bostwick is such a lousy shot. Two bullets and neither one hit a major organ. But the doctors had to dig the bullets out and stitch him up, so Dennis won't be clear-headed enough to talk until late tomorrow." Sean takes a swig of beer. "Frederic Bostwick is spending the night in Palmer County jail. I bet the guards are having quite a unique experience processing him."

"I feel sort of sorry for Frederic."

Sean's not having it. "He pointed a gun at your heart."

"True. I think the kid in Newark scared me more. Somehow I sensed Frederic wouldn't shoot me."

"What do you think Dennis said to Frederic that pushed him over the edge?" Sean asks me. "And how does Dennis know that Julius was a rapist? What proof could he possibly have?"

Just then my phone pings the announcement of a Facebook message.

Sean scowls. "For God's sake Audrey—this is no time for checking who's posted a new cat video."

Ignoring him, I squint at the screen. Someone has replied to my post in the Friends of Ebenezer Foight School Group:

Mrs. Willa Brantley.

But before she was Mrs. Brantley, she was Miss Simpson.

She was strict, but really a good teacher.

She left to be a principal somewhere else.

I turn the phone so Sean can see the screen. "One of the photos in the secret room showed a class picture from this school. I tracked it down on Facebook. The black teacher in the picture was named Miss Simpson! She *is* related to Maybelle."

Next step, Google Willa Simpson Brantley. The first thing that pops up is her obituary: BA and MS, Rutgers, distinguished educator, retired as Superintendent of Schools, Pine Crest, NJ. Survived by her son, Martin Simpson Brantley of Pine Crest and her daughter Mona Brantley Cox of Pine Crest. Three grandchildren, lots of nieces and nephews.

Next, I Google her son, Martin Simpson Brantley. He's a retired law professor who's written some books. "He has his own website," I tell Sean. "I can send him an email from here. I'm going to ask if he's related to Maybelle."

Sean puts a restraining hand on my arm. "Check to see if he's available, but don't tell him too much. I plan to take a little drive to the Jersey Shore tomorrow."

"I'm the one who tracked him down. You're not going without me."

Sean slides me my phone. "Okay, partner. I guess we're in this one together."

CHAPTER 42

AN EMAIL FROM MARTIN SIMPSON Bradley landed in my inbox long before I woke up. He says Maybelle Simpson was his great aunt, and he'd be happy to talk to me about her. Although the message is brief, there's something eager about it, as if he wants to meet me as much as I want to meet him.

So Sean and I set out on a two-hour road trip to the Jersey Shore. Martin lives in a manicured, fifty-five-plus development. There's a ramp leading up to his front door, and a van with handicapped plates sits in the driveway.

After we ring the doorbell, we hear a voice calling, "coming, coming." The door swings open, and we find ourselves looking down at a late middle-aged man in a wheel chair. He smiles warmly. "You must be my visitors from Palmyrton. I've been jumpy as a cat waiting for you."

He rolls backward to allow us to enter, and waves for us to follow him. "I thought we'd sit in my study. I made us some iced tea, and my niece brought me these cookies."

Sean shoots me a glance behind Martin's back. He had spent half the drive down here discussing strategies to get Martin to open up to us. Clearly, none of them will be needed. I guess the poor man is lonely and happy for visitors.

Once we're all settled in the book-lined room, I begin to speak. "As I explained, I'm the estate sale organizer clearing out the Tate Mansion. I don't know if you're aware, but the entire estate was bequeathed to the Rosa Parks Center in Palmyrton."

Martin nods. "Oh, yes—I read about that. An excellent choice!"

So, it doesn't seem he's conniving to get his hands on some of the money. I want to ask him if he knows why Vareena left her money there, but first things first. Let's establish the relationship. "Everyone said neither Vareena Tate nor Maybelle Simpson had relatives, but we found some photographs in the house. And it seems Maybelle Simpson was related to you, yes?"

"Yes," he says, "Maybelle was my great aunt." Martin sips from his iced tea. His gaze meets mine over the top of the glass. "So was Vareena."

CHAPTER 43

MARTIN SEEMS QUITE PLEASED WITH our slack-jawed reaction to his bombshell.

"Vareena and Maybelle were *sisters*?" I ask when I catch my breath. "I guess that explains why they dressed the same. We knew that Vareena was adopted. Is that how--?"

Martin sets his glass down and folds his hands in his lap. "It's a very long story. If you have the time, I'd like to tell it from the beginning."

I lean back in my chair. "Absolutely. There's nothing we'd like better."

Martin begins his tale. "My great-grandparents were Eula and Raymond Simpson, the maid and chauffeur for Julius Crawford and his wife, Sophia. They considered themselves very fortunate indeed. Two good jobs and an apartment over the garage on Julius's estate in which to raise their three children.

"In 1916, Sophia Crawford gave birth to her second son. She had a very difficult delivery and was weak and bedridden for months afterward. It fell to my great-grandmother to take care of the infant. She was just weaning her own toddler, and had milk enough for the newborn. She took to sleeping in a small storage room near the kitchen so she could take care of the Crawford baby at night."

Martin rolls his chair to the bookshelf to get a framed photo, which he hands to me. "This is the only photo ever taken of my great-grandmother."

In the faded daguerreotype, a tall, slender African American woman holds a white baby wearing a long, frilly gown. She looks at the camera somberly—people didn't smile for photos in those days—but her large dark eyes are friendly and lively. She has high cheekbones and chiseled features.

"She was lovely," I whisper.

"Yes, you're not the only one to have noticed."

I feel a squeeze of dread for what I suspect is coming.

"Julius Crawford lost patience with his wife's long recovery. One night, when Eula had just returned the baby to his crib, Julius decided that his cook and nursemaid could also fulfill the other responsibilities of a wife. He raped Eula in a room right down the hall from his wife's bed.

"That night, Eula returned to her own home above the garage. Her oldest daughter, Cassie, heard her enter, saw her trembling hands and tear-streaked face, and knew something was terribly wrong. However, Eula didn't tell her husband. What good would come of it? The police would not take her claim seriously, and if her husband took justice into his own hands, he would be the one who was executed.

"They had too much to lose—their jobs, their home, even their freedom. Eula stayed silent. She watched her back, careful never to be alone with Julius in the house again. Sophia Crawford had begun to regain her strength, and Eula turned the baby's care back over to the mother. Julius seemed preoccupied with his business, or perhaps he realized he'd been reckless. At any rate, he left my great-grandmother alone."

I can see where this is headed. "Eula got pregnant?"

Martin nods and continues the story. "Eula convinced herself that the baby had to be her husband's. Julius, of course, noticed her pregnancy as she worked in the kitchen. He asked Eula when the baby would arrive, ostensibly so he could prepare the other servants to fill in. But as Eula's time drew near, Julius sent Raymond on a long road trip to Detroit to pick up a new Ford roadster that Julius had custom-ordered.

"Eula got her first contractions just as she was serving dinner to the Crawford family. She went back to her own home to prepare. No one was around to help Eula except her daughter Cassie, who was thirteen. This being Eula's fourth child, the baby arrived in just two hours, with no problems."

Martin gazes out the window and speaks in a whisper. "A beautiful baby girl. Clear green eyes. Wavy brown hair. Light olive skin."

Vareena. Martin seems almost in a trance as he continues the story. He asks and answers his own questions.

"It wasn't long before Eula heard steps on the stairs that led up from the garage to their home. Julius Crawford had come to check on her.

"Since when does a wealthy white man care about the health of his pregnant black cook?

"He came to check on the baby.

"And he saw the truth immediately. He knew it would be impossible to explain this light-skinned child with golden brown hair—to his wife, to his staff, to his neighbors.

"To Raymond."

Martin snaps back to the here and now. He speaks directly to Sean and me.

"In the morning, the children learned the sad news. Their new sister had died in the night, shortly after her birth. But Cassie knew the truth. She had seen Julius Crawford carry the baby away, walking in the moonlight with a small bundle in his arms across the wide lawns of the estate."

CHAPTER 44

"CASSIE WAS YOUR GRANDMOTHER?" I ask. All these family relations are so hard to keep straight.

Martin nods. "I spent many hours with her when I was a child. First, while my mother was earning her degree, and later when she worked every day. I was a sickly child—had a bout of scarlet fever that kept me out of school and on bed rest for nearly a year. We didn't have TV, and I wasn't supposed to strain my eyes by reading, so my grandmother read aloud to me. But sometimes she ran out of books, and she would tell me stories. My grandmother told me the story of our people. She wanted me to know, so that the secrets wouldn't die with her. She told me the story like it was a Greek tragedy, with heroes and villains and a moral at the end." Martin smiles at us. "So, you'll forgive me if I tell the story to you in the same way. I've held it in for so long, but now that they're dead I can finally speak. I suppose I've just been waiting for my ideal audience."

I take a cookie and settle back for the ride. "You've found it, Martin. Did Cassie figure everything out on her own?"

Martin shakes his head. "The pain of giving up her baby was too much for Eula. She had to confide in someone, so soon she told Cassie as much as she knew: Julius had promised to give the baby to a Portuguese family in Newark. The man was a manager in one of Julius's factories. His wife had recently miscarried and was distraught because she couldn't have another baby. Julius would tell them that this baby had been born to an unmarried teenager who worked in one of his other factories. A Portuguese girl with olive skin and wavy brown hair just like them. Julius told Eula she was lucky—her daughter would be raised as a white girl. What better gift could she give the child?"

"That's horrible!" I protest. "Did Eula trust Julius? After all, he was a rapist. How could she be sure he hadn't killed the baby?"

Martin massages his temples. "She wasn't sure. She begged Julius for proof that the baby was safe and well loved. He showed her a photo of the baby with her new parents, taken at the child's baptism."

"I've seen that photo," I interrupt. "Loretta Bostwick, Julius's granddaughter found it." I scramble for my cell phone and call up the photo of the photo. "Here's Vareena as a baby."

Martin studies the image on the phone and his eyes fill with tears. "So these are the people who raised my aunt."

"But who is Maybelle?" Sean asks to get Martin talking again. "Cassie was thirteen years older than Vareena."

Martin continues his story. "After Julius took the baby away, Eula grew despondent. Of course, her husband thought she was mourning the death of their daughter, and he was sure that if Eula had another baby, her spirits would lift. And two years later, she did give birth to another child. A girl. A black girl. Her husband's daughter."

"And that was Maybelle."

Martin nods. "But only a few months after Maybelle's birth, a flu epidemic struck. Everyone in the family got sick, but they all got better. Except Eula. She left four motherless children. The youngest, Maybelle, was only five months old. My grandmother, Cassie, took over raising her siblings, and also took over her mother's job as the Crawford family cook. The boys were old enough to fend for themselves, but Cassie became the only mother Maybelle would ever know. But at the same time, they were still sisters. As Maybelle grew older, Cassie told her the story of their lost sister, a story that their father and brothers never knew. Eventually, Cassie married a young man who also worked for Julius Crawford. So the lives of the two families remained linked."

Martin adjusts the cushion on his wheelchair. "Then war broke out. I am a peace-loving man, but World War II turned the fortunes of my family for the better. Julius won several contracts to produce cleaning supplies and other chemical products for the military. At the same time that his business was booming, it became harder and harder to find men to work in the factories. All the able-bodied young men were enlisting."

"So he had to hire women," Sean says.

"Yes, he got so desperate, he even had to hire black women. By this time Maybelle was a teenager, helping her sister in the kitchen of the Crawford estate. But she despised housework, so Maybelle asked if she could work at Julius's factory in Newark. Everyone had to sacrifice for the war effort, even the Crawford family. They decided they could do with one less servant at home, and Maybelle got her wish to work in the big city."

Martin smiles.

"Maybelle had an ulterior motive?" I ask.

"She wanted to find the man who was her sister's adoptive father. Cassie was totally opposed. *Leave it alone. Don't stir up trouble.* But Maybelle was determined. She could never get her mother back, but she could find her sister. She wasn't sure what she would do when she found her. She would cross that bridge when she came to it."

Again Martin shifts into a trance as he recites the details of the story. It's as if he's forgotten we're there.

"Once Maybelle started working in the factory, she watched and listened to learn more about the managers. All of them were Portuguese, so nationality didn't narrow down her choices. But the general manager had eight kids and the shipping manager was a skinny, unmarried young man who walked with a limp. The assembly line supervisor had frequent loud, angry arguments with Julius. That left the accountant. His name was Roberto Soares. He worked in an office far from the factory floor, and Maybelle couldn't think of any reason why she should ever be over in that part of the building. Her prey so was close, but so far away.

"Then one payday, she got an idea. At that time, hourly workers received their pay in cash. One of the girls claimed she'd been shorted. The argument with the paymaster escalated until the girl was taken to Soares's office. The next day, the girl reported that the accountant had been very nice. He'd checked the records carefully and discovered there really was a discrepancy, and the dispute was settled in the worker's favor.

"This incident gave Maybelle an idea. She waited a couple of weeks, then made her way to Soares's office. She knocked on his door and told him she'd received an extra dollar in her pay and she was there to turn it in. Needless to say, Soares was stunned by her honesty. He counted the pay packet, into which she'd slipped a dollar saved from the week before."

"That must have been a big sacrifice."

"It was. That's how badly she wanted to find her sister," Martin tells me.

"Soares was a meticulous man, and while he searched his books fruitlessly, Maybelle sat in his office. A studio photograph of a young woman sat on his desk. She was beautiful—big eyes, a narrow nose, full lips, prominent cheekbones, a high forehead. Of course, Maybelle had never met her own mother, but she had seen this photo of Eula holding the Crawford baby that she had nursed. And of course, she knew Julius. The young woman in the photo on Soares's desk looked like a blend of Eula Simpson and Julius Crawford. She looked nothing like Maybelle and Cassie, who strongly favored their father, Raymond.

"Finally, Soares looked up from his search and saw Maybelle gazing at the photo. 'Is that your daughter? She's real pretty.' Maybelle asked.

"Soares smiled at the picture. 'Yes, that's my Vareena. Smart as a whip, but very headstrong.' That was the extent of their conversation.

"For a while, knowing that their sister was alive and that her adoptive father seemed to be a kind, honorable man was enough for Cassie and Maybelle. They speculated about her life. What was it like being Vareena Soares, growing up in the Portuguese community in Newark, that neighborhood they called The Ironbound? They knew that Soares wasn't extremely wealthy like Julius Crawford, but they were pretty sure he didn't live in a small apartment above a garage, as they did. In those days, black people couldn't walk down the street in a white neighborhood for no reason, but Maybelle had glimpsed the Ironbound neighborhood from the back window of the streetcar as she rode to and from work. She saw the children playing ball and the little corner stores selling fish and vegetables. She saw the streets lined with tidy brick and frame houses. Behind which door did her sister live?

"The more the two sisters talked, the more obsessed Maybelle became, and the more cautious Cassie grew. Cassie said their sister was a white girl now. There was no coming back. Why would she even want to? But Maybelle said Vareena was their kin. Soares said she was headstrong. Maybe that meant she wasn't happy. Did she even know she was adopted? Maybe she was longing for them just as they longed for her."

Martin sips from his glass of iced tea.

"Meanwhile, the war ground on. More and more men went off to serve. Julius Crawford's elder son joined the Navy, the younger served in military intelligence. Cassie's husband enlisted with the Army in a segregated tank battalion, and so did her two brothers. Men were shipping out every week, and there was a rash of hasty wartime weddings. Lovers knew they might never see each other again, so they rushed to tie the knot. Even the wealthy could not get enough ration tickets to put on an elaborate wedding with a long silk gown for the bride and a big feast for the guests. Weddings were quiet family affairs with an announcement sent to friends after the fact.

"It was just such an announcement that Cassie brought in with the mail as she was serving tea to Mrs. Crawford and two of her lady friends. When the envelope was opened and the announcement shared, a gasp went up among the ladies. Lawrence Tate had married before he shipped out to Germany.

"The ladies were astonished. Edgar Tate and his son Lawrence were prominent members of their circle. They hadn't heard of any courtship. Who had he married?

"My grandmother remembered Mrs. Crawford's hand shaking as she read from the printed card: Vareena Soares, daughter of Roberto and Emilia Soares of Newark, New Jersey."

Martin raises his voice an octave to imitate the society ladies. "Who in the world is that? The name sounds Portuguese! This would never have happened if Mrs. Tate were still alive!"

"Cassie slipped back into the kitchen absolutely thunderstruck. Her sister, the bastard daughter of a rich white rapist and a poor black servant had first been elevated to the white middle class, and now had ascended another huge step into the stratosphere of wealthy high society. Cassie was afraid to tell Maybelle, but she was so shaken by the news that she couldn't hold it in."

Martin leans toward us. "Now don't forget that Raymond, their father, was still Julius Crawford's chauffeur. He had driven Mr. Crawford to the Tate home many times, and while a chauffeur is waiting to take his employer back home, he goes around back and sits with the servants of the host family. So in this way, Raymond heard all about how Mr. Lawrence Tate's new bride was coming to live with Mr. Edgar Tate to await the return of her husband from the war."

"So now they knew exactly where their sister was living," I say. "But what made Maybelle decide to go to work for the Tates? And how did she tell her sister who she really was?"

"To understand that, we must go back to the Soares family. You may find this surprising, but they were not happy about their daughter's marriage to a man so far out of their social sphere, even though their new son-in-law was wealthy. The reason Vareena had even met Lawrence Tate was because she had defied her parents' wishes. Mr. Soares was an indulgent daddy, but Mrs. Soares had very strict notions about proper behavior for a nice Portuguese girl, and they didn't include training as a nurse and joining the Army. After a lot of arguing, the father relented as long as Vareena did not serve overseas. But her mother lashed out. She said her real daughter would not disregard her wishes. And in that moment of anger, the secret was revealed. Vareena was adopted."

"Vareena told Maybelle about this later?" Sean asks.

"Yes, much later. All Vareena knew at the time was this truth explained the distance and estrangement she'd always felt toward Emilia Soares. She now felt utterly free to go her own way. So Vareena ended up working at Newark Army Airfield, and she met Lawrence as he was preparing to ship out. Perhaps it was love at first sight, or perhaps it was a case of two young people who recognized in each other a desperate need to escape the limiting expectations of their respective families. Lawrence Tate was expected to take over his father's business even though he had no interest or aptitude for it. He wanted to become a doctor."

"Did she tell Lawrence that she was adopted?"

Martin shakes his head. "She never told her fiancé. You see, in those days, adoption was regarded as rather scandalous, and Vareena would have been ashamed that she was born out of wedlock. This notion of getting in touch with your birth parents was unheard of. Vareena knew her adoptive parents would keep her secret. After all, their friends also didn't know she was adopted because she had been adopted so soon after her adoptive mother miscarried."

"Lawrence promised Vareena that when he returned from the war, they would travel the world together and that he would never require her to be a dutiful housewife. He would go to medical school and she would work as a nurse by his side. Like all young people, they were full of dreams. Until he returned, Vareena could escape her mother and continue her work as a nurse by living at the Tate mansion. But the Tates' old housekeeper didn't take kindly to the notion of working for this unconventional young woman. She decided to retire, so…"

"Raymond brought home the news there was a job opening with the Tate family," I speculate.

Martin nods. "Maybelle applied without telling Cassie or anyone else. And of course, she got the job."

"Wasn't Julius suspicious that Maybelle took a job working for her half-sister?"

"You would think so, wouldn't you? But like many powerful men, he didn't take much notice of the doings of lesser mortals. He had solved his problem with Eula twenty years ago. He'd barely given the matter a thought since then. And he thought Eula had kept their secret. So if he noticed Maybelle's employment at all, he must have assumed it was an ironic coincidence."

"And what was Cassie's reaction?"

"Oh, she wasn't pleased, to be sure. But Maybelle promised she only wanted to get to know Vareena, and Cassie was preoccupied with other, more important matters. You remember I told you that World War II changed the fortunes of my family. Well, things changed both for the better and for the worse. With Cassie's husband and her two brothers serving in the military, Cassie had to hold together the extended family, which now included eight children under the age of ten. One sister-in-law was reliable, the other not so much. And then a series of terrible tragedies struck, one after the other."

On May 14, 1942 the Simpson family received the dreaded telegram: brother William was killed, leaving three young children. And after William, Cassie's husband was killed. And six months later, Brother Len returned, disabled and angry."

Martin sighs. "And finally, their father Raymond was seriously injured when a truck struck the car he was driving. Julius forced him to retire."

"So now everyone in the whole family was relying on Cassie and Maybelle."

"Everyone. Even Vareena. Because in 1943, a telegram was delivered to the Tate Mansion."

CHAPTER 45

MARTIN LEANS FORWARD, HIS EYES no longer focused on me but on a scene seventy years in the past. "Imagine the dread when the front door bell rang at a time when you weren't expecting a caller. Remember, at this time and in this neighborhood, deliveries of packages would be made to the back door. Only invited guests called at the front door. Guests, and the Western Union telegram delivery boy. Nowadays, the Army sends two officers to deliver the sorrowful news of a soldier killed in action. But in the darkest days of World War II, every officer was needed on the battleground. And so this terrible, sensitive job was entrusted to a boy, a mere child on a bike. Perhaps Maybelle looked out the window while she was dusting and saw the boy pedaling up the long driveway in the late afternoon sunshine.

"She raced to the door, and opened it before he even rang the bell. But the telegram was special delivery, and could not be handed to her. The boy must place it in the hands of the next of kin. So Maybelle went to fetch Vareena, who was resting in her bedroom after a tiring day working as a nurse. Mr. Tate was at his office.

"Imagine how heavy Maybelle's legs were as she trudged up the long staircase to bring her sister face-to-face with heartbreak. Yet she had to maintain the charade that she was merely a servant passing along a message. 'Mrs. Tate, there's a telegram for you.'

"The blood drained from Vareena's face and she began to scream, 'No, no!' You might think that surely every wife and parent understood this news was a possibility, but remember, Vareena was only twenty years old. The young never truly believe that death can touch them, even in times of war.

"So Maybelle half dragged, half carried Vareena to meet her doom. The boy placed the telegram in her trembling hands and escaped as quickly as possible. It was left to Vareena to read the terrible words."

Martin recites them from memory:

"THE ARMY AIR CORPS DEPARTMENT DEEPLY REGRETS TO INFORM YOU THAT YOUR HUSBAND, CAPTAIN LAWRENCE TATE, WAS KILLED IN THE PERFORMANCE OF HIS DUTY AND THE SERVICE OF HIS COUNTRY...."

"Vareena collapsed on the polished parquet floor of that magnificent house. In two short months, she had met the love of her life, a man who shared her dreams and valued her desire to serve others. She had quarreled with her parents and learned she was adopted, and defied them to marry her love. She had enjoyed two weeks of wedded bliss and then assumed the new and strange role as Mrs. Tate, mistress of a twenty-room mansion.

"And now she was a widow."

Martin takes a deep breath. "In the week after Lawrence's death, Vareena and her father-in-law avoided each other. Both were numb with grief, and there wasn't even a funeral to plan to help them move on because the body hadn't been recovered. Mr. Tate retreated to his office. Vareena holed up in her bedroom. She had no one to talk to, so she began to confide in Maybelle. She intended to move out of the mansion and volunteer to serve overseas as a nurse. She was all alone in the world; what did she have to lose? If she were lucky, she told Maybelle, she would be killed in action and be reunited with her husband in heaven."

Martin smiles. "Maybelle didn't like this talk one bit. It was time, she debated with Cassie, to tell Vareena the truth. She wasn't alone. She had kin who loved her.

"But Cassie cautioned restraint. The family was already in upheaval. If the truth came out, Cassie would lose her job with Julius Crawford and Maybelle might lose her job with Mr. Tate. Cassie promised Maybelle she would find a new job, then they would tell Vareena. But as Vareena was making her plans to move out of the mansion and request a transfer to active duty, she fell ill.

"Let me guess the symptoms," I say. "Light-headed. Exhausted. Nauseated."

Martin smiles at me. "Maybelle, having lived with plenty of pregnant women, recognized what was going on before Vareena did. She went home and told Cassie what she knew and together they stewed. There was a distinct possibility that the baby could be born with darker skin than its mother. How would Vareena explain it if she herself had no idea of her pedigree? What if Edgar Tate thought the baby wasn't his son's?

"Meanwhile, Vareena finally put two and two together about her symptoms. Overjoyed that she was carrying this little bit of her love within her, she shared the news with her father-in-law, and instantly his demeanor toward her changed. She was no longer the girl who had encouraged his son to turn his back on the family business and become a doctor. Now she was the mother of his grandson. He was, of course, positive that Vareena would have a boy.

"Every night, as Maybelle served dinner, she listened to the two of them plan for the child's future. It seemed that Mr. Tate had cancer, and he feared he wouldn't live to see the child born. But the impending birth gave him a reason to fight. The more he planned for the child's future, the more he grew to appreciate his daughter-in-law. His son had been right: she was smart and sensible. She would be a good mother to his heir. Edgar Tate was a man who prided himself on his judgment, his "gut" instinct. He called in the lawyers to make their plan legally sound. After his death, Vareena would hold a controlling interest in the company, in trust until the day she could turn it over to his grandson. The day-to-day operations would be handled by his managers, who would report to his executor and to Vareena. She would inherit the house and a living stipend outright. She would forfeit both if she married again or had other children.

"Vareena was satisfied with the plan. In her naiveté, she could not imagine ever being able to love another man. She fully intended to devote her entire life to raising Lawrence's child.

"The lawyers were not so happy. They warned against giving Vareena--a woman, a very young woman, a working class Portuguese woman--so much control. But Edgar Tate had made up his mind. His will would be done.

"Now Maybelle and Cassie argued continually about whether to tell Vareena the truth about her parentage. But Cassie won the battle. If they told Vareena the story of her birth, how could they prove it? The adoption had been done without any paperwork. Vareena would believe they were scheming to get her money.

So the days until the birth ticked away with Vareena in blissful ignorance and old Mr. Tate growing weaker. Vareena had decided that she would give birth at home, attended by her doctor, rather than in the hospital. In this way, Mr. Tate, who was clinging to life in his bedroom, would be able to immediately see the baby. As the due date drew near, Maybelle moved into the house to assist both the man on his way out and the woman about to bring in new life.

"On a rainy September day, Vareena's water broke. The doctor arrived and after a protracted and difficult labor, a baby boy was born. Maybelle hovered anxiously, eager to check her nephew's appearance. After his ordeal, the baby was dark red and prune-y with a dark fuzz covering his rather misshapen head. Maybelle was asked to carry the baby in to Mr. Tate so he could meet his grandson, Lawrence Tate, Jr.

"The old man lay in a stupor, but the baby's lusty cry roused him and he smiled as his grandson was placed in his arms.

"By morning, Edgar Tate was dead."

CHAPTER 46

BY THIS TIME, MARTIN HAS been speaking nonstop for over half an hour. Although his voice is growing hoarse, he seems to be drawing energy from telling the story. I don't want to mention that I already know the baby dies. I figure I'll let him get there in his own good time.

After taking a deep breath, Martin continues. "In the furor over Mr. Tate's funeral, no one other than Maybelle and Vareena took much interest in baby Larry. The lawyers and the executor had shown up for several intense meetings with Vareena, despite her weak condition.

"As the traces of his difficult passage into this world dissipated, one thing became abundantly clear to Maybelle: the heir to the Tate fortune bore a decided resemblance to his maternal grandmother, Eula.

"While Vareena napped, Maybelle carried the baby down to the kitchen to show the visiting Cassie."

Martin acts out the dialogue. "'Sweet Jesus,' Cassie murmured as she stroked the baby's café au lait arm.

" 'His hair's gonna be nappy,' Maybelle predicted as she touched her nephew's head.

"How could Vareena—raised as white, presented to the world as white, believing herself to be white—raise this little black baby?

" 'Has she noticed yet?' Cassie asked.

Maybelle shook her head. 'She's been too worn out. She wakes up to nurse him and falls back to sleep.'"

" 'Eventually she's going to notice. Maybe she won't want him.' "

Martin spreads his hands. "Imagine the sisters' dismay. They loved their nephew, but the last thing they needed was another orphaned child to look after.

" 'How does she treat you?' Cassie asked. It wasn't the first time she'd enquired about her younger sister's relationship with their half-sister. Maybelle tried to explain. Vareena wasn't like Mrs. Crawford and the other white women they'd worked for. Vareena had not been raised with servants. She and her mother had done their own cooking and cleaning, and Vareena always seemed uncomfortable asking Maybelle to do things for her. She was unfailingly polite. But at the same time, there was a distance between them. The year was 1943. Even though there were never official Jim Crow laws in New Jersey, segregation was a fact of life. White women simply did not have black friends. But they were two young women, alone together in that huge house. So despite the societal restraints, a bond was growing.

"If they told Vareena about her parentage, how would she react? Would she believe them, even with the evidence of the baby's appearance?

" 'I wish we had that photo of mama that the Crawfords took,' she told her sister.

"Cassie looked sheepish. "I have it. I took it with me when I quit as cook. I figured the Crawfords had plenty of pictures of their own kids, but this is the only picture we'll ever have of our mama. I figured they'd never miss it.'

"Now Maybelle's argument for full disclosure to their sister began to make sense. Armed with the photo of Eula, Maybelle could probably convince Vareena.

"But now Maybelle got cold feet. How could she bring up such an outlandish story out of the blue?

"The next week, Vareena gave her an opening. She had been growing stronger and now spent more time rocking the baby and gazing into her son's face. When Maybelle entered the nursery, Vareena looked up and asked her opinion. 'Who do you think he looks like?' "

" 'He doesn't resemble his daddy,' Maybelle agreed.

"'But I don't see much of myself in him either,' Vareena said.

" 'Must look like one of his grandparents,' Maybelle said, and Vareena looked perturbed. Of course, she didn't realize that

Maybelle knew she'd been adopted.

Maybelle took a deep breath and blurted out, 'I have something to show you.'"

She ran to get the photo before she had time to change her mind. By the time she returned to the nursery, Vareena was putting the baby down in his crib.

Maybelle handed over the photo and Vareena saw a darker version of her own face staring back at her. Her hand shook as she examined the picture. "Who is this?"

"Our mother."

CHAPTER 47

"THE HOURS THAT FOLLOWED WERE intensely emotional," Martin tells us. "Maybelle told Vareena the story of their mother's life, the story of her birth and adoption. Vareena never doubted her. It all made sense. She realized her adoptive parents hadn't been lying when they said they didn't know who her birth mother was. Clearly, they would never have agreed to take her if they had known.

"She knew that Julius Crawford was a friend of her father-in-law's but she had never met him. Her father was a rapist! A wealthy rapist. This seemed to shock her more than the fact that her mother was a black maid.

"As the shock receded, Vareena grew cheerful. She had sisters! She had a family after all. She was not alone. She and Maybelle embraced.

"Maybelle too felt as if a weight had been lifted from her. But she was more world-wise than Vareena. Their family reunion wasn't one of unmitigated joy. If the lawyers and the executor suspected baby Larry was part Negro, there would be grounds for challenging Edgar Tate's will. She had overheard old Mr. Tate grumbling about distant cousins and nephews angling for part of his fortune. The lawyers would claim the baby wasn't Lawrence Tate's. Or they would claim that Vareena had married him under false pretenses. How would Vareena support her child if she was stripped of her inheritance?

"Vareena pooh-poohed this. She had only been wealthy one year of her life. She didn't need the big house. She was a nurse and could work to support herself.

"Maybelle brought her back to reality. She had been a white

nurse. If she embraced her new family and acknowledged her son's ancestry, she would become a black nurse. Her employment opportunities would be limited to black hospitals, black doctor's offices. She could expect to struggle financially the rest of her life. Is that what she wanted for her son?

"The sisters went to bed exhausted, with no plan for the future.

"The next day Cassie arrived--at the back door, as always. Vareena met her older sister, the woman who'd witnessed her birth. Cassie told her how much Eula had loved her, but how she'd done what she hoped was best for her child and the rest of her family.

"Now Vareena wanted to meet her brother and her nieces and nephews. Maybelle and Cassie weren't sure how to handle this request. How could they explain the presence of a strange white woman in their home? None of them were ready to reveal the truth.

"Finally, they settled on a cover story. Since Vareena was a nurse, and one of their brother's children was always ailing, Vareena would visit as an angel of mercy, a white do-gooder.

"And so, brimming with excitement, Vareena went to visit her sisters' home, a tiny frame house in East Orange, New Jersey, that Maybelle and Cassie had scrimped and saved to buy. As Vareena walked down the street, she felt the eyes of every neighbor boring into her. Who was this white woman? The scent of unfamiliar foods—perhaps collards and ham hocks—drifted on the air. She passed a beer hall on the corner and some black men looked her up and down. She hurried along to her sisters' home.

"The house was tidy, but so lacking in creature comforts. And people—children and adults—seemed to be tumbling out of every room. How different from the huge, stately elegance of the Tate Mansion. How different even from the home of her adoptive parents, which had been modest but comfortable and very quiet.

"Her nieces and nephews clung shyly to their mothers, looking at the white lady in their living room like she was some exotic zoo animal who'd unaccountably turned up in their home.

"Vareena stayed less than an hour. She left much unhappier than she had come.

"How could she bridge this gap? Where did she belong? She

was an alien to her biological family, and soon would be a pariah to the family she had joined by marriage. How could she raise her son in this East Orange neighborhood? His grandfather intended for him to inherit the Tate business. His father would have wanted him to study any subject he chose and launch his own career. If Vareena brought him here, he wouldn't have either of those options.

"But how could she raise her brown-skinned boy among the Tates and Crawfords and their milieu?

"Like Eula, Vareena wanted what was best for her child. How could she provide it?"

Martin leans back and closes his eyes. He's been talking nonstop for over an hour. I know I should offer to leave to allow him to rest, but selfishly, I can't bring myself to do it. I'm dying to know how the story ends. What happened to Vareena's baby?

"Can I get you some more tea?" I offer.

Martin smiles slightly and his eyes open. "I'm not tired. I'm just traveling back in time. We're getting close to where I enter the story." He takes a deep breath and resumes.

"So, you may wonder why no one else noticed the baby's appearance. Well, consider Vareena's position. She was estranged from her adoptive family and felt awkward inviting her nurse friends to the Tate Mansion. Certainly those young women wouldn't "drop by" the mansion the way they might have if Vareena lived in a regular middle-class home like theirs. She had not made any new friends among her husband's and father-in-law's circle. It was not up to her to invite them. She was the newcomer; they should reach out to her. Until that happened, she spent her days and nights alone with Maybelle. And that solitude allowed her to postpone any decision about her son's future. How she loved taking care of the little fellow! He was plump and healthy and happy. But at the same time, Maybelle noted a cloud of sadness that never left her sister. It was as if she were waiting for the other shoe to drop.

"Then one day an invitation arrived. It was inevitable. After all, Vareena Tate was a young, widowed heiress. It's true that her pedigree left something to be desired, but the mothers of Palmyrton's high society could overlook that if it meant that one of their sons could marry the Tate fortune and the Tate business empire. Vareena's husband had been dead for almost a year, her father-in-law for three months. It was now appropriate to invite her to a small dinner party.

"Maybelle carried in the mail. She knew an invitation when she saw one and she knew who had issued this one: none other than Mrs. Julius Crawford. She stood in front of her sister and watched her open and read the card.

"'Are you going?' she asked.

"Vareena looked up at her. 'Yes. I want to meet my father.'"

"AS THE DAY OF THE party grew closer, Maybelle begged her sister not to go. No good could come of it. But Vareena assured Maybelle she had no intention of creating a scene. She simply wanted to meet the man who was her biological father. I'm told by friends who were adopted that this is a powerful drive, even if you know in advance the parent is not a kind, upstanding person."

"I understand," I murmur. When I thought there was a possibility my mother was alive, I certainly would have done anything in my power to meet her even though I was sure she'd abandoned me.

"On the afternoon of the party, Cassie came over to help Vareena get dressed. She told me many years later that on that day, Vareena was the most beautiful woman she'd ever seen. She wore her wavy hair swept up to reveal her high forehead and regal profile. Her dress was simple but elegant. Then Cassie began to cry because Vareena looked so much like Eula in the days when she was a happy young wife and mother. In the days before violence and loss cast a shadow over her.

"Cassie and Maybelle watched through the window as Vareena backed the Tate family's Buick out of the garage and drove off to meet her father.

"The dinner party was being held in honor of the Crawfords' younger son, who was home on leave. He had poor eyesight and couldn't serve in combat, but he held an important position in military intelligence in Washington. This was the child Eula had been caring for when Julius raped her.

"Did Julius know his wife had invited Vareena?"

Martin shrugs. "Probably. I imagine he realized that he would have to encounter Vareena someday. It's my speculation that he did not truly think of Vareena as his child. She was merely an inconvenience from the past. Men have the capacity to walk away from their offspring, but women don't. Even neglectful, cruel mothers have a hard time breaking the tie. So Julius wasn't concerned about his own paternal emotions. And he was confident that Vareena believed she was of Portuguese descent.

"But when Vareena walked into the Crawford's drawing room, Julius's indifference fell away. Vareena told her sisters it was like a current of electricity passed between them. From across the room, Julius's eyes widened at the resemblance to Eula. But when he shook Vareena's hand, his shock ran deeper. He could see in Vareena's eyes, green eyes that were so similar to his own, that she knew. Somehow, some way, she knew she was his daughter. All through dinner he was as jumpy as a cat—dropping his fork, chinking his wine glass, not following the conversation. Vareena took note of his consternation and Mrs. Crawford's puzzlement, but she carried on serenely, making polite conversation with the young men seated near her. At the end of the evening, her farewell lasted a moment longer than that of the other guests. She looked in Julius's eyes and squeezed his hand. "Thank you for a fascinating evening."

"THE NEXT DAY, JULIUS CRAWFORD paid a visit to the Tate Mansion. When the doorbell rang, Vareena told Maybelle to stay in the nursery with the baby. She descended the grand staircase and answered the door herself. Vareena met with her father in the study. After an hour, she led him upstairs to meet his grandson. Then they sat behind closed doors again. On that day, Larry's future was decided.

"Unbeknownst to Cassie and Maybelle, Vareena had already been working on a plan. But there was one aspect that she wasn't sure she could pull off. Julius's reappearance in her life allowed her to put the final piece in place.

"Remember I told you that Cassie had been looking for a new job so she would no longer be beholden to Julius Crawford. Well, a few months before Larry was born, Cassie found the perfect position: head cook at the Palmyrton Home for Retarded and Feeble Children."

"That's what it was called?" I ask. "How awful!"

"As you probably know, in those days people considered it for the best for children born with any sort of serious disability to be institutionalized. The babies and toddlers were turned over to large, impersonal "homes" to be raised by low-paid staff, while their parents and siblings were encouraged to forget the unfortunate birth had ever taken place.

"Cassie often came home from work full of heartbreaking stories about the children abandoned there. Many never received a visitor and were essentially dead to their families. Every few weeks, one of the children actually did die, perhaps from their maladies, perhaps from neglect, and often their families didn't even bother to claim the body. The child was buried in a pauper's unmarked grave."

I have a sickening feeling in the pit of my stomach. I have a glimmer now where the story is headed.

"Vareena had decided that the next time a baby boy of an appropriate age should pass away, she would bribe whatever staff members Cassie indicated and get the body. Then, this was the tricky part—she would need a real doctor to verify that this baby—her "son"—had died of natural causes so she could give it a proper funeral and bury him in the Tate plot. Then, she intended to turn over Larry to be raised by his aunts as a black boy. She would retain the Tate inheritance, and thus be able to provide her son with the best education available to African Americans at the time. And if her sisters objected, she was extending the benefit to all her nieces and nephews as well. All the descendants of Eula Simpson would have the best opportunities money could buy."

"And it was Julius's job to find the doctor who would seal the deal?" I asked.

"Exactly."

CHAPTER 48

I TELL MARTIN THAT I'VE SEEN baby Larry's grave in the cemetery behind St. Stephen's. But now I know that ornate grave contains the remains of some disabled child that no one wanted.

"The announcement of baby Larry's death shook Palmyrton high society. Many people murmured how tragedies always come in threes: Lawrence, Edgar and now little Larry. The doctor who was called to the house one dark night in March examined the baby and said he had died of complications of brain trauma sustained during Vareena's long labor and difficult birth. Since no one other than Maybelle and Cassie and Julius had ever seen the child, no one knew how robust and healthy he really was. Vareena had even laid the groundwork by telling a few ladies at the dinner party that her son was frail and that she worried about him. A small funeral was held at St. Stephen's Episcopal church."

"Who was the doctor?" I ask. "How did Julius get him to sign off on the death?"

Martin shrugs. "I don't know. He bribed the doctor, I imagine. Money makes all things possible. As Maybelle had predicted, lawyers for the distant relatives began circling, but Vareena hired her own lawyer and defended her inheritance. She received an excellent recommendation on legal representation from Julius."

"They became close after this?"

Martin shakes his head. "Vareena walked a fine line with Julius. She could not afford to be so contemptuous of her father as to make him into an enemy. Still, she maintained an unshakable aloofness and dignity in his presence that Julius, perversely, admired. He respected her, was oddly in awe of her, emotions that he was used to receiving, not giving. He never received them in return from his daughter, but I think that he desired her approval."

"And what about baby Larry? Did Vareena see him every day? Did he know she was his mother?"

Now Martin leans back in his chair and takes a long drink with a shaking hand.

"The sisters argued about this, but Vareena was unshakable. She could not risk Larry knowing the truth. A child will tell other children what he knows. So Larry was raised believing he was Larry Simpson, Cassie's cousin once removed, the child of a cousin from "down South." It's not uncommon in the African American community for a relative to bring up another woman's child in a time of need. The neighbors, the sisters-in-law, and the kids living at home all accepted this. Larry called Cassie his mama. My mother considered him her little brother. She was ten when he arrived."

"But did Vareena see him? Did Cassie bring him to the Tate Mansion?"

Martin nods. "For the first three years of his life, he came to the back door every day with Cassie. Thanks to the inheritance, Cassie no longer had to work at the Home for Retarded Children, thank goodness. But it would have looked suspicious to the neighbors and other family members if Cassie didn't work at all. So she told everyone that she too worked for Vareena Tate, and that Mrs. Tate didn't mind if she brought Larry along with her. He called Vareena VaVa, a term of endearment. A toddler does not question relationships. He just knew there were many people who loved him and whom he loved, and VaVa was one of them."

"But something happened...?"

Martin nods. "One day, Larry threw a huge tantrum. He did not want to go home. He clung to Vareena. He pushed Cassie away. Cassie stepped back. It was Vareena's call on how to handle this. But at that moment, Vareena knew. Cassie would never be able to parent the child when he was a teenager if she lost all authority over him now. He would run wild. She told Cassie to bring the boy less often. She distanced herself from him. Told him he must call her Mrs. Tate."

"That's so sad!"

"Vareena spent her time with him teaching him to read and

write so he would always be ahead of the others in school. She had Cassie bring the other children to the house as well, including my mother, and she ran tutoring sessions for them all, one or two at a time. She didn't treat Larry any differently than the others. This went on for years."

"But why didn't you ever spend time with Maybelle and Vareena?"

"In 1964, the year before I was born, the sisters had a falling out. It concerned another war."

1964! This is it—the year Vareena stopped leaving the house. The year she turned the accounts over to Maybelle.

"Vietnam," I say. "But I thought people didn't start protesting the war until the late sixties, early seventies."

"You're right--they weren't arguing about the politics of the war. In May of 1964, Larry fulfilled everyone's dreams by graduating from Princeton with a degree in chemistry. Vareena wanted him to immediately apply for medical school. Larry thought he should serve his country. Cassie didn't disagree—his father had served, although of course Larry didn't know that. His uncles had served. Some of his cousins had served."

I have a sinking feeling. I know where this is headed. "Cassie encouraged him to enlist and he was killed."

"She didn't encourage him, but Vareena said she should forbid the boy to enlist. But of course, he was a grown man—he didn't need anyone's permission. And Vareena of all people should have realized that young people will follow their own hearts."

"Even into disaster."

"Exactly. So Vareena blamed Cassie, and Cassie was angry and hurt at being blamed, especially since she too was devastated by Larry's death."

"And where did Maybelle stand?"

"Maybelle had an anti-authoritarian streak. Despite the fact that some of her nephews had used the military as a stepping-stone to a better life, she didn't want Larry to go. She spoke her mind to him, which Vareena saw as support for her position. But Cassie thought Maybelle's nagging just made Larry more set on enlisting. And then Larry's cousins weighed in."

"So everyone blamed everyone else. Sounds like my family," Sean says.

"The upshot of the feud was that a coolness set in between the Tate mansion in Palmyrton and the Simpson family home in East Orange. Vareena said she no longer had the patience to tutor the next generation of Simpson children, of which I was among the first. But she continued her financial support. Cassie took the money to help the kids, but she never visited the big house."

"Maybe Vareena was afraid of getting too attached to any of the children."

Martin nods. "I think that was it. She became more and more reclusive. She couldn't bear any more loss."

"What happened to Edgar Tate's business, Amalgamated Metals?" Sean asks.

"Vareena had the lawyers sell it. Years of neglect and mismanagement had eroded its worth. Vareena wasn't as rich as she had been in 1950, but she still had plenty."

I want to get back to the family drama. "But didn't Maybelle miss Cassie? You said Cassie was the only mother she ever knew."

"Maybelle visited the house in East Orange occasionally. Cassie gave her the latest pictures of the children. I remember Maybelle as rather dour, easily annoyed by the commotion at our house. By this time, she had lived with Vareena for over twenty-five years. She got used to peace and quiet and space. People become set in their ways. It's easier to avoid conflict than resolve it. So Maybelle and Cassie drifted further and further apart, until in 1975, Cassie got liver cancer. She was dead in a matter of months. As is often the case when there's a rift, Maybelle was hysterical with grief. She lashed out, blaming Cassie's children for not taking good care of their mother. Of course, that was preposterous. Liver cancer is deadly even now—in 1975, it was always incurable. So the break was complete. We never saw Maybelle or Vareena again."

CHAPTER 49

"SO THAT EXPLAINS WHY VAREENA didn't leave her money to your family. But do you know why she chose the Rosa Parks Center as her beneficiary?"

Martin shrugs. "It's an organization that helps young African Americans. I suppose she preferred to give the money locally, rather than to the NAACP or the United Negro College Fund."

Clearly, Martin doesn't care about the money. But I'm shocked that he could have known the story of his family all these years but stayed estranged from them. I know I'm prying into his personal emotions, but I have to ask. "So you always knew who Vareena and Maybelle were. Why didn't you ever get in touch with them after your mother died?"

Martin closes his eyes briefly, as if he's saying a private prayer. Then he speaks directly to me. "I'm sixty-eight years old, Audrey. Time and illness have mellowed me. But I came of age in the sixties and seventies, reading the works of Malcom X and Huey Newton. Martin Luther King was too tame for me. I reveled in my blackness and rejected white culture. Vareena was an embarrassment to me. A black woman masquerading as white, hiding her true identity. I could afford to be high and mighty about rejecting the blood money she had acquired by being raped by a white man. I told myself I had achieved my success entirely on my own, by virtue of my superior intellect. I certainly wasn't going to sneak around and enter the Tate Mansion through the back door! Not Martin Simpson Brantley, JD, PhD, professor of law." He slaps a fist into his palm.

"Like most men, I spent my forties and fifties climbing the career ladder. My wife and I never had children and eventually we divorced. Then illness struck—and I became disabled. I retired early and moved here to be close to my sister's family. And I had plenty of time to think. To think about the past and my family history, and those two old women in Palmyrton. Maybe if I still had my health, I would have driven up there and knocked on the front door and demanded to be admitted back into their lives. But my illness requires me to rely on others. I would have needed help to drive there, help to get up the steps into the house. And asking for help would have required an explanation to the helper. So I did nothing."

We all sit in silence for a while. The story has been fascinating, but there are still unanswered questions. I reach out for Martin's hand. "There's one more thing I'd like to know. Right after the end of World War II, the records show Vareena had a new kitchen built at the mansion, and above that kitchen, there was a secret room. Do you know anything about that?"

Martin chuckles. "Ah, the secret room! Maybelle complained plenty about that old kitchen with its coal stove and ice box. Once the sisters realized they really did control the Tate fortune, they decided to modernize. Vareena hired an architect to design the addition."

"The Palmyrton Library History Room has a copy of the plans, but they don't indicate any secret room." I interrupt Martin to hurry the story along.

Martin laughs again. "Well, it would hardly be secret if the most prominent architect in Palmyrton knew all about it. After the kitchen addition was built, Vareena realized there was a small, unfinished space above where the addition was tied into the main building. She wanted a place to keep her mementoes of Larry, a place away from prying eyes of workmen or visitors, where they'd never be discovered. So the sisters hired a carpenter, a man totally separate from the crew who'd built the kitchen, to turn the space into a secret room."

"That's where we found the picture of your mother and her class," I tell Martin.

"Vareena filled the room up with cards Larry made for her, the pictures he drew. Later, she collected his outstanding report cards and stories about his athletic and academic achievements that were published in the East Orange newspaper. All the little treasures a loving mother keeps. And she and Maybelle kept photos of the other kids as well."

Perplexed, I interrupt his story. "But when we found the room, there were no articles about Larry Simpson. If there were, we would have figured out the connection a lot sooner."

Martin looks surprised. "My grandmother told me that was the purpose of the room. A secret shrine to Vareena's son."

Whoever Ty walked in on in the secret room must have grabbed the scrapbook and photos of Larry. "Did the other kids know about the room?"

Martin shakes his head. "Only Maybelle and Vareena and Cassie. And Cassie told me."

"And you never told anyone else?" Sean asks.

"Never had a reason to until now."

"But one other person knew," I insist. "The carpenter who built the room. Do you have any idea who that was?"

"It was a young black man from Palmyrton. A fellow Maybelle was kind of sweet on for a time, according to Cassie." Martin gazes up at the ceiling trying to remember. "Sykes. I think his name was Sykes."

CHAPTER 50

SEAN DROVE BACK TO PALMYRTON in record time and went straight to the hospital to interrogate Dennis. Of course I couldn't go with him, but he's promised me a full report when he gets home. Ethel sprawls across my lap as we wait for him.

As I stroke her silky fur, I think of all the heartbroken mothers in this story, and the terrible sacrifices they were forced to make. Eula, who had to give up her baby girl to strangers to preserve the rest of her family. Vareena, who had to give away the dearest part of herself and her lost husband to protect her son from shame and poverty. And even Loretta, who knew her son was twisted, but loved him and wanted to protect him anyway.

I run a hand across my flat stomach. If I get pregnant, will I feel that kind of devotion? Is it automatic?

It wasn't for my own mother.

Ethel's ears prick up. She hears Sean's car before I do.

I run to greet him and hand him the glass of wine I have already poured. "Talk."

Sean performs a series of back and neck cracking stretches, then settles in to tell all he knows.

"First of all, Dennis is nobody's fool. He lawyered up as soon as he woke up from his surgery. He made a deal to give us what we need to know to settle Loretta's case and prove that Loretta gave Crawford the money to run. Dennis's lawyer and Frederic's lawyer have been working overtime. Dennis now claims the shooting was an accident. Frederic now claims Dennis simply requested a donation, no coercion involved."

"What?" I thump my chest. "What about me? I was an eyewitness, well, an ear witness, to the whole episode. Frederic pointed a gun at me and fired a shot at Mister Vargas."

"He fired a shot at the ceiling. His lawyer says the gun discharged accidentally. Both lawyers say you misunderstood. Without a recording, your testimony will be hearsay. Frederic will get charged with reckless endangerment and get off with probation. First offence, no prior history of violence."

"And a multi-million dollar net worth."

Sean offers a humorless smile. "Justice is different for the rich."

"What about Dennis? What will he be charged with?"

Sean takes a long gulp of wine. "That guy is too smart. I gotta trust that one day he'll trip himself up. But not today. He confessed to things that aren't crimes and denied everything that was a crime, knowing we didn't have enough other evidence to charge him."

"Did he pay that kid to steal my van?"

"I'm sure he did, but there's no proof. No fingerprints, and we can't find the kid. I'm sure Dennis wanted the van to get that ledger because he feared his grandfather's name would show up in the list of tradesmen."

"While you were at the hospital, I went to the library and looked at the ledger. There's no Sykes listed, and no expenditures that I could see that would be attributable to that room. The ladies kept it off the books. Dennis stole my van for nothing." I lean forward and grab Sean's hand. "But what was Dennis *doing*? Did you figure that out?"

"I think so, but I had to guess to fill in some blanks. When I got to the hospital, I told Dennis we'd talked to Martin Simpson and knew his grandfather had built the secret room. So with the lawyer there approving everything he said, Dennis told me this. When Dennis was a kid, his grandfather told him about a secret room he'd built in a big old house. It was a story Dennis had practically forgotten until the day the Parks Center inherited the Tate Mansion. When Dennis toured the mansion with the other Board members, the details of his grandfather's story came back to him, and he was sure this must be the house where his grandfather had built the room."

"Did Dennis know why the room was built?"

Sean gives me the evil eye. "Don't rush me, Audrey."

I run an imaginary zipper across my lips and nudge him to

continue.

"Everyone on the Board was trying to figure out why Vareena Tate left her money to the Parks Center. Dennis suspected he knew the reason—his grandfather had been friends with Levi Jefferson Senior, who founded the Parks Center in 1968."

I can't restrain myself. "Soon after Larry died!

Sean nods. "Maybelle and Grandpa Sykes stayed friends, although Sykes was quite a bit younger. They must've discussed the Civil Rights Movement, and how Levi Senior was doing his part right here in Palmyrton. And Maybelle must've carried that home to Vareena. So after the sisters fell out with the rest of their family, they must've decided to leave the money to the Rosa Parks Center. If Dennis's grandfather knew that was their plan, he never told anyone about it."

"So why didn't Dennis tell the others his theory?"

Sean arches his eyebrows. "This is where Dennis clammed up and we have to do some guesswork. I think Dennis saw an opportunity to play a long con that might bring the Parks Center even more money. He wasn't sure it would work, but he wanted the chance to gather more information. You see, he remembered that his grandfather had told him the room had been built to hold a family secret, a secret that would" Sean pauses to make air quotes " 'shake up all the high and mighty white folks in Palmyrton'. "

"So he wanted the chance to get inside the house and find the room before I did," I say.

"I think so. I bet he'd heard about your previous exploits discovering family secrets in the houses you clear. That's why he wanted Henry to have the job—Henry wouldn't be so curious, and Dennis would be able to come and go at the house, no questions asked. I suspect Dennis had copied Levi's key to the house and had been in there several nights looking for the secret room. Unfortunately for Dennis, the night he finally found it was the night Ty chose to study at the mansion. Dennis was exploring the room. He'd found the scrapbook about Larry Simpson. He found all the cards and drawings made out to VaVa, who must be Vareena. He noticed that Larry had much lighter skin than all the other family members whose pictures were displayed. And just as he was putting two and two together—"

"Ty came up and interrupted him."

"Yep. Dennis panicked. He hit first and realized whom he'd hit later. He shut Ty in the room and ran."

I'm outraged. "Dennis was going to leave him there? What if Henry and I hadn't found him? Ty could have died. Dennis should be charged with assault, attempted murder."

Sean chuckles. "Aren't you all high and mighty? Let's remember that at the time, you and Ty decided not to report the crime at all. And Ty didn't see who hit him. Nope, Dennis is free and clear on that one. If it's any consolation, the only time Dennis looked at all remorseful was when I questioned him about the attack on Ty."

"Humph. So Dennis knew Vareena was the mother of a black son. How did he find out who Vareena was, and that Julius had raped Eula?"

Sean leans forward with his elbows on his knees. "Don't forget, Dennis had overheard the argument between Loretta and Levi on the night of the fundraiser. He was willing to tell me all about that. Just as you overheard, Loretta was siphoning contributions to give to Crawford for his escape. Levi had been cooperating because Loretta promised him years of big, steady donations from her family foundation. But when Loretta told Levi how much she needed to take from the fundraiser profits, Levi panicked. He didn't think he could cover it up from Jared's sharp eye, and he needed an infusion of cash right away for the plumbing and roof repairs."

"Did Dennis actually see Levi push Loretta?"

"No, but Dennis said Levi was never the same after the party. He was a nervous wreck, and Dennis took advantage of that. He pressured Levi to tell him all he knew about Loretta. Dennis wanted to know why Loretta had suddenly taken an interest in the Parks Center. Turns out Levi had the same question when Loretta showed up on the scene. And when she approached Levi with her deal, Levi got her to admit that her grandfather had once done something that she felt required restorative justice."

"Restorative justice? That was the term she used?"

"Yes. But that's all Levi knew. So here's where Dennis was very clever. He went after the weakest link to get the rest of his information."

I think for a moment. "Crawford?"

Sean makes like he's playing a fiddle. "Dennis played him good. Told him he'd help him get the money Loretta had been lining up for him if Crawford could tell him more about what Julius had done."

"So that's why Crawford was looking for the photo at Birdie's house."

"Yes. His mother had mentioned something about it, but then Crawford couldn't find the evidence Dennis wanted."

"I guess Levi's suicide pushed Dennis into action," I say.

"Yep. Dennis turned around and used all the information he gathered from the son to blackmail the father. Either he would get more money for the Parks Center, or he'd get the opportunity to create a social media frenzy around the injustice done to Eula and Vareena. Win-win."

I study my husband. He seems strangely relaxed. "You're not making any arrests. Why aren't you agitated?"

"I've been reading up on life in Cambodia. High rates of dengue fever, malaria, typhoid, and sexually transmitted diseases. A really lousy health care system. Without a steady infusion of cash from home, Crawford will eventually get the punishment he deserves."

Then Sean offers his hands up to heaven. "And Dennis. Dennis is a con man. But he didn't do it to enrich himself. He really did want all the money to go to the Parks Center."

CHAPTER 51

A BANNER FLAPS IN THE AUTUMN breeze. **WELCOME TO THE GRAND REOPENING OF THE ROSA PARKS COMMUNITY CENTER** marches across the sturdy vinyl in perfectly designed type next to the new RPCC logo.

"That's a good-looking sign."

"It surely is. And look at that fancy new door."

The bake-sale ladies have gathered in a cluster on the repaved forecourt to admire the building before going inside for the festivities.

Sean holds open the door. "Have you ladies been cooking and baking for this party?"

"No, siree. It's *catered,* so we don't have to work and can just enjoy ourselves."

In the lobby, the mural of Rosa Parks has been retouched. She smiles down serenely with a whiter smile and a bluer dress. On the opposite wall, three new portraits now hang: Eula Simpson, Maybelle Simpson, and Vareena Simpson Soares Tate. Martin Simpson sits in his wheelchair right below them, the crowd milling around him.

Sean and I elbow our way through to join him. Together we gaze up in silence. The artist has captured Eula and Vareena quite effectively by using the photographs of them as inspiration. But we never did find a photo of Maybelle. Sean got the idea of using the police sketch artist to draw Maybelle from descriptions given by the few people who knew her: Martin, Joan the librarian, and old Mr. Hyler from the garage. The portrait artist has breathed some life into that rather grim sketch, creating a painting of a purposeful older woman with a direct gaze and hair drawn back in a bun. Looking at her image, I feel like I'm reuniting with a long-lost friend.

"What do you think? Does the painting look like Maybelle?"

Martin smiles wistfully. "Not precisely, but it captures her spirit very well. I think she'd approve."

A dais with a podium sits at the far side of the foyer. Beverly Masterson, wearing a snazzy cream and gold suit, adjusts the microphone. As the new Chairman of the Board of Directors, this is her show. "Welcome everyone to this glorious event!"

A smattering of applause, and the crowd falls silent.

Beverly lifts her right hand to the portraits. "We are here today to honor the lives of three unsung heroes. Their suffering, their sacrifice, and their resilience have made this day possible. We are shining a light into the dark alleys of the past in hopes of building a bright future."

Whoops and cheers from the crowd interrupt the speech.

Beverly continues, introducing the new Board of Directors, all business owners with roots in this neighborhood. She gushes on about their plans: branding, fundraising, a newsletter, career coaching, nutrition counseling, college readiness. It all sounds great, but penny-pincher that I am, I worry that the Parks Center will spend every cent it has inherited. "Did the sale of the mansion bring in enough to sustain all this?" I ask Sean.

He puts his hands on my shoulders and turns me so I'm forced to look at a corner of the room behind the dais. There stands a tall, thin man, hands clasped behind his back, eyes focused above the sea of faces.

"What's Frederic Bostwick doing here?"

Sean massages my shoulders. "Jared and Beverly just nailed down a half-million dollar grant, payable over the next five years..." he pauses for dramatic effect..."from the Scour-Brite Enterprises Foundation."

"Seriously? Frederic was willing to donate after all that's happened?"

"He went into seclusion after the episode with Dennis, but recently he's emerged and thrown himself into the work of the Foundation."

I glance around at the crowd. "Where *is* Dennis? Is he persona non grata here?"

Natalie glides up to us. "I believe Beverly made it clear he needed to find a new outlet for his…er…energies. Your father got an email from Dennis recently. He's working on grassroots campaigning and get-out-the-vote efforts for the next Congressional election."

"Dennis certainly has the sharp elbows required for politics." Sean guides us out of the crowd. "Let's go downstairs and see the rest of the building."

In the downstairs hallway, I can't resist looking up. The damage caused by the bullet that grazed the ceiling has been repaired. Then I look ahead and see a colorful sign: MATH EXPLORERS WELCOME. Two little girls about ten years old stand in the hallway peeking into the room where five or six older boys have gathered. The girl with pigtails pushes the one with braids. "Go ahead. You said you were going to do it."

"I didn't say for sure. I said maybe."

Dad appears in the doorway. "Hello, ladies. Would you like to learn more about Math Explorers?"

Pigtails shakes her head. "Not me. Her."

"Well, come on in, Janna."

Her face is a mixture of longing and doubt. "Is Math Explorers hard? I'm only in fifth grade."

"Math is challenging." Dad never sugarcoats the truth. "But I suspect you're a young woman who enjoys a challenge."

She shifts from one foot to the other.

Dad remains silent. Never one to coax.

Go in, Janna. Go. Does telepathy work?

I guess it must. Janna sways, then dashes into the room before she can change her mind.

I hear my father's voice happily projecting in lecture mode. "What do math and basketball have in common? Let's find out."

THE END

DEAR READER,

I hope you enjoyed *Treasure in Exile.* Please consider leaving a brief review to help other readers discover this book. Thanks so much!

Would you like to be notified when my next novel is released? Please join my mailing list. Don't worry—you'll only receive ONE email when a book is released.www.swhubbard.net/contact

OTHER BOOKS BY S.W. HUBBARD

Read all the **Palmyrton Estate Sale Mysteries**, available in paperback, Kindle, and audiobook:

Another Man's Treasure

Treasure of Darkness

This Bitter Treasure

If you've read all the **Palmyrton Estate Sale Mysteries**, it's time to try the **Frank Bennett Adirondack Mountain** mystery series:

Take the Bait

The Lure

Blood Knot

Dead Drift

False Cast

ABOUT THE AUTHOR

S.W. Hubbard is the author of the Palmyrton Estate Sale Mysteries, *Another Man's Treasure, Treasure of Darkness, This Bitter Treasure,* and *Treasure in Exile* She is also is the author of four Police Chief Frank Bennett mystery novels set in the Adirondack Mountains: *Take the Bait, The Lure (*originally published as *Swallow the Hook), Blood Knot,* and *False Cast,* as well as a short story collection featuring Frank Bennett, *Dead Drift.* Her short stories have appeared in *Alfred Hitchcock's Mystery Magazine* and the anthologies *Crimes by Moonlight, The Mystery Box,* and *Adirondack Mysteries.* She lives in Morristown, NJ, where she teaches creative writing to enthusiastic teens and adults, and expository writing to reluctant college freshmen. To contact her, join her mailing list, or read the first chapter of any of her books, visit: www. swhubbard.net.

Follow her on BookBub or like her Facebook author page. Connect with S.W. Hubbard on Twitter, Pinterest and Goodreads too.